HIGH SIERRA

Also by Adrienne Quintana

Eruption

Reclamation

HIGH SIERRA

Adrienne Quintana

pink umbrella
books

Thank you to my family and friends for their never-ending enthusiasm and support. Thank you to Yosemite National Park, where I was inspired to write this story during my own version of wilderness therapy. And thank you to God for always letting me know He's there and that He cares.
—Adrienne Quintana

Published by Pink Umbrella Books (www.pinkumbrellapublishing.com)
Adrienne Quintana- author

High Sierra / Adrienne Quintana
Library of Congress Control Number: 2019904961
Lyrics used with permission:
"I Am a Child of God" © By Intellectual Reserve, Inc.

One

The place was a total dive. Dirty log walls and rusting metal furniture gave off a homeless shelter vibe—nothing like the fat camp my mom sent me to last summer. I mean, that place looked and felt expensive. And the chunky, bald guy across the desk from me was no fitness instructor. Crooked, black framed certificates hung on the wall behind him. The seal on one of them said *American Psychological Association.*

Something wasn't right. My mom had been vague. She made it sound like she was sending me off to some kind of leadership camp, but the kids waiting outside this office didn't look like Model UN material. And what kind of leadership camp starts with a psych eval? My palms began to sweat.

I tried to keep my voice calm. "I think there might have been a mistake."

The man didn't look up from his notepad. Instead, he adjusted his suspenders and nodded absently.

Great. He wasn't even listening. He seemed to be thinking about something else—probably about what he was going to have for dinner, based on the size of his gut under that flannel shirt. Finally, he looked up and cleared his throat. "Let's start with introductions. Why don't you tell me a little bit about yourself?"

"Okay." I took a deep breath. "I'm Jasmine Fuentes. I'm 17 years old. I'm an honor student at Central High. I have a 3.96 GPA. *Unweighted.* I'm not sure what this place is, but I'm pretty sure I don't belong here."

He scratched something on the paper with his chewed-up pencil. Ridiculous. Nothing I said fazed him. Fluffy snowflakes started falling outside the wood-paned window. Snow in June? I was in the Twilight Zone or something. When my mom said California, I pictured palm trees and perfect weather. Why had she let me pack for the beach if she knew I was heading for the mountains? None of this made sense.

The man finally looked up. "Well, Jasmine, we're happy to have you in our program. It's a life-changing opportunity," he said. "We're going to give you a toolbox for success. All you have to do is accept the tools and learn to use them."

"What exactly is this program?"

"Your mom didn't tell you?" he asked.

I swallowed hard and slowly shook my head.

"High Sierra is one of the top-rated wilderness therapy programs in the entire world."

Oh, geez. It was like the two worst words on earth got together and had an ugly baby. Wilderness therapy? Like on the reality show my mom was obsessed with? Extreme rehab for troubled teenagers—kids with huge problems? Why would she…what had I…oh no, seriously, this had to be a mistake.

"I should introduce myself." He smiled and pointed to his nametag. "I'm Dave, and I'm going to be your shadow."

I raised my eyebrows. Shadow? Sounded super creepy, like a stalker.

"A shadow is more than a counselor," he explained. "More than a friend, even. I hope we become like family.

"For the next few months, you're going to learn to survive in the wilderness with very little besides the clothes on your back. You'll learn to find food and water. You'll learn to build shelter. And most importantly, you'll learn to make fire."

"Months?" I coughed out. "Therapy? Why? What do you think is wrong with me?"

He smiled and set down his pencil. "I don't think anything's wrong with you. You seem like a very intelligent, articulate girl."

"Right. Then why did my mom send me here?"

He picked the pencil back up. "Why don't you tell me why you think you're here?"

Oof. The weight of my situation pressed down on me, and my temples began to throb. Truthfully, it was just like my mom to send me away to some remote corner of the world to learn "new tools" that would help me cope with life. But she'd always been honest with me about the programs she'd signed me up for in the past.

I bit down on my lip to keep it from quivering. What if this wasn't a mistake? Maybe she'd just totally lost it. But no. Even if I knew the exact straw that had broken her back, I wasn't going to tell Jabba the Hillbilly Hutt about it. It was none of his business. And besides, he was almost guaranteed to believe the worst, just like my mom had. Adults suck like that.

Most of my friends had barely gotten a slap on the wrist after "the incident." Probably because their parents were normal—two people who liked each other enough to live in the same house. Even if they had a crazy mom like I did, they also had a dad who cared enough to talk some sense into her. What was the big deal anyway? Teenagers drink on prom night. It's a well-known fact. But I was the responsible one. I was the designated driver. I do wish I'd known about the open container law—that was unfortunate—but I'd never make the same mistake again.

I wasn't sure which had upset her more, the embarrassment of picking me up from the police station or the money she'd wasted calling her lawyer in. Sure, he'd negotiated it off my permanent record, but we'd all ended up with the same ten-day community service sentence. That was almost two months ago. Ancient history. I'd already paid for my mistake.

I folded my arms across my chest. "I already told you— I don't belong here. She must have been confused. She thought this was a leadership training camp. Just let me call my mom and we'll straighten this whole thing out."

He looked at me and blinked. "There's no mistake, Jasmine. I talked to your mom this morning. She's very excited for you to go through our program."

"So you're not going to let me call my mom?"

He shook his head.

Unbelievable. "I'm an American citizen. I have rights."

He looked me in the eyes. "You're a minor. Your mother has committed you to this program." He lifted a document from his desk, pushed it toward me, and pointed at my mother's signature at the bottom. "The sooner you accept it, the sooner you can start working toward going home again."

Committed me. I touched the swooping letters in her signature. Who was I kidding? She didn't make mistakes. My mom knew exactly what she was doing. She'd found something else she didn't like about me—and a program she thought would fix it. My fingers pressed hard into the paper until it crinkled.

"I guess if you're not going to listen to me, I'm done talking," I said.

He gave a half-smile and scratched another note on his paper. What could he be writing? Pressure and heat built in my face until I thought my head was going to explode.

He pushed his chair away from his desk and stood up. "Okay, Jasmine. I'm very pleased to have met you. I look forward to talking to you soon." Was he kidding? He really wasn't going to try harder than that to find out what my "issues" were? He moved over to the door and opened it. I reluctantly stood and followed him, guessing that whatever was waiting for me out there would be much worse than talking to Dave in his warm office. But I tried to act tough. What other option did I have? I was thousands of miles away from home with no phone.

"Monica, Jasmine is ready to get outfitted."

A girl on the other side of the room waved at me to come to her. In a daze, I brushed past Dave without shaking his outstretched hand through the crowd of waiting misfits.

"Hi Jasmine, I'm Monica," the blonde girl chirped. She was that annoying kind of "no makeup" pretty. Tall and willowy, she moved toward a closet while she sized me up with her soft blue eyes. "How tall are you? About five four?"

I nodded but squinted at her, mentally daring her to guess my weight.

"Where're ya from?" she asked.

"New Jersey," I muttered.

"Oh, really? What part?"

Was it exciting to be from New Jersey? "Newark."

"Nice," she replied. "Shoe size?"

"Eight."

She pushed a pair of hiking boots into the space between us as if I was supposed to take them. What would you even wear those with? I definitely didn't pack anything that would match them. Monica stood with her arms outstretched for several seconds before she set the boots on the ground at my feet.

"I was a nanny in East Brunswick last summer," she said. I shrugged.

She threw a green hiking backpack next to the boots and piled khaki cargo pants and a butter yellow dri-fit shirt on top of everything. "That's it. You can put your gear in cubby number twelve and take a seat. Orientation will start in a few minutes."

My gear? As in, I was supposed to wear this stuff? I raised one eyebrow.

She stared me down for a minute, her sincere smile slowly becoming plastic. She wanted me to cooperate so she could get on to her next victim. But if I picked up the clothes, that would be like agreeing that I was going to do this. Finally, she shrugged and turned her back on me, walking toward the big double doors to the lodge. She opened them, letting in a blast of cold air and stepped out, pulling the door closed after her.

A bright laugh rang out behind me, but it quickly turned into a hacking cough. I looked over my shoulder. It was the girl in the leather jacket with the platinum blonde pixie cut— the one I'd been sitting next to while waiting to go into Dave's office.

"You really showed her," the girl choked. She covered her mouth and coughed until it sounded like one of her lungs would dislodge itself and fall out of her mouth.

"Showed her?"

"Your little Gandhi, peaceful resistance move." She started laughing again. Laughing *at* me, not *with* me.

"I don't—" her laughing triggered another coughing fit. Even if I wanted to explain myself, Little Miss Emphysema wouldn't have been able to hear it anyway. I rolled my eyes and walked right past the hacker without making eye contact, all the way to the back of the room, and sat on an empty row. I had to figure out a way to talk to my mom before it was too late.

The room wasn't huge. Twelve folding chairs all faced a stone fireplace. Aside from the exit, four other doors led out of this room: one to Jabba's office, one to what sounded like an industrial kitchen with all of the metal clanking around, and the last two were restrooms. No phone anywhere in sight.

Man, there was nothing fancy about this place at all. I couldn't help wondering how much my mom had shelled out to send me here. What a waste. Didn't she realize that if she spent the same amount of money buying me a nice car instead of sending me to fat camps and reform-yourself wilderness programs, we wouldn't be having this communication crisis? I dug my fingernails into my upper arms to stop myself from screaming.

The doors blew open again, and Monica returned with a tall, scrawny kid. He had a disgusting lip caterpillar and saggy pants with no belt. His shoulders slumped forward, and he didn't look up from the floor.

Monica, the Backwoods Barbie, didn't look happy when she had to step over the pile of stuff I'd left on the floor in my rush to get away from Emphysema. She glanced at it, then scanned the room for me. I slid down in my chair a little.

Backwoods Barbie told the skinny kid something. He hesitated before slowly going into Jabba's office.

Without looking at me again, Backwoods Barbie bent down to pick up my gear. I fumbled to get up, accidentally kicking the leg of the metal folding chair in front of me. The other victims turned around, some with sympathetic faces, others annoyed. Their expressions seemed to say, "Get over yourself. You're not the only one who hates it here." And before I could stand up, Backwoods Barbie walked over to the cubbies where the other kids had put their stuff and hung mine in number twelve. My face burned with embarrassment.

Including the skinny kid, there were six of us. Three boys and three girls. Besides me and Emphysema, the only other girl was short with black hair and chalky white skin. Behind thick black liner, her eyes were bloodshot and puffy. She'd been crying. I looked away and blew out a long breath. What had she done to get herself sent here?

The two boys on the front row ribbed each other and laughed. They didn't look terrified. Either they'd been here longer than the rest of us, or they were already friends.

Jabba's office door squeaked open. He came out with his clipboard tucked under his arm, moved to the center of the room, and stood in front of the fireplace hearth. The skinny kid followed him and sat down on the end of the second row.

Jabba adjusted his suspenders. "Alright, everyone, it looks like we're ready to get going. Let's take a second to introduce ourselves. We'll start in the front and move to the back. Tell us your name and your trail name if you've earned one. Share how old you are and where you come from." He pointed to his name tag again. "I'll start. I'm Dave. Twenty-seven years ago, when I founded this program with my friend Samuel Chavis, he gave me a new name—Good Soaring Raven." Dave lifted his arms as if unfurling his raven feathers. *Plaid flannel feathers.* I snorted, trying to suppress my laughter. "Samuel and I walked the very trail you'll be walking today and reached the beautiful vistas you'll see. Since then, many young walkers have followed on their own journey of discovery—finding the elements missing from their lives in the basic gifts given by Mother Earth." He nodded toward the two boys on the front row.

They looked at each other, silently arguing about who had to go first. Finally, one of them stood up.

"I'm Todd Harper." There was a slight nasal twang when he said Harper. "I'm 17 years old and I come from Rexburg, Idaho. I thought moving sprinkler pipe was hard work until I came here." He paused, like he was momentarily frozen in thought. "But I've learned that I don't need some of the things I thought I needed before. My trail name is Quiet Wolf." He sat back down in his chair so quickly it seemed he was avoiding additional questions from Jabba or Good Soaring Raven, or whatever he thought we should call him.

The next kid stood up. "I'm Runs on Wind," he said. "I'm from West Palm Beach. I'm sixteen, and I really love spring onions."

The other kid cackled at this comment like it was some kind of hilarious inside joke, but Jabba cut off any more shenanigans. "And your name given by the folks back home?"

"Nathan Anderson," the kid said, dropping back into his folding chair with a thud.

Just then, the door opened again, and all heads turned toward it. The gust of cold wind took my breath away. My eyes watered, blinding me until the door closed. When I looked up, the newcomer strode by, glancing in my direction. Dressed in an olive shirt, khaki cargo pants, and weathered hiking boots, it was obvious he planned on walking today, but he didn't look like a teenager. Tall, with fair hair, tan skin, and broad shoulders, he belonged in an Abercrombie ad, not the wilderness. I sat up straight, pushing my windblown hair away from my face and the water from my cheeks. He tilted his head and his eyebrows knit together sympathetically. Wait, did he think I was crying?

Jabba nodded to the skinny kid with the lip caterpillar. Head hung down, his floppy hair fell forward exposing a lump on the back of his neck. He didn't stand up, clenching and unclenching his fists several times. The muscles in his jaw tightened and his chin pulled forward, emotion seeping out of his eyes like steam from a tea kettle.

Don't push him, Jabba, I thought. *He's had a rough day and he's ready to blow.*

Dave pushed his glasses up on his nose. "Just your name and where you come from," he said in that patronizing adult voice that's as painful as rubbing your butt against a cheese grater.

The boy pinched his eyes closed, holding perfectly still while we all waited.

Say something. Do Something. You're killing me.

Some of the others began to shift around after almost a full minute of weird silence. Why couldn't Jabba take a hint and move on already? The hunchback didn't want to talk. What difference did it make what his name was anyway?

Finally, Jabba cleared his throat and seemed like he was going to say something, but the newcomer, Abercrombie, stepped forward and preempted whatever psychological genius Jabba was going to bring out of his bag of tricks next.

"How about I go?" he said. This was an interesting development. Who was this guy?

Jabba turned his attention and gave his nod of approval to Abercrombie.

"I'm Firewalker." His deep voice was thick like Nutella. "I'm from Sandy, Utah, and I'm 21 years old." So he wasn't in the program. Did that mean he was a normal guy? If he was 21, that meant he was here of his own free will. Maybe not *completely* normal. "People in Utah call me Bryce Talmage. I'm lucky enough to get to take this walk with you as your spirit guide. I'll teach you the way of the Miwok. I'll help you learn to find the gifts Mother Earth has for you. This place is like a second home to me, and I'm so glad to be back."

"Bryce just got home from serving a two-year mission in Argentina," Jabba said. "You're his first group, and you're very lucky to have him. Ask him questions. Learn from his experience."

What did that mean, "serving a mission?" Like for the Peace Corps or something? Two years sounded like a long time to be in Argentina. I tried to picture Abercrombie digging wells in a small village full of children with no shoes. Would he be wearing a shirt in that scenario?

Jabba turned to Backwoods Barbie. "While we're at it, most of you have already met your other spirit guide, but why don't you introduce yourself, Monica?"

"Hi." She gave a stiff wave. The crooked arm, cheerleader wave. "I'm Monica Clark, and I'm so excited to be with you guys. I'm from Bothell, Washington and I'm 21. I'm a student at Washington State University, studying psychology. This is my sixth walking. Good Soaring Raven chose my favorite trail for this week. It's a bit of a climb, but the view at the end will make it worth every step."

Rah! Rah! Go team! She sounded like the fitness instructors at fat camp. I still had emotional scars from the hours I'd been forced to spend on the stair climber to give me a body my mom could stand to look at. Maybe I was wrong. Maybe it wasn't prom night that had gotten me here at all. Maybe this was passive-aggressive fat camp. Madness.

"Let's keep going," Jabba said, pointing to the pale girl next to the hunchback.

She stood up. "Michaela Meyers." Her voice was completely monotone, and she was staring at the wall behind Jabba. "I'm from Fresno. I'll be sixteen next week. I guess this was my birthday present." She sat down before she finished saying the last word.

What kind of jerk parents send their daughter off to the wilderness right before her sweet sixteen?

I folded my arms across my chest.

Suddenly, I realized everyone was staring at me. Abercrombie's gaze gave me butterflies.

I cleared my throat and stood up, throwing my shoulders back and lifting my chest. Like a marionette being pulled up by a string, my speech teacher had taught us. I took a deep breath in, expanding my chest even higher.

"Hello, my name is Jasmine Fuentes. I'm 17 years old and I'll be a senior at Central High in Newark, New Jersey, this fall. I was recently inducted into the National Honor Society. My toothbrush is yellow and I'm a Libra."

Abercrombie bent over to tie up his hiking boot. Backwoods Barbie stepped toward him and whispered something. They both smiled.

"Thanks, Jasmine." Jabba was already looking at Emphysema. She stood up before I sat back down.

"I'm Stormi Summers," her raspy voice managed without coughing. "I'm 17 years old and I would have been a senior at Hillcrest High School in Riverside, California, this fall. I was recently inducted into the National Dropout Society. I brush my teeth with Jack Daniels, and I hate puppies."

My face burned. How long would I be stuck hiking with this girl?

She sat back down, and Jabba shuffled the papers on his clipboard like he hadn't even heard her mocking me.

"Well, now you all know a little something about each other. Except for Noah." He looked at the hunchback, who was still staring at the floor, but his ears and cheeks weren't flushed anymore. "I've given you his name. See what you can do to help him feel comfortable telling you the rest."

Jabba looked at Monica, who took the floor and started explaining policies and procedures. My mind reeled, clawing desperately for any thought that could help me get myself out of this situation. As soon as we stepped outside this lodge, all hope of calling my mom would be lost. At this point, I was willing to promise her anything.

And just like that, everyone stood except me. That's it? Orientation was over? It was like a crushing weight held me down in the chair. This was really happening.

Two

It took everything I had to keep from trying to escape through the tiny bathroom window. But really, if I managed to squeeze through it, where would I run? The podunk town with the airport was miles away, and they probably had some kind of system in place that would notify the general population not to pick up hitchhikers. Like the warning signs you see near prisons.

Looking at myself in the mirror, I wondered who had picked out this monstrous combination of earth tone, light-weight fabrics. The khaki cargo pants were identical to the ones Backwoods Barbie had been wearing, but they looked much different hugging my curvy hips than they had on her long, skinny legs.

The metal stall door creaked open behind me, and the gothic chick stepped out. Michaela looked worse in her oversized t-shirt than I did in the fitted V-neck they'd given me, and her pale skin was only a few shades lighter than the grey pants she had on.

She stood next to me and neither of us moved for a few seconds, staring at our reflections while holding the wadded-up bundles of our former selves in front of us.

"Did you notice the drawstrings?" she finally asked, bending over and touching her pants near the knee. I looked down at my own pants. I hadn't noticed any drawstrings. I had been too distracted by the ugly zippers just above the knee. Who in their right mind would choose to zip off their pant legs in that exact spot? I generally didn't wear shorts, but when I did, they had to hit at the widest point on my upper thigh. Waist-to-hip ratio was very important for curvy girls. My mother taught me that you can never truly hide the negative, so it's better to try to accentuate the positive.

Michaela gave the drawstring on the side of her pants a tug, pulling the hem up until they were mid-calf length. I shuddered. The only thing in the world uglier than knee-length shorts: capris.

"Do you hike much?" Michaela's soft voice was tinged with fear.

I shook my head. "I mean, I walk, but not usually on actual dirt and stuff."

She pushed the pant leg back down until it covered the top of her stiff brown boots. "I guess it doesn't matter. We don't have a choice, do we?"

The slight tremor in Michaela's voice conveyed my own emotion exactly. I shook my head and turned away. I couldn't look at her. We were both in a fragile place.

Emphysema, wearing a black t-shirt, army green pants and a funky purple bandana wrapped up in her hair, slammed the other stall open. I blinked hard. I had to hold it together. There was no way I was going to let Emphysema see me cry.

Emphysema dropped her clothes in a heap on the floor between us and reached up to adjust her bandana.

"What?" she barked at Michaela, who was staring with her mouth open slightly.

"Nothing." Michaela turned toward her own reflection in the small space in the mirror Emphysema had left for her.

"If you're thinking something, just say it." Emphysema stepped toward her until Michaela backed away.

"Why don't you back off?" I said, pushing my way between them. "We're all dealing with a lot of pee in our Cheerios, so we don't need to make things worse for each other."

Emphysema scowled. "Let's get something straight right up front: your life will be a lot easier if you stay out of my way." She reached out with her fingertips and gave my collarbone a firm shove.

I grabbed her hand and squeezed, pushing it toward the floor. "Is that supposed to be a threat?"

Michaela took another step back, bumping into the stall. "Stop it!"

"Don't let her intimidate you." I looked over my shoulder. "Just because she looks butch doesn't mean she's tough."

Emphysema yanked her hand away. "You think your designer clothes and your National Honor Society make you better than everyone else, but guess what? You're here. Just like the rest of us."

It felt like she punched me in the gut. My mind was blank. No snappy comeback on the tip of my tongue. Emphysema didn't know me, but what she said unnerved me. *Just like the rest of us.*

No. I wasn't the same as the rest of these people. I didn't deserve to be here. I had just made a mistake. I should be at home, enjoying the first few lazy days of summer vacation.

Emphysema bent down to pick up her clothes, then turned around. She made her way toward the bathroom door, bumping me with her shoulder, then Michaela. With the same shoulder, she pushed against the door and stomped out.

"What a raging…" I started.

"You didn't have to do that," Michaela said, cutting me off. "I can take care of myself."

She was breathing like a freight train, and she didn't make eye contact with me. Wait a second. She was mad at me?

"Wow!" I replied. "I never said you couldn't. It's just that with girls like her, you have to let them know you mean business right away…that you have a spine."

She squinted her eyes slightly, but didn't respond, instead bending over to pick up her own black heap of clothes, piling her striped socks and purple Converse on top.

She blinked a few times. "I guess they're probably waiting on us."

It wasn't exactly an apology or the thank you I thought I deserved for my obvious offer of friendship, but I smiled anyway. She probably wasn't used to girls like me reaching out to her. She walked past me without looking up and followed Emphysema into the holding pen.

I stayed for another few seconds, staring at the mirror. *This isn't going to kill me*, I told myself. Maybe I hadn't survived this exact program before, but I'd been through enough of my mom's programs to know that I could. I smoothed out my long black hair. This would all be over soon, and the pain and humiliation could be tucked away in that special file in my brain reserved for the crap my mom did for "my own good".

That very, very large file.

Pushing open the restroom door, I saw everyone standing near their cubbies. As I approached the group, nobody looked at me. They were all busy checking over the gear in the backpacks we had been given. I hung up my clothes in the cubby and uncinched the top of my pack just so I'd look busy like everyone else. The sight of the tightly rolled sleeping bag at the bottom, and the down jacket didn't make me feel any better. I'd only slept outside a handful of times, and those had all been at a friend's backyard during the summertime.

"When you've double checked your gear, head into the kitchen to pick up your food. Bear canisters are on the counter behind the door." Backwoods Barbie said the words like they were a normal part of everyday life for her. Bears?

Everyone moved toward the double doors in a herd. After my mind unfroze, I fumbled to close my pack with trembling hands.

"Coming?" Abercrombie called across the room after everyone else passed through the kitchen doors.

I nodded, slinging the awkward green pack over one shoulder. He waited for me, holding the door open with a hint of a smirk on his face. Was he laughing at me? I tried to walk faster, but the buckles and straps from the pack kept slapping against my chest.

"Don't worry, you'll be a pro with all this gear in a few days," Abercrombie said.

"What was she saying about bear canisters?"

"You have to keep anything that has a scent inside one." He pointed to the black plastic containers sitting on the counter. "Yosemite has a good-sized black bear population. They're pretty harmless for the most part, but they like to help themselves to any food they can get their hands on." The kid with the hunchback picked one up. The container covered the area from his chin to his waist and was about half as wide as his torso. I moved in slowly and took the last one.

"You'll need around 2000 calories a day," Backwoods Barbie said. "We'll be resupplying in the Valley in a few days. Don't be afraid to try something new."

I watched the kids scatter to the different labeled boxes on the counters around the room. Stroganoff, red beans and rice, and granola were in the boxes closest to me. The calorie count was listed on each box.

"Don't be shy," Abercrombie said, tapping my back softly. "It might not sound good now, but believe me, it will be the best thing you've ever tasted around the fire tonight."

Something about his velvety voice was so soothing. Maybe this wouldn't be so bad if I pretended I was on a first date with him…a very long first date. As he moved away toward the hunchback, his arm brushed against mine. Tingles passed through me.

Quasimodo seemed even more hopelessly lost than I was.

"You should stock up on the garlic mashed potatoes. They're my favorite." Abercrombie's bicep flexed when he picked up a Ziploc bag full of white flakes, then tossed it to Quasimodo. The depressed kid caught it without changing his blank expression.

I turned away. Everyone else had moved quickly through the choices, throwing bags into their black canisters without much thought. It was like the sea of forbidden carbs. Macaroni and cheese, peanut M&Ms—pretty much every type of food I'd been taught to avoid last summer—now became my only choices. I shook my head and reached for a small bag of tortillas and the dehydrated refried beans sitting next to them. *Oh well*, I thought.

A few minutes later, we all stood at the counter with full canisters, passing a pocket knife around to twist the screws that locked the lids in place. Michaela was having trouble closing hers. Were the bears really that smart?

Three

Emphysema sat on the very back row of the 17-passenger van, so I sat in the front. I guessed Abercrombie would be driving with Backwoods Barbie riding shotgun, but I was wrong. They piled in with the rest of us. Abercrombie pushed his way to the back and slid into the seat right next to Emphysema. I couldn't hear what they were saying to each other over the chatter of the two boys, who parked themselves next to Michaela on one of the center benches. She ignored them, staring out the window at the overcast sky. Initially, it looked like Backwoods Barbie might sit next to me, but after a momentary pause, she sat down next to Quasimodo on the second row.

With everyone strapped in and ready to roll, I tried to tell myself I was glad I was sitting in the front all alone. I would have time to think. I wouldn't have to look at anyone. I could see the road from here. But after about ten minutes of listening to the conversations going on behind me, I wished I had placed myself in the center instead of cutting myself off. Emphysema was asking Abercrombie about the mission Jabba had mentioned, and I could only catch snatches of what he was saying over the stupid conversation the boys were having.

"What kind of food did you eat in Argentina?" Emphysema asked. What? Was she trying to interview him for her travel blog or something?

The kid behind me cut off the first part of Abercrombie's answer with a laugh that sounded like a goose in mating season.

"...steak with chimichurri sauce."

"It's hard to believe you used to be a vegetarian," Backwoods Barbie said, jumping into the conversation. "You've changed so much."

"I know," Abercrombie replied. "But when other people are feeding you, you eat whatever you're offered."

Wait. Why were people feeding him? Wouldn't it be the other way around if he was in the Peace Corps?

I folded my arms across my chest and watched the winding road ahead. The clouds parted and the sun broke through, shining down on the trees in patchy blocks. Without being able to feel the chill of the wind rustling through the trees and grass, it looked deceivingly like summer out there. The snow from earlier didn't belong here any more than I did.

"We're almost there," Backwoods Barbie said. "If you keep an eye out your window, you'll see El Capitan and Half Dome."

Everyone turned toward the left side of the van just as we passed an opening in a tunnel designed to give a short view of the rock formations in the distance.

"You guys probably recognize El Capitan from the movies," one of the boys said. "It's a pretty popular filming location."

"You keep saying that, but I seriously can't think of one movie it's been in," the other kid replied.

"Maybe you don't watch enough movies."

"I watch plenty of movies. Name one that's filmed here."

"*The Final Frontier*," he said, just a little too loud.

"*Star Trek 5*? Worst movie ever." Emphysema started laughing uncontrollably until her coughing cut her off. "It makes a lot of sense that you're a Trekkie," she said when she finally got the coughing under control. I turned around in my seat.

"It takes one to know one," the kid said. When he blushed, it turned his already too red complexion even brighter. I shook my head. This kid had serious skin issues. They were the painful looking kind of zits, erupting from the pore in a layered fountain of colors: first red, then white, and sometimes a little black at the tip.

"We're not too far from Yosemite Village," Backwoods Barbie informed us. "If everything goes as planned, we'll get to eat at Curry Village Pizza Patio in a few days."

The way she said it made me nervous. Why wouldn't things go according to plan?

"Good Soaring Raven wants me to drop you at the Bridalveil trailhead," the driver said. "You'll follow the road back this way until it splits off and then you'll stay on Old Wawona road."

"Ah, man!" Abercrombie leaned over Emphysema to look out the window. "Look at that."

We all looked out the windows at the massive rock formations.

"Did it change while you were gone?" Backwoods Barbie asked.

"No," he replied. "It's just like I left it, but I appreciate it even more now."

The driver followed a line of cars into a crowded parking lot. It was getting harder and harder to hold my breakfast down. A young mom and dad crossed in front of the van, hand in hand with a chubby toddler. She was wearing a bright pink bucket hat and brown hiking boots just like the ones I had on. She stopped and pulled her hands away. Reaching up toward her dad, she frantically opened and closed her fingers until he swung her up on his shoulders. She smiled. I looked away.

The group of teenagers standing around the open trunk of a Honda Civic was much easier to look at. They reminded me of my friends back home—attractive and fun. One of the boys threw back his head and laughed at something one of the girls said. I belonged with that group, not this one.

The driver pulled into a parking spot only two spaces away from the teenagers. Great. Now I was going to have to get out and be seen with my little chain gang. How embarrassing. Backwoods Barbie and the boys piled out first, followed by Michaela, who was looking surprisingly resolved. Quasimodo sat staring out the front window like he was in a trance.

"You coming?" Abercrombie asked.

Quasimodo didn't respond. I was kind of glad. He was testing the waters for me. What would they do if I refused to leave the van?

"C'mon, man. It's not as bad as you think. I know it seems like the end of the world right now, but give it a chance. You might end up loving it if you let yourself." Maybe it was because he was closer to our age, or maybe it was just because he was so incredibly good looking, but I almost believed him.

I took a deep breath and scooted over to the edge of the seat, turning around right when I was in front of Quasimodo so I blocked his view of the windshield.

"We have to do this," I said. "Our parents think this is supposed to scare us into submission. We've got to prove them wrong. We can't let them win."

His glossy eyes connected with mine, and he let the corner of his mouth drift up for a second. I saw Abercrombie's grin out of the corner of my eye.

"You people have parents?" Emphysema broke the spell from just outside the van.

Quasimodo hesitated another second, looking down at his shoes before nodding and sliding off the bench.

"After you," Abercrombie said, spreading a Nutella smile across his face.

The driver had already unloaded all of our packs. Was he in that big of a hurry to dump us off?

The other boys already had their packs on. A chilly breeze swept through the parking lot. I shivered, uncinching my pack to search for the down jacket.

"Are you sure you want that?" Backwoods Barbie asked.

I shrugged.

"It's just that once we get going, you'll warm up pretty quick."

Because she was suddenly an expert on my temperature preferences. She was seriously so irritating. I pulled my backpack onto my shoulders over the jacket and turned away from her. Quasimodo was still standing next to the van with his pack at his feet. Everyone else was occupied, so I decided to try my hand at encouraging him again.

"Does yours fit right?" I asked as I approached him, giving the strap on my pack a tug.

"Your belt is too low," the pizza face kid said, pushing past the other boy. "The buckle should be right over your belly button."

I rolled my eyes. Before I could protest, Pizza Face was adjusting the straps on my pack.

"Hmm…I guess you know your hiking gear," I said. "How long have you been here anyway?"

"I am a Boy Scout," he replied, stepping away from me to inspect his handiwork. "Or I guess I was."

"Wow. I've never met a Boy Scout. Is that a real thing?"

He smiled. "A real dumb thing, but yeah."

"Cool. Did they teach you anything about bears?"

"Bears?" He reached around and thumped the plastic canister inside my pack. "You're worried about them?"

"Aren't you?"

"They're just trying to scare us with these," he whispered. "So we won't try to run."

"Well, they're doing a good job," I whispered back.

"Everybody ready?" Abercrombie called. "Remember, this isn't a race." He looked meaningfully at the boys. "Enjoy the journey. There's beauty all around you, but you have to open your eyes and look at it."

He stopped talking and we all stood staring at him. He smiled at Backwoods Barbie. "Anything you want to add?"

"Nope."

Abercrombie nodded and turned unceremoniously toward the road. Pizza Face rejoined his buddy and fell into line right behind Abercrombie. Emphysema followed.

I hesitated. I wasn't ready for this. My pack already felt heavy on my shoulders, but after Abercrombie's little speech, strange excitement was growing inside me. As much as I hated that my mom had sent me here without consulting me, I was curious. Don't get me wrong, I didn't give a crap about the beauty we would find in nature. I just wanted to know what Abercrombie would say next.

Four

I shuffled along behind everyone else, listening to the crunching of gravel under our boots and the whoosh of passing cars. They slowed down as they passed us, probably because the shoulder was narrow and they didn't want to run us down, but I felt each driver's eyes on me.

It wasn't long before the narrow shoulder split off from the main road and Abercrombie led us onto a trail, away from the traffic. Pizza Face and the other kid moved out of single file when the path widened, but everyone else stayed in a line. The trail wasn't very well maintained, with old broken pavement and fallen trees creating obstacles to be stepped over or ducked below. After a while, I heard Abercrombie explaining that the trail was actually the old road that brought visitors into the Yosemite Valley before the new road was built. I looked around at the overgrown trees surrounding us, wondering how many years of neglect it had taken for the road to get this wrecked.

After hiking for only ten or fifteen minutes, I was already getting hot. Our pace was pretty slow, but the gradual uphill climb and the constant bending over and sidestepping, not to mention the weight of the pack, got my heart rate up like I was jogging at level seven on my mom's treadmill. I wanted to strip off the down jacket, but Backwoods Barbie walked behind me. If I took it off, she would know she was right. Instead, I unzipped it, leaving the bottom attached. For a few minutes, the breeze circulating inside my jacket cooled me down a little, but relief was only temporary. The climb continued, and beads of sweat began to roll down my chest, collecting in a pool.

Sandwiched between Backwoods Barbie and me, Quasimodo trudged along much more slowly than everyone else, forcing me to choose whether I would stay with the group ahead, or stay back and continue trying to bring him out of his shell. Emphysema had worked her way to the front of the pack and was making conversation with Abercrombie, which irritated the crap out of me. She was being so fake…acting like a real girl. I decided to try talking to Quasimodo. I had a feeling Abercrombie would notice and be all proud of me again. And if he didn't, maybe Backwoods Barbie would tell him about it later when they were comparing notes.

"So, Noah, what grade are you in?" I asked casually, acting like I totally expected him to answer.

When he didn't say anything, I wasn't surprised, but it was hard not to be annoyed. This was obviously going to take some work. I slowed down until we were walking side by side. He kept his eyes fixed a few feet in front of his shoes.

"I'm guessing you're going to be a sophomore. Am I right?" I was looking straight at him. There was no way he couldn't hear me.

He ignored me.

"You said you're going to be a senior?" Backwoods Barbie jumped in with an obvious rescue attempt.

Would she go away if I ignored her like Quasimodo was ignoring me? Probably not, but she might say something bad about me to Abercrombie.

"That's the plan," I answered.

"Do you know what you want to do after?"

I shrugged. "Not really."

"Hmmm. But you're a good student, you must have some idea what you want to be."

"It doesn't usually matter what I want," I muttered.

It was the kind of comment a counselor or therapist would pounce on, but Backwoods Barbie just raised her eyebrows and waited for me to elaborate. My friends at school sympathized and sided with me whenever I complained about my mom, but Backwoods Barbie basically worked for her. I didn't say anything else and took the next opportunity to catch up to the group when she stopped to wait with Quasimodo for a break.

The old road seemed to wind upward forever. Sometimes I caught glimpses of the new road that followed the same curves and bends, but was far below us. We'd settled into a steady pace now. Abercrombie must have been aware of the growing distance between Quasimodo, Backwoods Barbie, and the rest of us. Whenever we passed a new bend in the road, he would point out something for everyone to look at until they caught up. As soon as Quasimodo came around the corner, he would start moving again. I used one of these mini breaks as an opportunity to take off my jacket and stuff it in the top of my pack with just enough time to get it back on before Backwoods Barbie came into view.

"Look," I heard Abercrombie whisper, pointing up at one of the branches in the leafy canopy. Pizza Face and the other kid glanced up and quickly moved on, but the girls stood still, watching the light blue bird perched there.

"What kind is it? A blue jay?" Emphysema asked like she was some kind of bird expert.

Abercrombie put his finger to his lips and shook his head. The bird hopped from the branch it was on to the one below it, then flew up the hill.

"It was a bluebird. They're a little smaller. You're definitely going to see some jays, though. Keep your eyes open," Abercrombie said.

"So jays are bigger?" I said.

"Yep. The Steller's jays are probably the easiest to spot. Just look for the black mohawk. It really stands out." Abercrombie glanced over his shoulder at me.

All too soon, Quasimodo slunked around the bend. Abercrombie smiled at him, then turned back up the trail.

"Hang on," I said, I hoped not loud enough for Quasimodo to hear. I ran up a little until I was walking beside Abercrombie. "If we're only stopping long enough to let him catch up, when does he get a break?"

"Whenever he says he needs one." Abercrombie didn't stop walking or look at me.

"Right," I said. "I don't think that's going to happen."

"No?"

"Maybe you haven't noticed, but he hasn't said a word to anyone all day."

"I noticed."

I glanced over my shoulder. Quasimodo looked terrible. His feet were dragging. His complexion was pale.

"He doesn't look good," I said. "What happens if somebody needs medical attention while we're out here?"

"We have our first aid kits."

"Seriously?"

"Don't worry."

"Okay, sure. But, I mean, you do have some way to contact civilization just in case, right?"

"Don't worry, Jasmine," he repeated. "You're safe."

Easy for him to say. This wasn't his first time hiking. Or his first time sleeping in the woods. I decided to slow down and drop back, but I kept my eyes on his faded tan and blue backpack, worn at the seams, and covered in iron-on patches, some of which were beginning to peel away.

The clouds had almost completely dissipated now, leaving the blazing sun directly above us, trying to shrivel us into prunes. My water pack was almost empty, and my stomach wasn't much different. I hadn't seen Quasimodo and Backwoods Barbie in a long time, and the group stopped taking breaks to let them catch up.

Finally, we came to a fork in the road. A smaller trail turned left up the steep face of the mountain, another went right, leading down to the road below. When I reached the clearing, Pizza Face and the other kid were already sitting on a flat rock with their bear canisters out and open. Emphysema was unbuckling her pack and Michaela had just taken hers off, placing it on the ground next to the flat rock before wandering away toward the trees up the hill. She had the determined look of someone who needed to see a man about a horse. Maybe she'd already asked about the restroom. I needed it too. I quickly unstrapped myself and took my pack off to follow her.

"Is the little girl's room up the hill?" I asked the boys.

Pizza Face laughed. "It's anywhere you want it to be."

"At least 150 feet from the trail," the other kid added matter-of-factly.

"Seriously?" I froze, my back turned to them.

"Eight!" Michaela shouted in the distance.

I whipped my head around. "Did she just say eight?"

They both laughed. Pizza Face stood up and started walking farther down the trail in the direction we had been going. "Whenever you leave the group to do your business, you call out your number."

"What number?" I asked.

"The one on your cubbie back at the lodge," Pizza Face answered. "Weren't you paying attention at orientation?"

"Why?" I asked.

"To keep us from running," the other kid said.

Calling out a number from the woods while we "did our business." Could they be serious? How soon would it be before we reached a real restroom? I wasn't desperate yet, but I was definitely uncomfortable.

"How?" I asked.

"Were you expecting flush toilets? Or are you used to a bidet?" Emphysema chided.

I wasn't really expecting any of this! I wanted to scream. "I've been using flush toilets since I was 19 months old. Most civilized people do. But maybe you didn't have anyone to show you how."

Emphysema acted like she didn't hear what I'd said, stepping off into the brush herself.

"Twenty-six!" she yelled.

Was I the only one who didn't think it was normal to pee in the wilderness? I mean, how would you physically do it?

I turned back toward the flat rock where Pizza Face's buddy was sitting just as Quasimodo and Backwoods Barbie entered the clearing. He looked terrible, dragging his feet and creating a cloud of dust with every step.

"Looks like a great place to stop for lunch," Backwoods Barbie said, unhitching her pack and easily sliding it down on the flat rock. "What are you serving up?" she asked the kid.

"I'm not that hungry. I've been munching on the Peanut M&M's. I think I'll stick with jerky for now," he replied.

Backwoods Barbie nodded like he needed her approval, then took off into the woods.

Quasimodo and his dust stopped a few yards short of us. He stood next to another, smaller boulder, leaning his pack against it while he took a few deep breaths. It was obvious he was really struggling. What would Abercrombie and Backwoods Barbie do if Quasimodo collapsed right here on the side of the mountain?

Pizza Face wandered back and sat down next to the other kid.

"So what, we just eat whatever we want?" I asked.

Pizza Face squeezed a small packet of peanut butter onto a tortilla. "Enjoy it while it lasts," he said, rolling up the tortilla and shoving a bite into his mouth.

"What's that supposed to mean?" I asked, turning the screw on my own bear canister to open it.

The way he opened his mouth a crack while he was chewing was disgusting. "Just that this trail must get harder," he said, looking up at the cliff walls above.

"What are you talking about? How long have you been out here anyway?"

Pizza Face shrugged. "I'm just telling you that a bear canister full of dehydrated food is going to look great to you in about a week." He swallowed the mouthful of food he had been talking through and took another bite.

"I think they alternate easy hikes with more challenging ones. On the easier hikes, you don't take all of your gear and you forage for food." The other kid interpreted for Mr. No-Social-Skills-Or-Table-Manners.

Forage for food? I knew what it meant, but it was almost as hard to wrap my head around as the whole peeing in the wilderness thing. I opened my canister and looked at the mess of dried meals. I hadn't thought about how we were going to cook all of this. Opening the twisty tie from my tortilla bag, I opted to roll pepperoni inside instead of peanut butter. I had no idea what the calorie difference was, but peanut butter somehow seemed worse.

"You didn't answer my question," I said. "How long have you guys been out here?"

Pizza Face looked down at his last bite of tortilla and shoved it in his mouth. "Almost a month," he said.

A month. As in 30 days? My stomach dropped.

"I got here a week before Runs on Wind," the other kid said. He was the one who had said this was harder than moving sprinklers or something like that during orientation. From Idaho or someplace. His expression told me that he couldn't wait to get back to watering potatoes.

"So is that typical? How much longer do you have?" My life was literally flashing before my eyes. Summer vacation was only two and a half months long. Bonfires. Roller skating at Branch Brook Park. Tanning by Hilary's pool. Would I even get a summer vacation at all? "I mean…when do you get to go home?"

Pizza Face shrugged.

"It's on a case by case basis," Idaho Spud Boy whispered, looking over his shoulder.

"Talking about it doesn't help," Pizza Face said through gritted teeth. "I think it makes them add time on."

"You don't know that," Spud Boy said. The moment of frozen silence that followed was eerie. It was the first time all day that I felt like I shared anything in common with these two freaks. They both wanted to go home as much as I did, but they were both at least a month closer than I was. I looked down at my pepperoni sandwich. There was no way I could eat it now.

"You all look so serious. What are you guys talking about?" Backwoods Barbie asked, crunching through the leaves behind the rock.

"Quiet Wolf was just bragging that he's been here longer than me," Pizza Face said.

"I've taught him everything he knows about the Miwok ways." Spud Boy punched Pizza Face in the arm.

Backwoods Barbie smiled and sat herself down right in the middle of our lunch table. The serious conversation was obviously over. The boys were looking at me like I should jump in and act natural.

"Are you guys going to tell us how you got those cheesy names, or do we have to be initiated with some secret ceremony first?" I asked.

Backwoods Barbie raised her eyebrows. "People will be more likely to trust you with their story if you don't tell them right up front that you think it's going to be cheesy." She smiled like she hadn't just smacked my nose with a newspaper.

I folded my arms and leaned back against a tree trunk. "It's nothing personal against…you guys. I just think the whole Native American thing's a little over the top. I might feel different if somebody around here at least looked like a Native."

"Besides you, you mean?" Pizza Face mumbled.

Everyone glared at Pizza Face, but he didn't seem to notice.

When clueless people had the nerve to guess, they usually thought I was part Mexican, or Filipino. Once I'd gotten Hawaiian, but never Native American. The truth was that I had no clue. My mom had dark blonde hair and pasty white skin. She didn't like to talk about my dad, except to tell me that he was no good and we were better off without him. It wasn't until I was in second grade that I began to wonder what he looked like.

Backwoods Barbie started digging through her canister.

"I'll tell you my story." Pizza Face pushed a greasy strand of hair behind his ear. He was looking at Backwoods Barbie, not me. "It's kind of funny, actually."

Backwoods Barbie smiled. She'd found a bag of trail mix. "Cool. Let's hear it."

A twig snapped behind Pizza Face and we all turned around. Michaela was back. He waited until she sat down before starting his story.

"It was the second day of my spirit walk. I hadn't slept very well that first night. My shelter kept falling apart."

"Ha! That thing was a joke!" Spud Boy laughed.

"Yeah, I didn't have my ninja lashing skills yet, but that's not the point. Anyway, I was really tired, and I'd only had a handful of acorns and some spring onions to eat that morning, which is a *really* bad combination. When I heard we were only three miles from our pick up point, I kind of went nuts. I started running." He suppressed a laugh.

"But he was crop dusting all along the trail," Spud Boy added. Both of them started laughing like it was the funniest thing they had ever experienced.

"And that's how I got my trail name," he concluded as soon as he could breathe. Backwoods Barbie's teeth glowed through her broad smile. Michaela and I looked sideways at each other.

"I suggested 'Breaks Big Wind,' but Good Soaring Raven vetoed it," Spud Boy said, both of them bursting out in obnoxious laughter again.

"You guys are idiots," Emphysema said, coming up behind me from out of nowhere. She shoved her way in between them so she was sitting right next to Backwoods Barbie. Everyone continued eating, but Abercrombie was still MIA and Quasimodo had spread himself out on the rock, using his pack as a pillow, and appeared to be sleeping.

We'd hardly started this party and he was already out of steam. I didn't like being so far from civilization. The thought of being a helicopter ride away from a hospital was terrifying. What if one of us had an accident?

And speaking of accidents, the two liters of water I had already drunk were stretching my bladder beyond reasonable parameters. When Abercrombie finally reappeared,

Backwoods Barbie got up and started cleaning up her trash. Everyone else followed suit except for Quasimodo, who was snoring now. I panicked. If I was going to go, I had to do it now; otherwise, I would have to wait until we stopped again.

I looked left and right. The most heavily wooded area was up the hill, where Michaela had gone.

"Everything alright?" Abercrombie asked. Had he been watching me pace back and forth between my backpack and the tiny path Michaela had taken up the hill?

"Yep. Everything's fine," I said, throwing on a fake smile. "Are we ready to get going?" I glanced over at Quasimodo, now curled up in the fetal position.

"Yeah, we're trying to make it to Bridalveil Creek before sunset." He looked at Quasimodo too, then touched my shoulder for a second. "It's really cool that you're worried about Noah. The next few days are going to be really tough for him." He lifted his hand off my shoulder and I tried not to melt into a puddle on the ground…or create one, for that matter.

Abercrombie moved over to Quasimodo and shook him softly. "Hey, man. We gotta get going. Did you eat some food?"

Quasimodo didn't budge.

"Seriously, dude. You can sleep later. We've still got a couple of miles to go until we get to our first water source. We don't want to start running low in the heat of the afternoon."

His eyes twitched, but he didn't open them. Abercrombie took a step back, then looked over at Backwoods Barbie. She pointed to herself. He nodded, then walked quietly away.

Emphysema and Michaela started strapping their packs on. I guess my decision had been made for me. I would have to suffer until we stopped again. Maybe wherever we were stopping for water in a few miles would have a real bathroom. I slung my pack over my shoulder and fastened the belt, slightly higher this time so it wouldn't press too hard.

"Hey, Noah," Backwoods Barbie's sickly-sweet voice called when she was right next to him. "Everybody is ready. Are you ready to go too?"

He grunted.

"Nobody's going to force you to hike today, Noah. In fact, we're not going to force you to do anything. It's your decision. You can stay here as long as you want, but the tents are going on ahead." She touched his back. "If we stay here, we'll be on our own. And it'll get pretty cold tonight."

He squeezed his eyes even tighter then opened them. They looked more sunken than they had before his nap. I was no doctor, but Quasimodo obviously was in no condition to hike. He needed to be tucked in a soft bed where he could sleep for three or four weeks to get rid of those bags under his eyes.

"We still have a ways to go today, but we can take it at your pace, just like earlier. We'll stop when you need to stop." His eyes clouded over and he closed them, rolling away from Backwoods Barbie. I swallowed a lump in my throat. This was so humiliating for all of us.

She stayed there with her hand on his back. By now, everyone had gathered around Abercrombie, but we were all watching Quasimodo. I don't know about everyone else, but I was mentally willing him to stand up. Every minute he stayed lying there was another minute I would have to hold it. He needed to realize that this wasn't all just about him.

"Is she bluffing, or can we go on without him?" Emphysema asked. She didn't even try to whisper. She could at least pretend to have a little sympathy for him.

"What do you say, Noah?" Abercrombie asked. "Can you give it a go?"

"C'mon, man. You can do this," Pizza Face called, his voice overly full of emotion.

Finally, Quasimodo budged. He took his sweet time and kept his face turned away from us, but eventually he came to his feet and reached for his pack.

"Go ahead and get started," Backwoods Barbie said with a smile. "We'll bring up the rear again."

Even though the first few steps were painful and all I could think about was my aching bladder, I had never been so relieved to start moving in my whole life.

Five

The next three miles were sheer torture. As we moved steadily up the side of the cliff, the forest thickened. The view of the rock formations was mostly blocked out. All I could see were the trail and Pizza Face's dirty hiking boots and pants.

At one point, the trail got so steep that the chatter between Pizza Face and Quiet Wolf stopped completely. It was hard to guess how many miles we had covered, especially since they were straight uphill miles, but it felt like hours since we had stopped for lunch. Where was this water source Abercrombie had promised us? The intermittent rustling of wind through the leaves reminded me of water in a stream, which in turn made me feel like I was holding back Niagara Falls. My throat was completely parched, but I didn't dare take another sip of water for fear the dam would burst.

Finally, Abercrombie stopped at a switchback up ahead. I couldn't see what he was looking down at until I got a little closer. He took off his pack and moved to the side of the trail. A few steps closer and I saw it: a tiny trickle of water that pooled to the side of the trail then crossed over it.

"We're in a drought this year," Abercrombie explained. "This spring was about twice as big the last time I was through here."

I watched with fascination as he stooped down with the plastic water pouch from his backpack and disconnected it from the tube. It took almost a minute to fill up his pouch.

Wait a second, I thought. *This is the water source he was talking about?*

"Go ahead and get your bladders out," Abercrombie said.

I froze. That was a weird way to put it.

Emphysema and Michaela took out their plastic pouches. *Oh, bladders.* The boys had already taken theirs out of their packs and Pizza Face was detaching his tubing.

"Is that water safe to drink?" I asked. Sunlight streamed through the particles floating in Abercrombie's bag when he stood up to seal it.

"Not straight up, but with these filters, any water is drinkable." Abercrombie reconnected his tube and slid the pouch back in his bag.

I let my backpack slide to the ground, relieved temporarily to have the weight off my back. While Pizza Face and Quiet Wolf fought for the trickle of water, I looked around, desperate to find a place where I could be alone. To the left of the narrow trail, trees grew on an angle and there was a steep drop off only a few feet away. The right side of the trail wasn't much better. It would be an uphill climb. In either direction, I wasn't going to find a level surface to stand on. 150 feet from the trail. It didn't matter anymore. My situation was getting desperate.

The boys had finished filling up their pouches and Emphysema pushed her way in next.

"Want me to fill yours?" Pizza Face asked Michaela.

"Can you just show me how to get this thing off?" She gave the blue slide at the top of the pouch a little tug, but it didn't budge.

"It's easy," he said. "You just have to squeeze the button."

After resting my pack against a tree, I stepped over a fallen log on the side of the trail and continued up into the trees until I was sure I was way more than 150 feet away. Michaela and Pizza Face's voices were muffled, and I couldn't see anyone through the forest. I was dancing by now—the pressure almost unbearable. If I didn't find a place to do it soon, it was going to be eternally too late.

"Twelve!" I called out.

My mom had watched every episode of *Naked and Afraid*, but I'd only listened from the other room. Hadn't I heard someone mention squatting somewhere? Oh, oh, oh. Think!

Here goes nothing, I said to myself. Thoughts about how far down I needed to squat vanished as I finally let it all go. It was such a relief I thought I heard heavenly choirs singing above. But just before they finished the verse of the "Hallelujah Chorus", a twig snapped behind me. I jumped, tripping over myself to get my pants back up.

The snap was followed by rustling in the underbrush. Was it an animal, or had someone followed me up here? Whatever it was stood right behind me, staring at me. I could feel it, but I didn't dare turn around. Holding my breath, I waited for it to make another move. The hair on the back of my neck stood on end. Twigs began snapping again. One, two, three, four distinct movements. It was big, and it was walking on all fours.

Bear!

"Help!" The word came hurtling out of my mouth. My feet tumbled over branches and tall weeds, rolling me back down the hill toward the trail.

"What is it?" Abercrombie came around a tree just in time for my face to plow right into his chest. He grunted and stumbled backward. "What happened?" he asked, regaining his footing. "Are you okay?"

The sky spun above me, and jagged waves in my vision made it hard to see straight. "It was…there was…I heard…" I sucked in a deep breath. "Something behind me." I turned around and pointed back up the hill.

Abercrombie pushed his arm protectively between me and whatever was up there. The noise was faint now. Moving away.

"Did you see it?" he whispered.

I shook my head.

"Shhh. It's over there now."

My eyes darted back and forth between Abercrombie and the trees. What was he looking at? Whatever it was must be much smaller than the giant grizzly I had imagined.

Finally, I spotted it. The deer's coat matched the bark of the trees almost exactly. Very clever, Mother Nature.

"I thought it was a bear," I tried to explain, but I was still short of breath. Now that the immediate danger had passed, I became keenly aware that my pants were resting mid-hip, still unbuttoned and unzipped. I hoped my long t-shirt was hiding it, but I couldn't draw attention to the situation by looking down.

Abercrombie and the deer's eyes were locked in an intense stare-down. After a few seconds a smile spread across his lips.

"In Miwok legend, the bear is the deer's sister-in-law," he whispered. The deer blinked right on cue, like it was confirming what Abercrombie said.

I reached slowly for the waistband of my pants and stepped to my right so I wasn't in Abercrombie's full peripheral vision anymore. "Sister-in-law?"

He kept his eyes on the deer, but she turned away and continued grazing on the leaves and grass around her like she didn't even know we were talking about her ancestors.

"We can learn a lot from watching how four-legged animals interact with each other and Mother Earth," Abercrombie continued, still whispering.

I had just managed to zip up my pants. "Huh?"

Laughter erupted from the trail below, startling the deer. She leapt through the long grass, an instant later disappearing into the thick trees. For a second, I thought Pizza Face and Spud Boy were laughing at us, but when I looked down, I realized they were still several yards away, hidden from view.

The magical power the deer had wielded over Abercrombie vanished. He shoved his hands in his pockets and looked at me.

"Most of the two-legged animals I know aren't even trying to live in harmony with their own species, let alone the other animals."

"You mean people?"

"The bears don't want to hurt you," he said. "If we respect their space, they'll respect ours."

He smiled. Sympathy smile? You're an idiot smile? It was hard to tell.

My sun-kissed face already felt hot, but now I was all out blushing. "Are you going to tell everyone what happened?" I whispered. "Did they hear me call for help?"

"It's not a big deal." Abercrombie smiled. "It's okay to ask for help."

"But it's embarrassing. Especially when you don't really need it."

"Never be embarrassed to ask for help. Even when the dangers are only in your mind." He was talking in the smooth voice again and every trace of *you're an idiot* had disappeared from his expression. "We need each other. That's why we're all here."

I nodded. *We need each other.* That sounded nice. Abercrombie started walking toward the trail.

"Okay, we all need each other, but was that a 'yes' or 'no' on telling everyone?"

"You're the keeper of your own legends. Tell them whatever you want."

"Thanks," I said, just as we stepped onto the path.

Emphysema coughed when she saw us. "What happened? Did you fall in? We thought we heard you call for help."

"Me?" I asked, giving her the stink eye. "You must have been hearing things."

She and the boys already had their packs on. Michaela looked like she was struggling to reconnect the tubes. Abercrombie left me to go help her.

"It wasn't you?" Emphysema continued. "I could have sworn I heard your prissy voice."

I ignored her and opened my pack. Figuring out how to disconnect my water pouch from the tubes wasn't as hard as I thought it would be. While I filled the bag in the tiny spring, my eyes drifted down the trail. Where were Quasimodo and Backwoods Barbie?

Abercrombie didn't seem concerned. He'd finished putting Michaela's water in her bag and was now strapping himself back into his pack.

"Almost ready?" he asked as I struggled to squeeze my pouch back in my bag.

"What about…Noah?" I asked.

"They're coming," he said. "We need to keep moving if we're going to make it before dark."

"How do you know they're coming? We haven't seen them for hours."

Abercrombie didn't respond. He stood looking over my head down the trail with ultra-focused eyes. I turned and tried to see what he was looking at.

"See?" he asked.

I shook my head.

He nodded toward the last switchback below. Finally, I spotted the red top of Quasimodo's pack.

"Let's get going," Abercrombie called to the others.

"But shouldn't we wait to make sure they've at least seen us?"

"Monica knows the trail," he said, already walking away.

I finished closing my pack and stood up. My legs felt like Jell-O. How many more miles did we have to go today? Admittedly, part of the reason I wanted to wait was so my legs could solidify again, but seriously, didn't anyone want to see how Quasimodo was doing?

Nope. Abercrombie was off. Falling in line behind the others, I took up the rear again. Quasimodo still hadn't made it to the spring by the time it disappeared from my view.

The climb continued. My legs ached, my back hurt, and my eyes and nose were full of dust. Completely zoning out, I tried to think about something, anything less painful than this…like having my wisdom teeth ripped out of my head during Christmas break, or watching my middle school crush make out with my ex-best friend in the hallway at school.

Six

After a while the forest thinned out significantly. The climb steepened. The path became rocky. Suddenly, Pizza Face and Spud Boy took off like someone had lit them on fire. They wove their way through the low gnarled bushes, disappearing over the crest of the hill. Abercrombie and Emphysema were only a few paces behind. When I caught up to Michaela, I saw the rusty sign that had apparently prompted the 40-yard dash.

Stanford Point was at the top of this hill. Crocker Point was less than a mile away. The sign listed Dewey, Taft, and Glacier points, but Bridalveil Creek wasn't even on it.

"I wish this was where we were stopping for the night," Michaela said.

"Come check this out," Spud Boy called back down to us. "You're going to wish you had a camera."

Michaela raised her eyebrows at me and sighed, then we both trudged up the hill. The boys were standing uncomfortably close to a huge drop off. The late afternoon sun cast dramatic shadows over the jagged rock walls we had seen from below in the van earlier in the day. *Stanford Point, elevation 6659*, another rusty sign informed me.

"This is just a quick pit-stop," Abercrombie said. "We've got to keep moving."

Emphysema dropped her arms to her sides. "I thought you wanted us to stop and look at the beauty around us."

"Absolutely. Just don't look too long. You'll miss the most spectacular sunset you've ever seen."

"How much farther to camp?" Michaela asked.

Abercrombie looked back down the trail. "We might have to change plans. It's getting late, and we're slower than I thought we'd be."

"You mean Noah's slowing us down?" Emphysema said. "Why don't they group us according to ability?"

Abercrombie didn't reply. I wanted him to give her the same speech he'd given me about how we all needed each other. I wanted him to say something to shut her up for good about Noah, but he didn't. He didn't even look like he wanted to.

"Let's get going. It's less than a mile to Crocker Point but we're losing daylight. We don't want to set up camp in the dark."

Glancing down the trail again and hoping to see some sign of Noah and Backwoods Barbie, I followed Abercrombie into the woods. Emphysema tried to pass me, but the trail became narrow and I wouldn't let her. Pizza Face and Quiet Wolf fell into line, still full of energy, and Michaela walked several paces behind.

My legs burned out after only a short time. I had to rest. Everyone passed me except Michaela. She was struggling too.

She sat down on a big boulder to the side of the path. I continued up the trail a few feet, then found a fallen log to sit on.

"You don't have to wait for me," she called.

"I know," I said.

"You don't want to miss the sunset."

She sounded determined to release me from any obligation to keep her company. I rolled my eyes. She must not have noticed that I hadn't spoken a word to her since we left Crocker Point.

I wasn't ready to move yet, and I didn't really care about seeing the sunset, but I didn't want Michaela to think I was waiting around for her. I swiveled on the log and prepared myself to try to get up.

Taking a deep breath, I rocked forward, but before I could lift myself onto my feet, I heard a distinct sniff come from Michaela.

"I can't do this," she muttered. Her voice cracked in the most disturbing way. Then she sniffed again. Wait. Was she full-on crying? No. She couldn't. I couldn't let her. Other people crying made me cry.

I took a deep breath and looked up at the sky. It was starting to turn all kinds of crazy shades of orange and pink.

"C'mon," I said, standing up. "You've gotta see the sunset too. We all need each other…" or whatever. My voice trailed off at the end. It didn't sound so poetic when I said it. "You've gotta get out of your own head. Go to your happy place."

"What happy place?" she croaked. "They sent me here to get rid of me…because…they don't want to deal with me anymore."

The chain reaction of sobs and sniffs made me wish I'd just walked away.

"How can they say they love you…then send you into the wilderness alone?"

What would Abercrombie say? Looking desperately up the trail, I considered yelling for help. Would he hear me?

"How's this…how's hiking supposed to fix…me?"

I bit my lip when it began to tremble.

She was right. Programs don't fix people. They don't make parents love you more. I would know. There was no program that would magically turn me into what my mom wanted me to be.

I threw my pack down then marched toward Michaela and sat next to her on the rock.

"Whatever, Michaela," I said loud enough for Abercrombie, or Backwoods Barbie, or Sasquatch to hear if they were listening. "Go ahead and cry! The sign said we're at 6000 feet, but I'd say it doesn't get any lower than this. This is by far the worst thing a parent could do to a child." I took another breath. "Except for maybe eating their young…that might actually be worse."

Michaela's back stopped shaking for a second, and then she let out three short breaths. Her face was still smashed into her backpack, but after a pause, then another spurt of short breaths, I realized she was laughing instead of crying. Not in a normal, "very funny, ha ha," way. She was laughing in a desperate, "I can't breathe," kind of way. I started laughing maniacally too. I couldn't help it. Crazy was as contagious as misery.

When the moment passed, Michaela was quiet, except for the occasional sniff. "I think I have about ten blisters, but I've been too afraid to take my boots off to look."

"Seriously?" I said, slapping her back softly. "You know Abercrombie has been dying to pull out his first aid kit all day. Why didn't you tell him?"

"Abercrombie?"

Oops. I looked around to make sure he wasn't hiding in the bushes. "I mean Bryce. But don't you think he looks like an Abercrombie model?"

Michaela sat up and glared at me through smeared eyeliner that would scare the crap out of KISS. "Please don't tell me you shop there."

The truth was I'd never actually bought anything there other than the obligatory A&F sweatshirt, but it wasn't because I hadn't tried. They just didn't cater to the curvy crowd. I could live a long and happy life inside that store, where everyone is the perfect size, with washboard abs, wind tossed hair, and really white teeth—not to mention the earthy scent that was even more enticing than Auntie Anne's pretzels.

"You do, don't you?" she accused when I took too long to answer.

"I mean, you make it sound like one of the deadly sins or something."

She was serious, wiping her face with the sleeve of her t-shirt. "It kind of says a lot about a person."

Unbelievable. Here we were, sharing a Hallmark Hall of Fame moment, and now she was going to unfriend me because I had a weakness for faded denim with perfectly placed rips.

"I'm not trying to hurt your feelings," she continued, "but Abercrombie is kind of the epitome of capitalist materialism."

I shrugged. "I don't see how it's worse than any other store in the mall."

"Hmm," Michaela said. "You wouldn't."

What was that supposed to mean? I looked away. The sun was growing larger by the second, partially shrouded by wispy, golden clouds. "We'd better get going."

"I really don't think I'm going to make it by sunset," Michaela said. "You should go ahead. I'll rest here until Monica and Noah come."

"You don't know how far behind they are. You're going to be sitting here alone in the dark."

"You said yourself it's not that far. If it gets too dark before they come, I'll find you guys."

Fine. I couldn't really take any more drama for the day. I'd done my best to drag Michaela up the hill with me, but none of my capitalist, materialistic tricks were going to work on her.

"Okay," I said, slowly raising myself from the stump. "If you're sure."

"Go ahead," she urged. "I'll be fine."

I shrugged, hefting my backpack onto my shoulders. The sleeping bag and dehydrated food felt like they had turned to dumbbells and a bowling ball. Something in the pit of my stomach told me that leaving Michaela alone was not going to win me brownie points, but then again, hadn't Abercrombie been leaving people behind all day? Maybe it was the Miwok way.

It was only another five minutes of moderately paced hiking before I reached the vista. Everyone had dropped their packs near a hollow log and stood on a narrow, natural bridge that jutted out over the canyon below. With the sky lit up behind them in cotton candy blues, yellows, and pinks, the crew looked surprisingly beautiful. A light breeze tousled Spud Boy's hair, and the golden sun rays brought out his farmer's tan. Emphysema's complexion looked warm instead of dull. And Pizza Face...well, his back was turned to me, which was an improvement anyway, but with his pack off and his shoulders pulled back, taking in a deep breath of the mountain air, he looked almost like a real man, instead of the man child he actually was.

And then I saw Abercrombie. Perched on the very tip of the overhang, mostly in the shadow of the boulder behind him, he drank in the view with so much rapture I could feel it from fifty yards away.

I didn't move any closer. Staying where I was in the bushes just below the overhang, I watched the sun turn blood red then slip below the horizon.

"Jasmine!" Pizza Face spotted me first, just after the light show ended. "Did you see it? Where's Michaela?"

Nodding my head to answer the first question, I slowly unbuckled my pack and let it slide down to my feet. Emphysema started coughing and sat on one of the logs near a rock fire ring. Pizza Face came at me like a freight train.

"Did Michaela see it too?" he asked when he was a bit closer.

"She's a little ways back. Her feet were hurting, and she decided to wait for Noah and Monica."

"You left her alone?"

I shrugged. "She told me to."

He raised his eyebrows and looked at me out of the corner of his eyes. *What?* I wanted to yell. If I wasn't allowed to enjoy the sunset because I had to babysit Emo Pixie Chick, somebody should have spelled out the rules clearly.

Or maybe Backwoods Barbie had during her orientation. What else had I missed?

Seven

"Hey, Firewalker!" Pizza Face called back over his shoulder. "Michaela's having trouble. I'm going to go carry her pack the rest of the way up."

Abercrombie smiled and threw him a thumbs up. "We'll get things set up so we can eat some dinner. Everybody's got to be starving."

Pizza Face started down the trail with his head still turned toward the others, bumping my arm when he passed me.

Spud Boy and Emphysema both looked pretty comfortable. I mean, for being outside in the dark. On the edge of a cliff. By the time I wandered up the hill, they were gathered around the fire ring. Spud Boy was demonstrating how to use a little wooden bow against a plank of wood to start the fire. Abercrombie looked on but didn't interrupt.

"You've gotta protect it from the wind. Get it going as fast as you can," Spud Boy said. Emphysema worked hard, pulling the drill against the stick. Pretty soon, smoke began to rise up from the plank. "You got it!" He pushed Emphysema aside while he dropped a little glowing spark into a small nest of twigs and branches. "Then you want to give it some air," he said, blowing on it softly.

After just a few seconds, the spark ignited the nest. Spud Boy looked pleased with himself.

Emphysema clapped her hands. "Right on! That was so easy."

"You had a good teacher." Abercrombie slapped Spud Boy on the back.

Within minutes, they had a roaring fire going. Abercrombie went down to the packs and came back with a few small pots and his bear canister.

"Where do you want us to set up the tents?" Spud Boy asked.

"There's a nice flat area down there between the big trees," Abercrombie said.

"Okay, cool," Spud Boy said. With that, he and Emphysema marched down to start setting up tents, while I stood awkwardly between the fire and the cliff. My eyes were on the horizon, but I glanced at Abercrombie now and then. I guess I was waiting for someone to tell me what I was supposed to do. I had no idea how to set up a tent, and I didn't really cook anything outside of reheating in the microwave. All I really wanted to do was sit down.

Finally, after Abercrombie finished filling up the pots with water and rigging them on a rock near the flames, he acknowledged me. "Is this your first time camping?"

"No," I answered. I'd been "camping" before. But the KOA in Cape May had cabins and flush toilets. Still, it wasn't like I'd never left the city. "Why?"

"Just wondered. I've never been to New Jersey. Isn't Newark right by New York City?"

I stepped a little closer to the fire. "Yeah. Just over the bridge. My mom actually works in Manhattan."

"Nice," he said, poking the logs in the fire with a stick. "What does she do?"

"She's in advertising," I said. "The youngest VP at Sigmond and Bray."

One of the logs in the fire snapped and sparks flew above the flames. I stepped back.

"What about your dad?" Abercrombie asked.

"It's hard to explain what he does," I said.

"Try me." He looked up from the fire with that smile of his.

Great. Now what was I supposed to say? Most people accepted that answer and never asked about him again. I mean, who really cares what your parents do? It's just polite small talk. I stepped over to one of the gnarled logs and sat down. Was there any point in being vague with him? It was Abercrombie's job to discover my issues, but would my mom have already disclosed all of her dirty laundry to them? She didn't usually talk about it.

"Firewalker!" Pizza Face's cry from the trail below sounded urgent. *Oh, good.*

Abercrombie stood up and searched the shadows. He dropped his stick in the fire and turned on his headlamp. "I'll be back. Keep an eye on the water. Take it off the flames when it starts boiling."

I nodded, taking his position as soon as he started down the hill. It was too dark to see much, but Pizza Face had definitely made it back with Michaela. They were moving slowly, and she was limping, using Pizza Face as a crutch. Spud Boy and Emphysema dropped what they were doing and went to help. A huge knot grew in my stomach. I should have stayed with her. I'd apparently broken another one of the rules I hadn't paid attention to during orientation, and now it looked like I was totally selfish and heartless. She wasn't going to tell anyone about the encouragement I'd given her, or my offer to stay.

So I just sat there. Watching the pots. Which were in no immediate danger of boiling.

Trying to distinguish the voices below, I listened for my name. A few minutes of nervous tension passed, then I heard laughter. Whatever had happened couldn't be too serious. It would be nice if someone thought to bring the conversation up here. Where I could be part of it.

Several more minutes passed. The wind was getting a bit chilly. I should have grabbed my jacket. Maybe I could run down the hill and get it. Would the water boil before I got back? More laughter rang out from below. What were they talking about?

I picked up Abercrombie's stick and poked the pot. C'mon. Boil already. I blew out a long breath.

Finally, I heard the crunch of rocks as someone came up the hill. The water was steaming now, but the tiny bubbles at the bottom of the pot hadn't started rolling to the top.

"Hey, how's the water coming?" It was Spud Boy.

"Almost ready, but not yet," I responded, feeling unreasonably happy to have a human voice addressing me.

"Cool. Firewalker told me to help you take the pots off when they boil."

Because he didn't think I was capable of doing it myself? *Ouch.*

He sat his bear canister on the ground next to me and took a pocket knife out to open it.

"I think we should all have beef stew tonight since we don't have a place to wash dishes."

I shrugged. While I didn't care what we ate, his mention of water made me nervous. "There's no water around here?"

"No. That's why Firewalker wanted to get to Bridalveil. We still have a couple of miles to go."

"So we only have the water in our packs?"

Spud Boy nodded. "But don't worry. We're all at least half full, and Firewalker has two extra liters in his bag."

Where did Abercrombie have room for everything in his bag?

A few minutes later, the others joined us—first Emphysema, followed by Michaela, who was supported on both sides by Abercrombie and Pizza Face. She had been doctored up with moleskin on one foot and an Ace bandage wrapped around the other. Her face had been wiped clean of all eyeliner and even though her eyes were still red and puffy, she looked much better.

Spud Boy took the boiling water off the fire and dumped a bag of dried food into it.

"I should have come with Jasmine, but I thought Monica and Noah would catch up sooner. Sorry I worried everyone."

"Stop apologizing," said Abercrombie. "It's not your fault."

Pizza Face glanced at me. I turned away.

Everyone settled in around the fire and waited for the food to cook, or hydrate, or whatever it was doing in the covered pots. Spud Boy and Pizza Face talked incessantly about nothing important while the girls all sat staring at the flames. Finally, Spud Boy lifted the lid off of the pot and declared the stew ready to eat.

Abercrombie passed around large plastic utensils with forks on one end and spoons on the other. Then we each got a plastic mug. Spud boy filled up our cups with the steaming stew.

"Even though we didn't find this food on the trail, I highly recommend taking a moment to thank the Great Creator for giving it to us," Abercrombie said. Spud Boy and Pizza Face bowed their heads and closed their eyes while Michaela, Emphysema and I all stared at each other. Emphysema had already lifted a spoonful of stew but hadn't put it in her open mouth yet. After a second, I closed my eyes, just like Abercrombie, and tried to imagine what this Great Creator would look like if there really was one. Was he talking about the Creator in the Christian God sense, or was he referring to Miwok folklore?

I waited until I heard movement then opened my eyes. Abercrombie was already eating a bite.

Everyone ate the first cup of stew in silence. With wind rustling through the trees and the crackling of the fire as a soundtrack, the first stars made an appearance in the sky. By the end of my second cup, the sky was filled with twinkling light. More stars than I knew existed. Tiny ones nestled between the brighter constellations I recognized.

When the boys finished eating, they immediately picked up one of the lame threads of conversation they had been carrying on earlier in the day.

"Toilet papering doesn't really count," Spud Boy said. "I mean real pranks this time. What's the closest you ever got to getting caught?"

Pizza Face glanced at Abercrombie to gage his reaction to this line of conversation before proceeding. Abercrombie smiled.

"My brothers and I egged our principal's house. We were almost back to our car when we heard the sirens outside the gated community. We ended up leaving the car and jumping fences until we got back to our neighborhood. It was so dark my brother fell into a pool. Try explaining *that* to your parents."

"Not bad," said Spud Boy.

"What about you?" Pizza Face laughed, sounding a little too excited to hear what mischief Spud Boy had been guilty of in Idaho.

"Heard of cow tipping?" He looked around at all of us.

"I thought that was an urban legend," Emphysema said.

"Have you ever even seen a real cow, or do you think they are urban legends too?" Spud Boy came back all defensive.

She rolled her eyes. "You're saying you've tipped a cow? How? They just stand there and let you do it?"

"They aren't awake," Spud Boy said, like it was so obvious. "You do it at night."

"Doesn't it hurt the cows?" Michaela said. "What did they ever do to you?"

"Most of the time they don't even fall over. I've watched so many of my buddies plow into a cow and they're the ones who end up on the ground. In fact, I've only actually seen two cows go over."

"Is this like a weekend ritual or something? How often do you go?" You could almost hear the wheels spinning in Pizza Face's head. Maybe he should go to college in Idaho where a whole new world of pranks existed.

"No. Nothing like that. I've only been a few times…and my tipping days are done."

"Why? What happened? Did you get caught?" asked Pizza Face.

"No. Worse than that. The one time I actually tipped one, my friend James and I did it together. It wasn't a huge cow, and instead of falling on its side, somehow it ended up upside down in an irrigation ditch. The farmer had to come in with a tractor to get it out."

"Was it okay?" Michaela asked.

"It drowned."

Emphysema started laughing. "That's too weird to be a lie."

"That is the most disturbing thing I've ever heard." Michaela looked like she was going to be sick.

I wrapped my arms around myself as the breeze whistled past. *Surreal.* Was I really sitting on the edge of a cliff listening to some random teenager confess to bovine homicide?

"Are we going to have a talking circle tonight?" Pizza Face asked Abercrombie, who was staring into the fire with a faraway expression.

"We'll see. Maybe when everyone gets here if it's not too late," he said, looking over his shoulder toward the trail.

How far behind were they? We hadn't seen them since we had filled up our water at the spring. That was hours ago.

"What's a talking circle?" Emphysema asked.

"It's pretty cool," Pizza Face said. "The Miwok do it to solve their communication problems. Everyone sits around the fire, and there's a special stick you hold. Whoever has the stick has the floor. Nobody can interrupt them."

"Except if you want to agree or disagree. But you are limited to noise you can make through your nose." Spud Boy demonstrated by grunting softly. "Runs on Wind loves the talking circle because he can go on and on forever and nobody can interrupt him."

Abercrombie laughed. "Not entirely true. In Miwok culture, if somebody goes on too long, they cough to let the person know."

"Group therapy," Emphysema said. It looked like the words left a bitter taste in her mouth.

They did something similar at fat camp, only you didn't have to hold a stick to talk. Everyone just sat around sharing their feelings, jumping in whenever they felt like it to "support" each other.

They were crazy if they thought I was going to talk about my problems here. The only person I trusted with my secrets was Hilary, and she probably had no idea where I was right now. I blinked hard, rubbing my eyes, then pretended to fan the smoke away.

"We should probably rinse these out before they harden," said Spud Boy, tapping his mug against a rock.

"Good thought," Abercrombie said. "Remember to conserve. We should have plenty if we get going early in the morning, but we don't want to waste."

I was getting really chilly by now, and I wanted to go get my jacket from my pack, but the headlamp they had given me was in my bag, too. There was no way I was going to go down the hill by myself in the dark to get it, and I didn't want to ask someone to go with me. I decided my only option was to tough it out until someone decided to go down, then follow them.

My opportunity came after a few more minutes of staring alternately between the stars and the fire. The moon was just starting to rise. It wasn't full, but magnified by its position on the horizon, it added an eerie glow to the woods around us.

"I think I'm ready to crash," said Emphysema. "Any special bedtime procedures? Ankle bracelets or something?"

Abercrombie smiled and shook his head. "Nope. Sleep tight. Good walking today."

"Not to mention my fire building," she said. "I guess I'm kind of a natural at this wilderness stuff."

"Are you sure this is your first walking?" Pizza Face asked.

"Hey, if you're good, you're good." Emphysema stood up and dusted off the seat of her pants.

"I think I'll head to bed too," I said.

Nobody looked at me or commented. Emphysema was already stepping away from the fire ring so I didn't have much time to analyze the silence, but it stung a bit. Where was Abercrombie's praise and encouragement of my walking? Or hadn't I earned any because I'd left Michaela behind?

"Goodnight, Jasmine," he said when I was a few steps away from the fire.

"'Night," I said, barely looking back as I followed Emphysema down the hill.

Emphysema and Spud Boy had set up two teepee-style tents about twenty feet apart. After kicking her shoes off outside the door of one of them, Emphysema turned, blinding me with her light.

"I tried to put my stuff with Quiet Wolf and Runs on Wind, but apparently the tents aren't coed. I'm stuck with you." She and her light disappeared inside the tent. "You'd better not snore," she added.

With only the tinted glow of her light from the tent, I was left to fish through my pack for my headlamp in the dark.

For as heavy as it felt, my pack was surprisingly empty. Inside a gallon size Ziploc bag, I found a few basic hygiene supplies: a small bag of moist towelettes, which must have been what Michaela had used to remove her makeup, a tiny travel toothbrush, a strange brand of biodegradable toothpaste I'd never heard of, and a tiny roll of camping toilet paper. I took a moment and washed my face, neck and arms with the wipes, then brushed my teeth. I wanted to use the toilet paper too, but there was no way I was going one hundred fifty feet from the trail or the camp in the dark. It would have to wait until morning.

With my sleeping bag in hand, I was about to follow Emphysema into the tent when I heard the shuffling of feet against rocks in the distance. I listened for a few seconds as the sound came closer. They were moving painfully slowly.

"See the fire up there, Noah?" Backwoods Barbie said. "You made it."

The movement stopped.

"Are you hungry? We'll get some hot dinner. Firewalker has everything set up and ready for us," she continued.

He didn't reply. Man, it would suck to be Backwoods Barbie. I couldn't imagine spending all day with Quasimodo.

Eventually, the shuffling started up again and two headlamps came into view, bobbing up and down and blinking in and out like fireflies as they passed the trees. After a minute, Noah and Backwoods Barbie reached the point where we had all dropped our packs and Abercrombie came striding down to meet them.

"Hey!" he called. "So glad you guys made it. I was starting to get a little worried."

I kind of wanted to show Noah I cared that he'd made it, even if he wouldn't acknowledge me. But after taking a few steps toward the trail, I stopped myself. *Wait, would it seem weird to come back after saying goodnight to everyone?*

"It was a tough day, but Noah really pushed through," Backwoods Barbie said.

"Good job, man! I'm really proud of you." Abercrombie gave Quasimodo a solid pat on the back. Even in the dim light, I could see Quasimodo's hunchback straighten out and his whole body stiffen.

"I think what we both need now is some hot food and a good night's sleep," Backwoods Barbie said.

"Totally," said Abercrombie. "I had Quiet Wolf start some water boiling as soon as I saw your lights. It should be ready any minute." This was addressed to Quasimodo more than Backwoods Barbie, but he still just stood there, frozen.

"Go ahead and go on up, Noah. I'm going to get my stuff set up a bit before I join you." I didn't blame Backwoods Barbie for wanting to be alone for a few minutes after the day she'd had.

Now seemed like the best time to bust into the conversation, so I took the necessary fifteen or so steps to bring me from the tent to the trail. I tucked the sleeping bag I was still holding under my arm.

"Hey, Noah!" I said, like I'd just realized he was there. I wasn't sure how to follow up my greeting. *Glad you made it*, or anything like that would sound patronizing and lame.

Naturally, Quasimodo left me hanging.

"Hi, Jasmine," Backwoods Barbie said. "Looks like you guys got the tents all set up." She nodded over my head. "I can't wait to crash."

Quasimodo took a step away from Abercrombie.

"Yeah, I think we should all get to bed early. We've got another long day tomorrow," said Abercrombie.

"You still want to try to make it all the way down?" Backwoods Barbie asked.

"We'll see how we do," Abercrombie replied. "We'll make it as far as the bridge and see where we're at."

Could they shut up about tomorrow already? The thought of hiking again was killing me, and I'd been resting for at least an hour. How was Quasimodo supposed to feel?

Quasimodo started walking away, but not toward the fire. Instead, he crunched through the underbrush into the woods. We all stood there, watching him. What was there to say? My best guess was that he was off to answer nature's call, but it would have been nice if he had at least said something so we'd know he wasn't going to go find the nearest cliff to jump off.

"Go ahead and do what you need to do," Abercrombie said softly to Backwoods Barbie. "I'll radio backup and let them know you're here, and I've got the night shift."

Backwoods Barbie responded by throwing her arms around Abercrombie's neck, letting her cheek rest against his chest for a second. "Thanks, Bryce. You have no idea how glad I am you're back."

Well, that's not awkward, I thought. *Hello, I'm standing right here.* I tried to step back quietly, but Mother Earth had placed a huge rock just a few inches behind me. My heel smacked into it and I almost tumbled to the ground, but somehow caught myself through a series of clumsy steps while my sleeping bag went flying through the air, landing at Backwoods Barbie's feet.

"Jasmine?" Abercrombie said.

"Are you okay?" Backwoods Barbie asked.

"I'm fine," I said, my face burning from…embarrassment. *Yeah. We'll go with that.* It wouldn't make sense for a teenage girl in a program full of misfits to be jealous that two normal people were allowed to like each other. "We have rocks in New Jersey," I said. "But we also have street lights."

Backwoods Barbie laughed. "True. You have to be extra careful out here at night. Were you headed to bed?"

"Yeah. I'm really tired," I said, trying to keep the emotion out of my voice.

"Would you mind throwing my sleeping bag out for me?" she asked, already reaching into her pack for it.

I shrugged, but no one could see it in the dark. Again, it didn't matter what I wanted. Tonight I would sleep in a teepee, sandwiched between a bully who hated me for no reason, and the girl who was everything my mom wanted me to be. Not to mention Michaela, who thought I was the spawn of Satan. Where was she going to sleep? The tent didn't look big enough for the four of us.

Backwoods Barbie handed both of the sleeping bags to me. "Sleep tight," she said.

I took them and made my way back to the tent. Abercrombie had gone the other direction toward the boys' tent. In the distance, I heard him talking to someone on a crackling radio. Well, that was a relief. He could have told me they had a way to get a hold of civilization earlier when I was so worried about medical emergencies.

Spread out on a bed of twigs and pine needles, my exhausted body couldn't get comfortable enough to fall asleep. After a while, I stopped trying. Emphysema's buzzsaw snoring and the muffled conversations at the campfire competed against the noise in my brain.

Finally, the others came to bed. With the friendly noise of human voices gone and the flashlights extinguished, the chilly night air was alive with unfamiliar sounds. Leaves rustling in the wind. An owl hooting in the distance. And insects. They seemed to be everywhere. Buzzing, chirping, I could even hear them crawling on the outside of the tent. Or at least I hoped they were outside.

Eventually, I must have drifted off, but my senses woke me sometime later. The leaves and brush rustled near the tent, but the wind wasn't blowing anymore. The hair on the back of my neck stood on end. Over the sound of Emphysema's congested breathing, I heard it again. The bushes moved and twigs and leaves snapped and crackled. Was somebody walking around outside the tent?

I listened more intently, but it was hard to hear over my thumping heart. *Maybe it's just another deer.* I pinched my eyes closed, hoping whatever it was would go away. But the noise came closer. It was just outside the tent now.

I held my breath. It was sniffing around. Did deer sniff?

∞ ∞ ∞

The soft light of dawn barely touched the tent when nature began screaming in my ears. Backwoods Barbie and the other girls were entombed inside their mummy bags, Emphysema still wheezing like a ninety-year-old. I carefully unzipped myself, letting the frigid air in. Stepping over them awkwardly, I tried to unzip all of the screens and flaps that kept me from escaping without waking anyone up. When I finally did, I wasn't taking time to admire the wispy golden clouds on the horizon. I made a beeline for the camping toilet paper and a secluded spot in the woods.

Every part of my body ached. My quads were the worst, but my back and shoulders also hurt from carrying the pack and sleeping on the hard ground. Each individual toe felt raw, and when I took my sock off to investigate, I found a small blister between my baby toe and the one next to it.

I hobbled toward the tents but realized I didn't want to crawl back into my sleeping bag when I reached the door. It would hurt too much to bend down, and it probably wouldn't be long before I'd have to hoist myself up again. Instead, I moved like a sloth up the hill.

The chilly morning air was surprisingly invigorating, and the sun painted the sky behind the cliffs in the distance soft shades of pink and purple. Birds chirped in the distance. I took a deep breath and pushed my stiff muscles up the last few steps. It was nice to be up here alone. A nice break from feeling awkward.

When I reached the top of the hill, I walked slowly toward the sheer drop off. A safe distance from the edge of the precipice, I found a smooth, flat rock to sit on. The clouds on the horizon turned slowly from deep purple to bright pink and orange, until finally, the shape of the sun pushed its way above them, instantly warming my face with its rays.

67

As the sun moved higher in the sky, the chorus of birds chirping grew louder. Based on what Abercrombie and Backwoods Barbie had said, a little village was waiting for us at the bottom of these cliffs, but I couldn't see any signs of civilization from here. While I scanned the valley, something caught my eye from the overhang where we'd watched the sunset the night before. With the blinding sun right in line with it, I couldn't tell what it was. It wasn't moving, but it looked human. Or maybe half human, because it wasn't tall enough to be a full-sized person. I brought my hand up to shade my eyes.

Okay. Definitely human. It was Abercrombie. Perched only a few feet from the edge of the cliff, he was kneeling on the rocks, with his arms folded just above his waist. I held my breath, waiting for him to move. Had he seen me?

Seconds turned into minutes. What was he doing there? His chin was touching his chest. Was he examining the rock, or practicing some ancient Native American yoga or something? Fully conscious that all he had to do was look over his shoulder to see me staring at him, I continued to gawk. How long had he been out there like that?

Finally, he uncrossed his arms and slowly stood up. I spun to the right so my back was facing him, which made no sense because now it looked like I had been sitting here on the edge of the cliff, enjoying the view of a weird, prickly bush.

"Morning," he called when he saw me.

I pretended to look around like I didn't know where the voice had come from. "Oh, hey," I said when I finally locked eyes with him.

"Great view, isn't it?"

I smiled and gave him a thumbs up.

"Do you have sunrises like this in New Jersey?" he asked.

"I've been told that the sun rises everywhere," I yelled back.

He smiled and took a step back, then disappeared behind a boulder, reappearing again a few seconds later on the path headed in my direction. I guess the giant chasm between us wasn't great for conversation, but for some reason, this made my palms start to sweat. I tried to tell myself to get a grip. Today was a new day. Abercrombie hadn't seen me with my pants down, or tripping all over myself yet. Maybe I could pretend yesterday had never happened.

"How'd you sleep?" he asked when he was close enough to talk without raising his voice.

"Not too bad."

"Stay warm enough?" He sat down on the rock next to me.

"Surprisingly."

"You always a morning person?" He looked at my hair and smiled.

I touched my matted locks. *Seriously.* Mother Earth didn't have a mirror in her great outdoor bathroom. I hadn't even considered what a wreck I must look like.

"Not really," I said, running my fingers through the tangles.

"I didn't used to be either. But you kind of can't help becoming one out here, can you?"

I nodded. I liked the way he smiled at me after he said that.

"We'll get a fire going soon, but I think we'll wait until some of the others wake up," he said.

Glancing over my shoulder at the tents, I wondered how long that would be. I hoped not too soon.

"Good Soaring Raven said we'd all learn to make fire. Is that one of the requirements to graduate from the program?" I asked in what I thought was a really sincere tone of voice.

His smile vanished. "That's not really the best way to think of your experience out here."

"How exactly *am* I supposed to think about it?" I said, kicking at the pebbles under my shoes.

Abercrombie picked up a rock and stacked it on top of the one sitting next to it. "I can't tell you how to think," he said. "But in my experience, true happiness comes from gaining knowledge and experience, not from earning a reward or certificate."

So I was supposed to learn true happiness from this program? Hmm. I doubted it. He didn't understand what I was dealing with. He didn't understand what it was like to have all of his choices made for him. He didn't understand that the only thing that made my mom happy was a certificate, or award, or trophy.

"Okay," I said. "But can you see how this is a little frustrating? I mean, it would be nice if somebody passed out a syllabus at the beginning so we'd know what we need to do to ace this thing."

I took a deep breath and let it out.

"Yeah. I can see that you're frustrated. It's pretty obvious."

"Well, wouldn't you be, if our roles were reversed?"

He didn't answer. He picked up another stone and stacked it on top of the other two. Really? Can't answer that one, eh?

The exaggerated pause and the cold wind blowing my hair away from my face made me shiver.

"So are you going to teach me how to make fire, or do I have to pass a test first to prove my motives are pure?"

He stood up, smiling down on me, but his eyes didn't have the usual warm glow.

"I think maybe we'll skip a fire this morning. We're probably better off eating protein bars instead of oatmeal to conserve water anyway." He turned and walked toward the tree line. "I'll be back in a while."

With that, he trudged off into the woods, leaving me standing alone in the wind.

I hated my life, and I hated Abercrombie for just walking away like that. He had the completely wrong idea about me. I wanted to cooperate. I wanted to do whatever it took to get through this. How was I going to show Jabba I was ready to go home if Abercrombie wouldn't teach me what I needed to know?

I grabbed a bandana and comb from my pack and started braiding my hair, watching the spot where Abercrombie had disappeared into the woods.

After a while, Spud Boy and Pizza Face stumbled out of their tent. Michaela emerged a few minutes later when the noise the boys made became louder than the birds. I wandered down with my pack.

"Firewalker said we're supposed to eat protein bars or whatever doesn't need to be cooked this morning," I said.

"Yeah. Makes sense to conserve water," said Spud Boy.

Michaela completely ignored me, wandering off into the woods.

Backwoods Barbie unzipped the tent and stepped out, looking as perfect as she had when she went to bed. Didn't she move when she slept?

Michaela came back a few minutes later and right away asked Backwoods Barbie to take a look at her blisters. She was limping, even though the sandals she wore weren't coming into contact with the bandages.

Emphysema and Quasimodo were still sleeping when Abercrombie came down the trail carrying a bunch of acorns he'd gathered.

"I've never heard of people eating acorns," said Michaela. "Can I try one?"

"Everyone can try them tonight," Abercrombie said. "They need to be ground up and leached first."

"It takes forever," said Spud Boy. "Enjoy the protein bars while you can."

"We should wake Stormi and Noah so we can pack up," Backwoods Barbie said. "It's going to be warm today." She looked up at the sun in the now cloudless sky.

Abercrombie agreed. He dropped the acorns into a pouch on the hip of his pack and began the process of trying to coax Noah out of his cocoon. Emphysema got right up, but I wished she hadn't. She looked worse than I did, and she was already in a foul mood.

"What are you looking at?" she snapped, purposely bumping into me to get to her pack.

"Just realizing how much makeup it takes to fix the hot mess you've got going on," I said.

The boys snorted, then laughed until her evil glare shut them up.

"Well, nothing can fix an ugly personality," she replied.

Whatever. If Abercrombie hadn't taken a sudden interest in what was going on, I would have told Emphysema that her personality made Bigfoot's armpit look attractive. But today was a new day, and I wasn't going to let her make me look bad.

I rolled my eyes and walked away.

Noah finally came out of the tent. He looked worse than yesterday, which was scary. It was hard to say if his skin was more yellow or grey. When he picked up his shoes, his hands trembled, and he was sweating like crazy.

Backwoods Barbie and Abercrombie were either ignoring Noah's flu-like symptoms, or they just thought they were no big deal. Whenever he sat down to rest for a second, they coaxed him to keep packing up his stuff.

With everything finally packed up and Michaela's blisters stuffed back into her shoes, we set out at a much slower pace than we had the day before. This time Backwoods Barbie took up the lead and Abercrombie stayed at the rear with Noah. I placed myself in the middle of the pack.

My legs were stiff and sore starting out, but once I got going, they loosened up. I guess all those hours on the stair climber had paid off. Michaela and Noah weren't so fortunate. The steep climb was killing them. Michaela had to stop every ten steps or so to rest, and Noah had already fallen so far behind I couldn't see him or Abercrombie at all.

Despite my aches and pains, I was getting into a rhythm with the hiking. Following my own advice, I started to find ways to zone out. Instead of focusing on the trail in front of me, I let my mind wander back to the conversation I'd had with Abercrombie that morning. Why was it so wrong for me to want to know what I needed to do to finish the program? I was pretty sure I would enjoy the journey much more if I knew how and when it would end. I came to a bend in the trail and found a log to sit on while I sipped at my water.

Michaela came around the corner and sat down next to me.

"We should play name that tune," I suggested.

"Why?" she asked.

"I usually zone out listening to music, but since we don't have any, maybe playing a game will help us pass the time."

She shrugged.

"I'll go first," I said. "This one will be obvious…start us off easy." I hummed the first few notes of the song that had been stuck in my head since we started hiking. My favorite radio station had it on heavy rotation. I waited for Michaela to guess.

She raised her eyebrows. "I'm supposed to know what that was?"

I was a decent singer. She just wasn't used to playing. I patiently hummed the notes again, this time a little slower. I even added on a few bars.

"No idea," she said.

"Seriously," I said, "you're not even trying. Think about it. It's top forty. This song is huge right now."

Michaela rolled her eyes. "Do I look like I listen to top forty?"

"Okay, fine. You go first." I had no idea what Michaela listened to, but I was pretty well rounded. I knew the classics too.

"I don't think this game is going to work for us," she said smugly.

"Try me."

"If you can name one song by Portishead or Grizzly Bear, I'll play."

I couldn't tell if she had picked the two most obscure bands in the world, or if she had just made up two ridiculous sounding names to shut me up. Either way, I was annoyed.

"Okay," I said, "it's obvious we don't have the same taste in music, but maybe we could play the Beatles version. Everyone likes the Beatles."

"You can't argue with that," Abercrombie said, coming around the corner. He stopped when he got to the stump, looking back to wait for Noah to catch up. "What are you guys doing?"

"I wanted to play name that tune, but Michaela and I have really different taste," I said.

Abercrombie smiled. "I'll play." Noah shuffled around the corner. "I bet I can even guess what kind of music you all listen to."

If Noah cared even a little bit, his face didn't show it. But he didn't look angry anymore. All I could see now was defeat.

Abercrombie knew a lot about music. He knew who the bands were that Michaela mentioned and could even sing the best hits from both. His voice was nice, which shouldn't have been a surprise.

"I thought you said yesterday that you couldn't listen to music or watch television and stuff for the last two years," Michaela said.

"Right," he replied, "I didn't. But I've been home for three months, and my siblings have made sure to catch me up on pop culture."

"You didn't listen to music for two years?" I asked. "Why not?"

"Mission rules," he said.

I couldn't interpret the strange tone of voice he used when he said it. Almost like he was talking about rules to a board game that nobody understood how to play.

"What about Noah?" Michaela said. "You didn't guess what he listens to yet."

Abercrombie looked at Noah and brought his fist up to his chin, rubbing his knuckles against his stubble. "I'm going to have to go with rap, but I can't tell just by looking if he's into gangsta or classic hip-hop."

Okay, Abercrombie didn't ever need to say the word "gangsta" again. I was trying to be polite, holding back the laughter at how white he sounded, when Noah suddenly pursed his lips and gave one little nod. Unbelievable. Abercrombie was right?

For the next thirty minutes or so, we all hiked at Noah's pace while Abercrombie took turns playing name that tune with us. Sometimes he tried to get Noah to play too, giving him songs to guess. He didn't seem to care how ridiculous he sounded beatboxing the music. Noah never responded, but Michaela and I couldn't help laughing. I completely forgot we were hiking for a while.

But the game stopped when the trail got steep again and Noah fell behind.

After a while, Michaela looked over her shoulder and asked, "Do you think Noah's going to be alright?"

I looked back too, just in time to see Noah lean over a fallen log on the side of the trail. Luckily, I didn't see what he was throwing up. Watching his body convulse was bad enough.

"Yesterday was too much for him," I whispered. "How can they keep making him hike while he's sick? This program is deranged."

Michaela shook her head. "I guess this is one way to force us to deal with our issues, but I don't see how it's going to help in the long run. When he goes back, he's just going to start using again."

Using again? *Withdrawals.* I nodded like I'd totally been thinking the same thing.

"Why would a parent send their child out in the wilderness to detox?" I said, after watching Noah's second round of convulsions.

Michaela tugged her sleeves down at the wrists and shrugged. "I think we're wasting our time trying to figure out why they sent us here. There are definitely a million other options that don't involve hiking."

As soon as Noah stood up, Michaela started up the trail again and I followed her. It felt awkward enough watching him in such a vulnerable position. Neither of us wanted to talk to him about it. What would we say?

Fortunately, the trail leveled out only a few minutes later, and pretty soon, we heard the soft but distinct sound of water rushing over rock in the distance. When we reached the wooden footbridge that crossed Bridalveil Creek, Emphysema, Pizza Face, and Spud Boy had already changed into their swimsuits and stood waist high in the water. Backwoods Barbie's pack sat in the shade of a tree next to the others, but she was nowhere in sight.

"Come on in," Pizza Face called. "It'll feel good to soak your blisters."

Michaela looked at me. "Where do we change?"

I shrugged. "150 feet from the trail?"

It must have been close to noon, and the sun was beating down, baking the sweat and dust from the trail into my skin. Michaela and I dropped our packs and fished through for our suits before heading in opposite directions to change.

I made it back to the bridge before she did, just as Abercrombie and Noah came down the hill. I felt a bit self-conscious in the unflattering, sporty one-piece they'd picked out for me. Paired with hiking sandals, it was a fashion tragedy, but then again, I wasn't alone. Michaela came out of the woods wearing her purple swirled Speedo, only she'd kept her long-sleeved shirt on over the top like a rash guard. With only her glow-in-the-dark legs showing, I was pretty sure nobody would be looking at me if I stood next to her.

Backwoods Barbie met Abercrombie halfway down the hill. The noise of the water drowned out their conversation, but I imagined Abercrombie was bringing her up to date on Noah's little episode in the woods. The two of them surveyed the area around the trail, then Abercrombie pointed to the left and they both nodded.

Noah had parked himself on the closest fallen log and was laying with his head against his backpack.

"You coming in?" Michaela asked, heading toward the bridge.

"I'll be right there," I said. But first, I dropped my clothes inside my bag and walked up the hill to Noah.

"Hey," I called softly when I was a few feet away. His eyes twitched but he didn't open them. "I know you're not feeling well. I just wanted to see if I can get anything for you? Do you need your water refilled or anything?"

He didn't answer, pinching his eyes closed even tighter.

"It's okay," I said, reaching out to touch his arm. "I can totally understand why you don't want to talk to anyone. I don't blame you."

No answer, but he didn't pull away from my touch.

"But I'm here for you if you need anything," I whispered.

Creases formed in his forehead and his breathing became uneven.

"It's not you," he groaned.

I nodded, giving his arm a little squeeze, then turned away. Before I reached the bottom of the hill, I heard him retching in the bushes behind me.

I felt terrible for him, but I couldn't help smiling. Noah had finally talked. And he had talked to *me*.

Suddenly, out of nowhere, Abercrombie appeared on the path in front of me. My smile disappeared as soon as we locked eyes. Following his gaze up the hill, I saw Noah doubled over in the bushes. Abercrombie raised his eyebrows slightly, but he didn't say anything, instead continuing up the hill to Noah.

Wait. Did he think I'd been smiling or laughing at Noah?

∞ ∞ ∞

The others spent the rest of the afternoon swimming in the stream, rinsing out their clothes and sunning on the rocks. I washed my clothes in the freezing cold water, but kept to myself, laying out everything to dry on the opposite side of the bridge from everyone else. My separation didn't seem to bother anyone. If they noticed, nobody came over to invite me to join them.

Abercrombie came wandering down after a while.

"So what's the verdict?" asked Spud Boy. "Are we moving on, or staying the night?"

"Noah's not feeling so well. We'll stay here."

"Do you want us to get things set up?" I heard Pizza Face ask.

"I set up our tent already. You can help the girls set theirs up later if they need it. We have plenty of time before it gets dark."

Backwoods Barbie appeared on the bridge above us, dressed in the same purple Speedo I was wearing, but it looked much different on her flawless figure. She looked over everyone for a few seconds before coming down to join us. I slid down on my warm rock so I was more camouflaged by the surrounding bushes.

"Noah's sleeping now," Backwoods Barbie reported when she reached Abercrombie. "He drank some water. Hopefully he can keep it down,"

Abercrombie smiled at her. "It'll be good for everyone to rehydrate and rest before we get going again tomorrow. Yesterday was tough."

"Today too," Michaela added. "I'm glad it wasn't as long. This is the hardest thing I've ever done."

"You should be proud of yourself," Abercrombie said. "You've got a great attitude and determination."

What? I raised my head up slightly to see Abercrombie patting Michaela on the back. Was her attitude really so much better than mine?

"How are your blisters looking?" Backwoods Barbie asked.

"I still can't believe you walked all day with those." Abercrombie said, "Your pain threshold must be through the roof."

Ugh! They were acting like her blisters were some kind of mark of bravery. Like she deserved a Purple Heart for them or something. I rolled over on my rock and picked up my clothes. If I showed them my blisters, would that give me points?

With my stuff under one arm, I made my way back up to the path. The clothes weren't completely dry, so I pulled some of the paracord out of my backpack and rigged up a clothesline between two branches.

The boys' tent was set up a few feet from a small fire pit. The flaps were open, so the breeze flowed through the mesh netting. I peeked in when I walked past. Noah was curled in a ball on top of his sleeping bag. He still looked horrible, but his breathing was steady and rhythmic. Hopefully some sleep would help.

The other tent was still in its bag a few yards away on a flat spot where they probably intended to set it up later. The entire area was surrounded by fallen logs in the shape of a square. I sat down on one of them, looking up at the sky overhead. This might go down as the longest day in the history of the world. What were we supposed to do out here all day? I almost wished we were hiking again, just to kill time. I knew exactly what my friends were doing right now. We'd been planning it for months—the first pool party of the season at Hilary's house. Warm sun, cold drinks, and a lounge chair.

A giant horsefly buzzed past my ear and landed on my shirt. Jumping to my feet, I brushed it off, dancing around and swatting at it until it left the area.

"This sucks!" I said under my breath. My friends were sitting around a luxurious pool with fruity drinks with umbrellas, while I was being attacked by bugs the size of birds. And they were probably talking about me right now.

I couldn't take it anymore. I felt like I was going to explode and the kids down in the stream were splashing around and laughing like this was the best thing that had ever happened to them.

I stopped pacing in front of the ground cover and tent waiting to be set up by someone who knew how to do it. Could it really be that hard? I didn't need Pizza Face or Spud Boy or Abercrombie to teach me how to survive in the wilderness. I'd passed AP Physics on my own.

With fiery determination that would put Michaela's to shame, I began spreading the ground cover and removing the tent from its bag. Besides the actual tent, the only other pieces were a single pole I remember holding everything up, placed in the center of the tent, and a bunch of long metal nails with hooks on the ends. I wasn't paying attention to how those had been used. It didn't matter. I'd figure it out.

I'd just finished unrolling the tent when Spud Boy and Emphysema came up from the stream.

"Oh, wow," Emphysema said, "Jasmine's turned all domestic on us." She plucked the paracord like a guitar string when she walked by and my clothes bounced up and down. "Need any help?"

I had actually just reached a point where I wasn't sure what to do next. The tent only had one pole that went right in the center, but holding it in my hand now, it seemed to be about one third of the size it had been last night. Was I missing something?

"Nope," I said without looking at her. "I've got it."

"Oh, really?" she said. "I had no idea you were so outdoorsy. You seemed kinda lost last night."

"There's a difference between looking lost and wishing someone would get lost. You might have been confused." I stood up and rested my hands on my hips.

"So tough," she mocked. "Looks like we're off the hook, Quiet Wolf."

"Are you sure you don't want help?" Spud Boy asked, looking more sympathetic than Emphysema. "Firewalker asked us to come set this up. It's much easier with more than one set of hands."

Of course Abercrombie had sent them to do it. He probably hadn't even noticed I had left the stream. Maybe he hadn't even noticed I'd been down there at all.

"I don't need your help," I said, unzipping the door of the tent.

"Great," Emphysema said, parking herself on a tree stump right in my line of sight. "We can just relax and watch."

Spud Boy didn't move for a minute, watching as I stepped inside the open tent and lifted the walls with the pole in my hand. While I was twisting the pole, trying to figure out what to do with it, it began expanding until a notch clicked into place. Nice. It totally looked like I knew it was going to do that.

"C'mon," Spud Boy said. "Why don't we gather wood and get a fire started?"

Emphysema buzzed her lips. "Sure you wanna miss this?" she said, nodding toward me.

"Looks like she has things under control," Spud Boy said.

Yeah! I have things under control! I wanted to shout. *Go take a long walk off a short cliff!*

Emphysema stood up and followed Spud Boy toward the trees but kept her eye on me for an unreasonable amount of time, while I pretended to be positioning the pole in the exact center of the tent.

When they were finally gone, I examined my handiwork. It still wasn't right. The pole wasn't tall enough to allow me to stand inside the tent, and the bottom of the tent wasn't staying in place. Maybe the weight of Emphysema's sleeping bag had kept it down last night.

Pulling on the pole again, I expanded it upward until it was as tall as I was. I let go of the pole when it seemed balanced and stepped away. I smiled and reached for my backpack, in search of my sleeping bag.

My back had only been turned for a second when I sensed that the pole was tipping. I turned back just as a small gust of wind filled the tent with air and the whole thing lifted off the ground. *Crap!* I immediately chased after it, almost catching it when it landed briefly, but another gust picked it up again, filling it like a hot-air balloon. It sailed above the trees, coming down toward the bridge. Abercrombie and Backwoods Barbie were just coming up the hill from the stream below.

"What the…" Abercrombie dropped his hiking shoes and socks and ran toward the tent, capturing it just before it sailed into the water. Backwoods Barbie and I got there from opposite sides a few seconds later, each reaching for a corner of the tent.

"You've got it," Abercrombie called to Backwoods Barbie. "We've got to pull the pole out, so it'll collapse when the wind lets up."

She nodded, planting her feet while he reached inside and grasped the pole. With the tension gone, the top whipped left and right before slowly caving in on itself and the whole thing fell to the ground.

"What happened?" Abercrombie asked. "Where are Quiet Wolf and Stormi?"

Even if I'd had a clue what to say, I was out of breath and couldn't answer.

Ten

atching how easily Backwoods Barbie and Abercrombie set the tent up was humiliating. How was I supposed to know that the nails were meant to be pounded into the ground through the loops on the bottom of the tent? And nobody I knew would think of using a rock as a hammer. I was still stewing about it when the sun dropped behind the trees and we all sat around the fire, being eaten alive by mosquitoes.

Noah had slept all afternoon, but Backwoods Barbie insisted on waking him up when the red bean and Spanish rice concoction was ready.

"You need to keep eating and drinking," she told him. "Even if it's just a little bit."

He staggered over and plopped down on the log next to me. Maybe it was because he considered me a friend, or maybe it was because I was sitting the farthest away from everyone on a huge log that gave him plenty of space to lay down.

Backwoods Barbie set a mug full of steaming food in front of Noah, but he already had his eyes closed again. I was hungry, but the food didn't appeal to me at all. I wanted large fries and a Frosty. Comfort food. I forced myself to eat a few bites, and left the rest sitting at the bottom of my mug.

"I think we should definitely have a talking circle tonight," Pizza Face said while Abercrombie boiled water to wash the dishes.

"Great idea," said Backwoods Barbie. "I have a talking stick we can use, unless you have something?" She addressed this to Abercrombie.

"First group," Abercrombie reminded her. "I'll have to make one."

Backwoods Barbie went to her pack and came back a minute later with a ghetto-looking stick. With faded red paint, and feathers attached on both ends with small strips of leather, it looked like a cross between an Indian drumstick and a feather pen.

"Who wants to go first?" Backwoods Barbie asked. "Runs on Wind, it was your idea. You must have something you want to say to get the ball rolling."

Pizza Face nodded his head, looking around at each of us with uncharacteristic seriousness. Backwoods Barbie handed him the stick and then sat down next to Abercrombie. He held the stick, turning it over a few times before saying anything. The suspense was killing me. I wasn't really looking forward to hearing Pizza Face's innermost feelings, but I was curious whether he was going to share about his life before wilderness therapy or talk about how much he hated us or hiking.

"I just want to start out by saying that it's really cool to be in this group, and not just because it's smaller than our last group." He looked around at each of us, but his eyes stopped extra long on Michaela. "I just feel like we're already gelling…working well together." He paused for a second. "I was never much of a leader back at home, so the last two days have been awesome. I finally feel like I know enough that I can help other people…which is a surprisingly good feeling." He paused again, staring down at the stick. With the light from the fire dancing on his face he looked a little elfish. "On a slightly different note, I think we need to talk about the tension that's been going on between Jasmine and Stormi. We can all feel it, and I think it needs to be addressed before it festers."

Completely unprepared to be called out like that, I felt like the wind had been knocked out of me. My face was glowing, and I didn't dare look up, especially to see how Emphysema had reacted.

The dirt crunched under Pizza Face's feet, and before I knew it, he was standing in front of me, shoving the stupid talking stick in my face. I took it from him but waited until he was back to his log before looking up at the faces in the circle. I had no desire to talk to any of them right now about anything, but especially not to Emphysema about our "tension." She wasn't the kind of girl that would stop being a jerk just because I told her to. She would probably be worse after this, even if I didn't say anything.

I must have looked like a deer in headlights because Abercrombie smiled at me. The first warm, reassuring smile he'd given me since our conversation at sunrise.

"I don't really have anything to say right now," I said. "I'm not really sure what tension you're talking about."

"I think he means the way you look like you want to claw my eyes out every time I say anything to you," Emphysema said.

"Shhhh," Pizza Face brought his finger to his lips. "You can't talk until you have the stick."

Emphysema rolled her eyes and folded her arms. I sat there staring at the stick. What was I supposed to say now? I couldn't just pass the stick on when she was so obviously going to spin this tension to look like it was all coming from me. The way I saw it, I couldn't really win. Pizza Face must have thought I was the one causing problems, or he would have handed the stick to Emphysema. Did everyone else think it was my fault too? I looked around the circle and tried to swallow the lump in my throat.

These people still didn't realize that I wasn't one of them. I didn't deserve to be here. I wasn't addicted to any illegal substances. I didn't have any real psychological or behavioral issues. I looked down at Noah, who could at least pretend to be oblivious to all of this. I didn't agree that this was the best treatment option for him, but we could all agree that he needed some kind of treatment. I didn't need to be treated. I was just a normal teenager. There was no reason for me to be here.

"Well, okay," I finally said, looking up at Pizza Face, "you gave me the stick, but didn't you say that when I'm holding it, I can talk about whatever I want?"

He nodded, grunting softly.

"Well, I guess I'll just come right out and say what probably seems really obvious to all of you…" I took a deep breath. "I'm not like the rest of you. You're all here to try to overcome some addiction or behavior that's keeping you from having a good life. My life is just fine. I don't have any big issues I need this program to fix for me. I'm only here because of a misunderstanding…and because my mom loves programs. I don't think she realized what this program was or who it's really for. I don't belong here."

Abercrombie coughed and I looked up from the fire into his eyes. I couldn't tell what emotion was dancing in them with the reflection of the flames, but it definitely wasn't like warm Nutella. He'd said something last night about Miwok traditions and the talking circle. The cough was supposed to signal something. I couldn't remember what, but his eyes seemed to be inviting me to shut up and pass the stick on to someone else.

Fine. I'd already said what I wanted to say, but I wasn't passing the stick on to Emphysema. I didn't want to hear her snarky comments. I didn't want to know right away what she thought about what I'd said. I passed the stick to Michaela, who was seated to my right. She didn't make eye contact or smile.

She sat there holding the stick while we all stared into the crackling fire for several minutes. *Who cares?* I thought. *Silence is golden.* But as the silence wore on, the words I had just spoken kept replaying in my head. *I'm not like the rest of you…My life is just fine…I don't belong here.* My head started pounding.

"It must be nice to be so perfect and have such a perfect life," Michaela finally said, voice full of emotion. "I've never felt that way. I can't remember ever feeling like things were just fine. My family is messed up. My childhood was messed up. Things happened to me that should never happen to an adult, let alone a little kid. So yeah. I belong here, but I don't think this program is going to fix my problems. No program can make me forget." Her eyes drifted up from the dirt to Spud Boy and Pizza Face. "I'll go home, and I'll remember. Everything and everyone there will remind me, and I'll have to do something to control the pain."

The tremor in Michaela's voice was too much. Glancing across the flames through the smoke, I saw Spud Boy and Pizza Face's eyes glistening. Emphysema pulled her knees up to her chest and rested her cheek against them, her expression completely unreadable.

"I don't think anyone or anything can fix my problems," Michaela whispered. "But part of me hopes that somehow, someday I'll be able to forget."

She looked around the circle, obviously finished talking. Her eyes locked on Emphysema and she rocked forward like she was going to stand up, but at the last second, she changed her mind and handed the stick to Abercrombie, who was sitting right next to her.

He held the stick, letting his eyes drift shut for a brief moment. When he opened them again warmth and compassion poured out on Michaela, now trying to cover the tears streaming down her face with the palms of her hands. I instantly wanted to take the stick back and unsay everything I had said. I didn't belong here, but my life wasn't perfect either.

"This land we walk across is sacred. The voices of the ancients cry through the trees with the wind, trying to speak to us. To give us their wisdom." A log snapped in the fire, and all eyes watched the sparks fly above it. Abercrombie held the talking stick over his heart. "If you listen, you'll hear them telling you that being here at this time…in this place…together…is no program. It is the plan of the Great Creator. The same Creator who put the sun in the sky to warm us and the stars to guide our journey."

I lifted my eyes to the sky. The billions of twinkling lights blurred together in my misty vision. How had the ancients been so sure that all of this was made by a Creator? I didn't buy it.

"We all have problems. We all know about pain and suffering. We're all carrying burdens that slow us down and keep us from enjoying our walking. But the Miwok knew that everything they needed to sustain and heal them could be found on the land." He looked around at the darkness behind us. "The Creator has given us everything we need. We just have to learn how to live in harmony with nature and each other."

Abercrombie said it with such feeling. He obviously believed what he was saying. I didn't have any issue with the idea of living in harmony with nature. Except for the horsefly and the mosquitos, nature and I were getting along just fine. I looked across the flames at Emphysema, who was still hugging her knees. How was I supposed to live in harmony with someone who hated me before she'd even given me a chance? She didn't even know anything about me.

After he let his words sink in, Abercrombie stood and walked the talking stick around to Emphysema, but when he tried to give it to her, she closed her eyes and shook her head. Without hesitation, Abercrombie accepted her refusal to talk, and gave the stick to Spud Boy.

"I like what Firewalker said about how everything on the land is put here to help us heal. Like how areas that have poisonous plants sometimes have the antidote growing close by. Wasn't it stinging nettle and dock plants?" He turned to Pizza Face for confirmation, but he only nodded his head, ever vigilant about following the talking circle rules. "Well, yeah," he continued. "Don't feel bad, Michaela. Most of us are trying to forget something. At least for you it's stuff that happened to you, instead of just stupid stuff you've done." *Most of us.* I didn't like the way he said that. He wasn't looking at me, but I felt the sting. Whatever. The whole thought was a misfire, trying to make whatever horrific abuse Michaela had suffered land somewhere in the same ballpark of pain as Spud Boy's cow tipping mishaps. Someone take the talking stick away from him. "I guess if I had to sum up what I've been learning, I'd say maybe we don't have to forget to heal. Healing just means you don't feel the pain anymore…even if you can still see the scar."

Hmmm. That was a pretty deep thought.

Spud Boy looked around the circle. Noah was still pretending to be asleep, although it seemed impossible since he was laying on the same log that was currently causing butt paralysis for me, and Backwoods Barbie was the only one who hadn't yet been offered the stick. He only had to lean forward to reach his long arms across the circle.

Backwoods Barbie held the stick, and just like everyone else, took a few seconds to collect her thoughts before proceeding. "I just want to say that I really love you guys." Her perky voice cracked slightly, making it obvious she'd been tuned in to the emotion of the circle, but was choosing to cut it off with her little ray of sunshine. She'd only known us for two days. We'd hardly talked at all. I knew for sure I hadn't given her anything to love, and I doubted anyone else had had time to give her much to work with either.

Emphysema coughed. "So is that it?" she asked. "Can we go to bed now?"

Abercrombie and Backwoods Barbie looked at each other, then down to Noah, and nodded. "We'll get an early start tomorrow," Abercrombie said. "We want to make it into the village before the Pizza Patio closes."

"How many miles to the village?" I asked as the other kids gathered up the last of the dinner dishes.

Abercrombie stood up. "It's not the number of miles that count, but the direction you're headed." He grinned at me. "That's the answer to number eight on the test to prove if your motives are pure."

He said it playfully, but my face was as hot as the flames in the fire. Turning toward the tent, I walked away. I was done asking for information from the King of Pure Motives.

∞ ∞ ∞

The ground wasn't soft or level, and I couldn't fall asleep in the same tent as Emphysema and Michaela, especially since neither of them had spoken a word to me since the talking circle. In fact, neither of them had even looked at me. Backwoods Barbie was as chipper as ever, but she'd been more concerned about getting Noah comfortable before going to bed than anything else.

While I lay there, waiting to fall asleep, I couldn't stop thinking about Abercrombie's faith in a Great Creator. I had a feeling there was more to it than just a belief in Miwok legends.

I didn't know what to believe. I mean, I had thought about it before, but it wasn't the kind of thing you talk about with your friends, and my mom was completely closed off on the subject. The few times I'd brought up religion casually, she'd made it sound like she'd been forced to go to church every week with her siblings. She'd stopped going when she left for college. She said her family kind of disowned her when she wasn't living the zealot lifestyle taught by their religion. It was impossible to verify this with her family though, since she was the black sheep, and none of them ever came to visit. Her two sisters lived in California, and her brother lived in Utah. I'd only met them once when I was pretty young at her grandma's funeral.

My grandparents called fairly frequently when I was little, but my mom had refused any offers to have me come stay with them, and even avoided a visit from them when they were traveling to New York one time. But they did send me a birthday card every year with money to buy myself a gift. I treasured and saved the envelopes in a neat stack in my top drawer. all except the one they sent me for my eighth birthday. My mom gave me the money without the card that year.

"Where's the card?" I had asked.

"It wasn't really appropriate," she'd said, waving me off as if she didn't want to discuss it further.

I was confused. My mom usually used that word when something I said or did was bad or wrong. "You mean it talked about boogers or something?" I'd asked.

She had laughed and rumpled my hair. "No, nothing like that. It just talks about their feelings about God, and I don't want anyone to force their beliefs on you. When you're old enough, you can decide for yourself what you believe."

I didn't argue with her, but I was always curious about what they had written. Secretly, I hunted through her desk looking for the card. I searched her underwear drawer, the junk mail pile on the kitchen counter, and even the recycle bin, but I never found it. My stack of envelopes with the Utah return address would always be missing that one card.

Grandparents who only existed in cards and letters. A father who only existed in the small bits of information my mom had given me about him. A God who may or may not exist at all. Was I old enough to decide for myself yet? My mom hadn't made it easy for me to believe in much of anything.

Eleven

Quiet rain started tapping against the tent sometime in the middle of the night. I drifted off into uncomfortable sleep a few times, only to be ripped back to my awful reality by the hundreds of terrifying noises happening just outside the tent.

Those crunching leaves had to be the wind, right? I scooted down lower in my sleeping bag until my head was completely covered. But the bag only muffled the sounds. I squeezed my eyes shut and tried to picture myself lying on the beach. Somewhere far away from here. Eventually, I must have drifted off to sleep.

"We've got to pack up and get going, ladies," Backwoods Barbie said, shaking each of our sleeping bags in turn. "It doesn't look like this weather is going to let up."

"In the rain?" Michaela asked.

"Rain, sleet, snow, or hail," Backwoods Barbie said. "High Sierra is more regular than the post office."

Emphysema groaned and rolled over in her bag.

The rain had slowed to a steady drip. I stuffed my sleeping bag inside my pack and combed and rebraided my hair. Abercrombie had a fire going, but it was smaller and smokier than the night before. Spud Boy and Pizza Face were stuffing their tent inside its bag, and Noah sat by the fire with Abercrombie, eating something steaming from his mug. He actually had a little bit of color in his cheeks, and the whites of his eyes looked clear instead of dull.

Still annoyed at Abercrombie, I avoided eye contact. With the heavy clouds dampening the sun, everyone seemed somber and subdued. We packed up our tent and ate oatmeal in relative silence. It was too much effort to talk over the trickling stream and the wind and rain.

Watching the others, I discovered the purpose of the giant trash bag in the bottom of my pack. It was a giant poncho with a hood. It was big enough to cover both hiker and backpack, but it looked ridiculous.

With my thermals under my clothes and the down jacket on top of everything, I had almost been warm enough standing next to the fire, but waiting for everyone on the trail with my pack covered with the trash bag poncho, I was already shivering. Hopefully when we started walking, the exertion would heat me up.

"About half of the hike today is going to be downhill," Abercrombie told us.

"But this morning is my favorite part of the trail," Backwoods Barbie interjected. "If you thought the view from Crocker Point was spectacular, just wait."

"Is everyone comfortable? Packs are secure?" Abercrombie asked. I didn't like the way he was looking at us. He hadn't asked about our packs yesterday or the day before. "So this morning, we're going to do something a little different. I need you guys to go down to the creek and pick up three stones…about this size." He lifted his hands up like he was holding an invisible bacon cheeseburger.

Moving his hands, he rounded out the full shape. Okay, so not a Junior Bacon Cheeseburger, more like the Baconator.

Spud Boy and Pizza Face looked at each other and shrugged.

"What for?" Pizza Face asked.

"I'll explain when you get back," Abercrombie promised.

"Three stones?" Spud Boy repeated.

Abercrombie nodded.

"Each of us?" Emphysema asked.

"Yeah. Everyone," Abercrombie said. "Take your time. Look for stones that appeal to you. Maybe some that look like they could represent who you are as a person."

"Or just hurry up and pick some," Emphysema said. "Didn't you say we're trying to get somewhere before it closes?"

For once, I kind of agreed with Emphysema. It was raining, and we had a long hike ahead. What was with Abercrombie's sudden interest in geology?

"We'll get there," Abercrombie said. "This is important."

Could we have done this before we put our packs on at least? The boys shrugged again and then led the way down the small hill to the creek. Emphysema picked up the first three rocks she saw and turned back toward the trail. The boys looked around a little before selecting their stones, but Michaela seemed to be taking it all very seriously, picking up and then discarding several before she finally settled on her three. Noah and I stood watching everyone else until Abercrombie spoke.

"What are you waiting for?" he asked.

I looked down at the rocks near my feet. Most of them fit the size criteria, but I wasn't sure how I was supposed to decide which ones represented me. All of the stones were smooth and clean from the rain. The color variation seemed more distinct than yesterday when they had been washed out by the sunlight and covered with dust.

Would I be a perfectly rounded rock, or a more interesting shape? Would I be smooth or rough? Straight or jagged? Whole or broken?

Noah bent down and picked up three rocks. They were all different. One was light brown, smooth and round. Another white and sparkly, but broken and jagged, and the third was oddly shaped with one pointy edge.

I liked that idea. Pick a variety. Those personality tests that tried to lump you into a category based on the answers you chose were so stupid. We were individuals. Human beings, not rocks. Stones had nothing to do with who we were. I picked up the other half of Noah's white sparkly one, then found a jagged one that looked sort of like the state of Kentucky. My third one was shiny and black, round and smooth, just about the size of a Magic Eight Ball.

Carrying them up the hill in my arms like oversized juggling balls, I tried not to drop one on my toe. They were awkward, and heavier than they looked.

"Cool," Abercrombie said, leading us all out onto the bridge. "Michaela and Quiet Wolf both mentioned things that were weighing them down. Things they are trying to forget or heal from."

The rain began falling gently again. We were a pitiful sight, standing in a line with our trash bag ponchos, holding our stones in the freezing cold.

Get to the point, Abercrombie!

"So you're going to carry these today. Carry them however you want."

"Seriously? That's about fifteen pounds of extra weight." Spud Boy sounded like he'd been asked to carry twice as much.

"You're right. Think about what they represent. They're not really part of you. They're just something extra you've picked up."

"Because you told us to," Emphysema said.

"Because I told you to." Abercrombie nodded his head. "But we mentioned last night that not all of our problems come because of choices we make. Sometimes our burdens come because of circumstances or other people's choices. They're just handed to us." He started walking over the water-glossed, wood bridge, turning back when he was half-way across. "I'll take your stones. You can give them to me anytime you want today. All you have to do is tell me what they represent when you hand them over. What's holding you back? What's weighing you down?"

"Tell everyone, or just tell you?" Emphysema asked.

"Just me," Abercrombie said. "I'll take them from you whenever you get tired of carrying them."

Backwoods Barbie led everyone again. Spud Boy and Pizza face dropped the stones in each other's packs before falling into line behind Michaela and Emphysema, who had each placed the stones in the mesh side pockets of the pack, making them more easily accessible.

I placed my stones in the side pockets too. It was surprising how much weight the three stones added to the pack. Had Abercrombie picked the odd number on purpose? I was off balance with two stones in one side pocket and the Kentucky rock in the other.

The rain covered the meadow in a gloomy filter. Heavy from the weight of the water, purple and red flowers bent over in beds of bright green along the sides of the muddy trail. The sounds that had become white noise to me over the last two days were muted too. At first, I thought it was because of the crackling of the trash bag over my ears, but after a while I realized that the birds and insects were in hiding.

It wasn't long before Bridalveil Creek and the flat terrain of the meadow disappeared behind us and we were climbing again. The two rocks in my left side pocket clacked against each other with every step.

I was toward the middle of the pack. Noah fell back until he was just in front of me with only Michaela and Abercrombie behind. Had Michaela handed over any of her stones yet? She was the only one that could have. I resisted the urge to look back.

I caught up to Noah when he was resting on a rock. He'd taken his pack off and it was sitting on the log next to him.

"How are you feeling today?" I asked. "You look a lot better."

He nodded, taking a sip of his water.

I sat down next to him. "How are those stones treating you?"

He stood up. Reaching inside his pack, he pulled out the stones and quietly set them on the ground behind the log.

My heart sank. Maybe the assignment was stupid, but the student of the month side of me would never let me completely ignore directions. That would be cheating.

Noah cinched up his pack and put it on without looking at me. Abercrombie and Michaela came up the trail behind us, walking side by side, talking like old friends.

"Do you think she gave him her rocks yet?" I asked Noah, wishing he would get a clue that his little defiance was causing a major moral dilemma for me.

He ignored me, clicking the buckle on his chest strap. Before Abercrombie and Michaela reached us, Noah shuffled away. I could hear snatches of their conversation. Michaela was telling a story about someone called Maggie who had introduced her to thrift store shopping.

"All of the ties I took on my mission came from the DI." Abercrombie told her.

"What's that?" Michaela asked.

I looked back and forth between Noah moving up the trail and Abercrombie. Should I say something about the discarded rocks?

"It's a local thrift store. I guess they don't have them everywhere."

It wasn't really my job to babysit Noah. I stood up and fell into line behind Abercrombie and Michaela, happy to be distracted from my misery with snatches of their small talk.

∞ ∞ ∞

We made it to Dewey Point a little while later. Backwoods Barbie and the others had dropped their packs under a tree for a small break. The boys were looking at the view, while Emphysema was calling out her number from the woods. Noah and I took off our packs and joined the others. The rock formations and valley floor below looked pretty dismal in the shadow of the low hanging clouds. Would it still be raining when we reached it? It looked so far away.

Abercrombie and Michaela came into the clearing, still talking. Her serene face contrasted the bleak weather just like the wildflowers in the field had. She wiped her eyes with her sleeve. Had she shared more details about her painful childhood? Had she given him her rocks?

Emphysema came back out of the woods just as Abercrombie was taking off his pack.

"I'm ready to ditch my dead weight," she said, hefting the stones out of her pack.

"Cool," Abercrombie said. "Whatch'ya got for me?"

I turned toward the view and tried to pretend I wasn't listening, but Emphysema didn't seem to care. She was talking full voice. "This one represents sex," she said, handing him one rock, "and obviously the other two are drugs and rock and roll."

"Okay," Abercrombie said, undaunted by her obvious disregard for the seriousness of this exercise. "I can see how all three of those things can hold you back from living a healthy, happy life." I turned around just as he took the stones from her. Abercrombie blinked, rain drops falling from his lashes to his cheeks. Emphysema looked as surprised as I was that he took them so easily. "Thanks for giving them to me. Now that you've given them away, you don't have to worry about those things anymore. They're not part of who you are, and you don't have to carry them ever again."

Really? What was he going to do next? Slap her on the forehead and tell her she was healed like those televangelists? Abercrombie was losing credibility with me pretty fast. Emphysema and I both watched as Abercrombie turned back toward his pack, carrying the rocks. Emphysema shrugged and walked away, joining Pizza Face and Spud Boy at the overlook. I kept my eye on Abercrombie. He'd stopped at his pack, setting the rocks aside while he opened the top. Did he already have Michaela's rocks inside? If he took all of our stones, he would be carrying an extra ninety pounds for the rest of the day. Why would he choose to do this? What was it supposed to prove? Emphysema hadn't learned anything from it.

Just then, Pizza Face approached Abercrombie in the distance, before he had time to put his pack back on. I was too far away to hear a word he said, but I watched him hand over each of his stones. Abercrombie just listened and smiled. They exchanged a bro hug when the transaction was completed.

I took a moment to look at the view with everyone else, but I was still thinking about Abercrombie. Was this exercise part of the program, or just something Abercrombie made up himself? What were we supposed to learn from this little life metaphor? That it's easy to give up your vices? False.

That just telling someone about your problems would make them go away? C'mon. That's crazy. That we weren't supposed to feel bad that Abercrombie had to carry around our baggage for the rest of the day? Selfish.

We mounted back up a few minutes later. It was only a fifteen pound difference, but Michaela and Pizza Face's packs looked much lighter. Nice for them, not so nice for Abercrombie. His pack was already bulging at the seams, and he still had stones to collect from four other people.

The light rain turned into a downpour for the next few miles. Trudging uphill with mud sticking to the bottom of my boots added to the injustice of it all. I really hated this place. I hated the rain. I hated this program. I hated hiking and I hated my mom for sending me here. She never would have put up with the crap I'd been dealing with since I got here. This place was against everything she valued. She couldn't go a day without makeup. And the thought of what the wilderness would do to her manicure was just too horrific. She wouldn't last one day out here.

It was still pouring when we reached the next outlook point. This one had actual guard rails…and wait, something we hadn't seen in two days. I walked right up to the rails and watched the two dots out on the cliff in the distance. People. Two hikers in rain gear were taking pictures.

"You did it, guys!" Backwoods Barbie cried as Abercrombie and Noah joined the rest of us. "It's all downhill from here."

Noah was completely out of breath from the steep climb.

"Yep," Abercrombie agreed. "The rest of the trail is easy compared to what you guys have already done. And we've got hot pizza waiting for us."

"So I guess we're not stopping here for lunch," Spud Boy said.

"You're hungry? It's only been two hours since breakfast," Pizza Face said. How did he know that? As far as I knew, none of us had a watch, and the sun was no help…if it was even still up there. I looked up at the heavy clouds. I wasn't really hungry yet, but it felt like we had been hiking forever. "I'm not dying or anything. I think we're just burning more fuel, carrying around this extra weight. And with the rain too."

"Go ahead and grab something if you're hungry," Backwoods Barbie said. "I can bring up the rear and stay behind for anybody who needs a little breather."

Abercrombie glanced at Noah, who was breathing normally now, but looked a little pale. "Fair enough. We just need to try to keep a reasonable pace. The switchbacks on Four Mile are going to be a little tricky if it's still raining like this."

Backwoods Barbie nodded. "Why don't we find a spot to sit down under a tree for a minute," she said, touching Noah's arm.

He jerked it away. Turning around in the mud, he started back toward the trail.

Abercrombie and Backwoods Barbie exchanged concerned glances, and then Abercrombie chased Noah. "Let's get going, guys," he said as he passed the others. "Think about pizza…fresh out of the oven. It's waiting for us."

I had a decision to make. Pizza Face was taking off his pack on a relatively dry log under the cover of some trees, and Backwoods Barbie stood close by. Michaela stayed with them too. Would I rather sit and rest for a few minutes, or push ahead through the sludge? If it had been Abercrombie staying behind, I might have made another decision, but my feet pointed themselves in the direction he was headed, and I followed in spite of my weary body.

The trail flattened out pretty quickly, and the trees overhead blocked some of the rain, but I was still miserable. How is it physically possible to have your nose and toes freezing cold while the rest of your body is sweating and suffocating under the plastic that is supposed to be keeping you dry? This mystery was taking up so much brain power that I completely stopped pondering the meaning of the rocks until I saw Abercrombie stopped on the trail up ahead.

He and Spud Boy were talking. It looked solemn. When I got a little closer, I saw rocks exchanging hands. Ugh. What was he saying? More animal felonies to confess to? I pushed myself a little faster, but they stopped talking when I was in range to hear what they were saying.

"Thanks, man," Spud Boy said, just before I passed them. Abercrombie put his pack on a large rock and set the stones down next to it. He smiled at me as I passed. I looked away, pretending I hadn't been trying to listen in. The rain had let up a little. Abercrombie didn't put the rocks in his pack right away, instead he took a detour into the woods, while Spud Boy followed me up the trail.

"Still have your stones?" he asked.

"Yep."

"I'd get rid of them before we get to Four Mile trail if I were you," he said.

I glanced over my shoulder at him and slowed down enough to let him catch up. "What's Four Mile trail?"

"Firewalker was just telling me that it's the last stretch of trail before we hit the Valley floor. He said it's pretty steep switchbacks all the way down."

"Downhill?" I said. "Shouldn't that be easier?"

"It's going to be slick in this weather, and you'll be surprised how much it'll beat up your toes. Fifteen pounds lighter will make a huge difference. You're going to feel it."

And what about Abercrombie? Wouldn't he feel it too?

"I'll keep that in mind," I said.

"I'm going on ahead to catch up with Stormi. Firewalker wants her to slow down a little."

I nodded, and Spud Boy stepped by, splashing up mud from a puddle in the middle of the trail as he passed. The rain started again when he was only a few yards away.

Everyone seemed to think handing off the rocks was the point of this little exercise. I still wasn't sure. Could it be that simple? If Spud Boy was right, and the trail was going to be harder going down, I should really think about what I would say if I decided to give Abercrombie my rocks. I had to think of something that sounded serious enough that he wouldn't think I was mocking the program, but I didn't want to make something up, just so I could get rid of them. Aside from the prom night incident, my record was squeaky clean…to the point of seeming boring. I didn't even have any egging, toilet papering, or cow tipping experience to fall back on.

For a split second I considered telling him about the family sized bag of Doritos I kept in a box on the shelf at the top of my closet. Sadly, I turned to my emergency bag whenever my mom said something especially hurtful about my weight.

I loved the salty taste. I loved the crunch. I could completely block out sad thoughts while I was eating them. Sometimes I would eat the whole bag in one sitting, but they never filled me up. Doritos were like an old friend, but they'd weighed me down for years. I'd gone to them for comfort, but they'd only contributed to the problems with my mom. In fact they made them worse.

My stomach rumbled. *No!* What was I thinking? My Doritos obsession was something I hadn't even talked about at fat camp. There was no way I was going to tell Abercrombie about it now. Besides, I hadn't touched them in over a year.

"How's it going?" Abercrombie caught up with me.

I didn't look back at him, afraid he'd see my face and somehow know what I'd been thinking.

"Fine," I said.

"Feet staying dry?" he asked.

I looked down at my hiking boots. The toes were much darker than the rest of the shoe from the rain and puddles. I guess it made sense that my socks were damp inside. I hadn't dissected the individual reasons for my general discomfort.

I shrugged. "I guess they're wet."

"Are they rubbing at all?" he asked. "You should put on a dry pair of socks when we get to Glacier Point. Wet feet and blisters tend to go together."

I caught his smile out of the corner of my eye. The Nutella smile. He didn't want me to get blisters. He'd hurried to catch up with me to make sure I was doing okay. I let the warmth of this thought fill me for a second. I even smiled back at him.

"Four Mile trail is really cool, but we're going to lose the same elevation we've gained in the last three days in about two hours." he said, looking directly at my backpack.

Or he just wanted an excuse to bring up the terrifying Four Mile trail so he could convince me to give him my rocks. Too bad. It wasn't going to work.

"Did you hike a lot growing up in Utah?" I asked, changing the subject like I didn't know what he was trying to get me to do.

"Not much," Abercrombie said. "My family isn't very outdoorsy."

"Really?" I asked. "But I mean, you've always liked it?"

"Not really," he answered.

He said it so matter-of-factly, but I found it kind of hard to believe.

"Hmm," I said. "For some reason I pictured your dad strapping a backpack on you as soon as you could walk."

"Maybe he did. I can't remember that far back." He laughed, but it was weird—not his normal laugh. "He used to be into hunting and fishing when I was little, but he kind of gave all that up a long time ago."

Was he speeding up? I suddenly felt like I was jogging to keep up with Abercrombie. Had I said something wrong? Hiking seemed like a pretty safe topic. We were catching up to the others fast and my time alone with him was coming to an end. I looked over at his pack again under his clear plastic poncho. Why did he carry a pack that was so weather beaten and worn? Everyone else, including Backwoods Barbie, had a brand new-looking pack.

"You get paid to work here, right?"

He looked a little surprised by this question. "Yes. This is a job."

"I just wondered because of your pack. Thought maybe you couldn't afford a newer one."

He laughed. "Nah. I'm doing okay for money. This pack just has a lot of sentimental value. Kind of one of those things that you don't want to replace, even though you know you'll have to eventually."

I glanced at the pack again. Had the buttons and patches and faded sharpie tattoos all been put there by people Abercrombie knew? Maybe other kids like us? Had he carried their rocks for them?

The kids stopped up ahead in the middle of the trail. Abercrombie had already taken their rocks. Didn't they feel at least a little bit guilty that he was carrying forty-five extra pounds because of them? They smiled as we got closer like they totally didn't care.

"Check it out," Spud Boy whispered, pointing into the woods. Abercrombie and I both turned and saw two deer and a fawn walking through the brush only about fifteen yards from the trail. Standing there next to Abercrombie watching the deer, I couldn't help thinking back to my first wildlife encounter two days before. It felt like a year ago.

We stood completely still, watching until the deer were out of sight.

"So cool," said Emphysema. "A little family."

It didn't sound like she was being sarcastic for once. The others must have noticed too, because everyone was staring at her.

"What?" she said, shoving Spud Boy away.

"Nothing," he said. "You just sounded so sentimental."

"Yeah, well that happens when you see something beautiful that you don't have." Emphysema started walking up the trail again.

"You don't have deer?" Spud Boy asked, taking off after her.

"I don't have a family, idiot." I heard her say. "I grew up in foster care."

Spud Boy was silent for a second. "But a foster family is still a kind of family, right?" he finally said.

"I guess, theoretically," Emphysema answered. "I just never stayed in one long enough to know."

We hiked in silence for a few minutes. The rain was slowing down, but now the wind picked up. Spud Boy must have been pondering his next question. I had to strain to hear it through the wind. "I guess they cared about you enough to send you here."

"Not really." Emphysema glanced over her shoulder at us.

"Enough to pay for it." Spud Boy pressed. "This program isn't cheap."

"They don't know I'm here," Emphysema said, stopping on the trail. "I haven't seen them for about eight months."

Nobody knew what to say to that. We were all dying to know how she ended up here, but nobody had the guts to ask her.

"Sounds like you've had it rough," Abercrombie finally said. "I know you already gave me your stones, but I'd say not having a family is something you were handed that has been weighing you down. Maybe more than rock and roll?"

"Yeah," Emphysema agreed, "but not exactly a vice you can just give up for Lent."

The rain stopped completely, and a sliver of light broke through the clouds in the distance. I caught sight of a rusty sign up ahead. We were coming to another outlook point or something.

"I didn't ask you for vices. I asked you for burdens," Abercrombie said. "Things that are weighing you down. Things that keep you from being happy."

Emphysema was quiet. Her shoulders fell forward slightly, but she didn't turn around. We reached the metal sign and a fork in the trail. One path would take us to Sentinel Dome, and the other to Glacier Point.

"Yeah, I guess 'no family' would even come before drugs and sex when you put it that way," Emphysema said. "Which direction are we heading?"

"Glacier," Abercrombie responded. The rest of us were quiet, waiting for Abercrombie to offer Emphysema some sage advice from the ancients, but he just smiled at her then walked past, leading us up the trail again.

"You know, Mother Earth has a way of balancing things out and giving you what you need," Spud Boy said. "I discovered that on my Spirit Walk. Right when you think you can't go another step because you're dying from hunger, you find a meadow with a bunch of edible leaves and wild onions."

"So what?" Emphysema said. "You think Mother Earth is just going to lead me to a meadow where I can pick a family like wild onions or something?"

"I don't know. I guess not exactly like that," Spud Boy said. "But can't a family just mean a group of people who really care about you?"

"That's not what it says if you look it up in the dictionary," she replied.

"Well, sometimes you have to make up your own definition," said Spud Boy. "And if you think about it that way, then Mother Earth is giving you a family right now."

Wow. Quiet Wolf. Maybe he didn't talk much, but when he did, it could be profound. Emphysema didn't say anything, but she must have felt it too.

More and more sun started breaking through the dark clouds as we walked. Could the rain really be over? We were getting close to Glacier Point when I heard voices behind us. Backwoods Barbie, Pizza Face and Michaela had caught up with us. Everyone seemed to feel the excitement of reaching civilization.

"We can stop to use the outhouses," Backwoods Barbie said.

High fives were passed among those of us who were close enough to each other, and everyone else gave their own personal cheer.

"We'll need to stay together," Abercrombie told us. "And we're not stopping for long."

Nobody cheered about this.

The sun had completely pushed out of the heavy clouds by now and everyone started taking off their ghetto ponchos. I pulled mine off too. The cool breeze felt good against my smothered skin. I wadded up my trash bag and tried to shove it in my left side pocket like Pizza Face had, but it wouldn't fit. My rocks were still there, taking up space. I'd forgotten them for a while, but as soon as I touched them, my pack seemed to triple in weight.

My eyes darted from hiker to hiker. They'd all given up their stones. They were all carrying less weight than I was.

Except for Abercrombie. His bulging pack looked like it was filled to capacity. Even if I wanted to tell him what was weighing me down, he didn't have room for my stones.

Glacier Point had a full-on visitor center with a gift shop and restaurant. A tour bus had just unloaded and the lines for the outhouses were long. The tourists all looked so clean, but none of them seemed concerned that they were standing in line with a bunch of juvenile delinquents. I guess maybe they couldn't tell just by looking at us. Maybe Quiet Wolf was right. Maybe we could pass for a family or something.

Standing in line behind Backwoods Barbie, I considered giving her my rocks. She hadn't picked up any stones at the river. It wouldn't be adding an unfair burden like it would be if I gave them to Abercrombie. It would just mean she would carry the extra fifteen pounds instead of me. She was a more experienced hiker. And she was being paid to do this.

Everyone else had taken their turn. I was the last one in line. If I was going to give up my stones, I had to do it as soon as Backwoods Barbie came out. It was the perfect opportunity. I could give her a lame, short list just like Emphysema had done. She wasn't going to question me or try to delve further into my psyche with a bunch of old people standing around, waiting to use the bathroom.

I glanced at the rest of the group, who'd already finished and were strapping back into their packs on the side of the paved parking lot. Abercrombie caught my eye and glanced at my pack. Was he thinking about the stones too? Wondering why I hadn't given them to him yet?

The lock turned on the stall Backwoods Barbie was in and her door opened, letting a horrendous smell waft out. My gag reflex was triggered, but nothing came up. My mind went completely blank and I let Backwoods Barbie walk right past me.

Forget about the stones. In four more miles, I could give them back without any obligation to tell Abercrombie anything. I didn't need him, or Backwoods Barbie, or anyone else to carry them for me.

<h1 style="text-align:center">Twelve</h1>

The next four miles were sheer torture. My legs were so used to going uphill that the constant pressure on my knees made them start to shake after only a short distance. I understood what Quiet Wolf had been saying about my toes now. Each step pushed my feet straight to the ends of my shoes, with the full force of my body weight, plus my pack.

The sky had cleared up, with the sun directly overhead, beating down on me. This trail was different than anything we had seen before. The view of the valley was almost completely unobstructed most of the way down, with very little foliage for shade. The boys let momentum carry them down the hill at high speed, with Emphysema close behind. Michaela walked at a more cautious pace just in front of Backwoods Barbie, and I lagged several yards behind, reaching one switch back just as everyone else rounded the corner ahead.

I couldn't stop thinking about Emphysema's sad life. What would it be like to be bounced from one home to another? My mom was crazy and dysfunctional, but I was biologically bound to her. No matter how many programs she'd dropped me off at, from daycare to fat camp, I'd never been afraid she wouldn't pick me up at the end.

So what exactly was it that was holding me back? Anybody looking at my resume would say "nothing". I was on the road to success. In a year, I would be headed to college, most likely with a scholarship. But was I happy? Had I ever been happy?

Just then, my toe struck a big rock in the trail and I tripped. But this time I didn't catch myself, falling straight forward onto the damp earth. My palms hit just before my knees, and then my pack smashed me flat into the ground.

"Are you okay?" Backwoods Barbie called, running back up the trail just as I managed to flip myself over.

I looked down at my clothes. My forearms and chest were completely covered with mud. "No, I'm not okay," I huffed.

"Hold on," she said, extending her hand when she reached me to try to help me back up. "How did you fall? Is anything broken?"

"I'm fine," I croaked. "Don't touch me."

"You're bleeding," she said.

I looked down at myself again. I didn't see any blood until it dripped from my chin onto my shirt. Where was it coming from? Touching my face, it was impossible to tell. It was covered in mud too.

"Just sit back. Let's get you cleaned off. It looks like you hit a rock."

Defiant, I tried to stand up, but my head started throbbing.

"Firewalker!" I heard Michaela, still a few yards away, yelling down the trail.

No. I didn't want Abercrombie to see me like this. And I didn't need him swooping in to save the day. My eyes blurred with tears.

"I'm going to clean you off so we can see how bad the gash is," Backwoods Barbie said, just before she sprayed me in the face with her water tube. I pinched my eyes and mouth shut, but I was screaming inside. *I don't need your help! I don't want it.*

"What happened?" Abercrombie's velvety voice called as the sound of his boots came running up the hill.

"She hit her head on a rock," Backwoods Barbie said, leaving out *she's super clumsy and she tripped over her own feet.* But I was sure she was thinking it. She was probably giving Abercrombie some kind of condescending look or signal or something, but I couldn't tell because she was still spraying me in the face.

"It doesn't look too bad," Abercrombie said. I heard the click of his pack buckle. "Are you okay, Jasmine? Can you hear me?"

Backwoods Barbie stopped spraying and I blinked the water out of my eyes. I could feel the gash now. It was above my left eye, between the brow and my hairline.

"I'm fine," I said, trying to get up again.

"Just relax," Abercrombie put his hand on my shoulder. "Michaela, can you tell everyone to sit tight?"

"Sure," she replied, immediately taking off to tell the others what an idiot I was.

"Let me take a look at that," Abercrombie said, peering deep into my eyes before shifting his focus to the cut. He pushed some hair that had fallen out of my braid away, and then ran his thumb under the cut. "It doesn't look too deep. I don't think it'll leave a scar if I close it up with liquid bandage."

Backwoods Barbie tore open a small package of gauze and handed it to Abercrombie. He pressed it firmly against my forehead.

"It works kind of like Super Glue, but it stings like crazy," Backwoods Barbie said.

Wait. Why did she say that like she was announcing that I had just won a new car?

"Are you hurt anywhere else?" Abercrombie asked, his eyes doing a quick sweep over my muddy mess.

"Not really." I rubbed my hands together before folding my arms in front of me. Abercrombie took the stinging glue from Backwoods Barbie, dabbing my forehead several times with the gauze. He was so close to me, and his clear, caramel colored eyes kept coming back to mine, full of concern. The butterflies almost convinced me he really cared.

"There," he said, handing the gauze back to Backwoods Barbie. "How many fingers am I holding up?"

Backwoods Barbie disposed of the gauze and leaned over Abercrombie to look in my eyes too, placing her hand on his shoulder. She killed the butterflies instantly. Abercrombie hadn't been trying to make a connection with his lingering eye contact, he'd been checking my pupils to see if I had a concussion.

"I'm fine," I said through gritted teeth. "Two fingers. Can you get on with it?"

Backwoods Barbie didn't take her hand off his shoulder. I'm not sure who she thought she was helping by standing so close like that. It was suffocating me. Finally, Abercrombie painted the gash with the liquid bandage and pressed his thumbs on both sides of it, blowing softly to help it dry. I closed my eyes to hide the tears, but it wasn't the sting of the cut that put them there. How much humiliation could one person take? Was it possible to die from it?

Before I knew it, Abercrombie's hands were off of my forehead, and his shadow wasn't blocking the sun anymore. I opened my eyes, and he smiled at me, offering me his hand.

"Can you stand up?" he asked.

I nodded. "I think so."

His hand was rough, but warm. The warmth spread from his hand to mine, clear up my arm until it reached my cheeks. He gently lifted me to my feet. "How does your head feel? Are you dizzy?"

I took a second to evaluate, looking down over the valley. My head pounded, and the cut stung, but my vision was clear. And he was still holding my hand. I looked back up to his face, sucked in again by his warm eyes.

"I'm perfect," I said in a weird, dreamy voice I didn't even recognize as mine.

His eyebrows came together, and his smile disappeared. Was he thinking about the stones? Wondering if they'd thrown me off balance? Blaming himself?

He dropped my hand like a hot potato.

Wait. Did I just say, *"I'm perfect?"* I meant *"perfectly fine"*.

"Why don't you drink some water, and we'll get going again," he said, turning away.

No. I didn't mean what you think I said. My mind was like jello.

"Let's slow down a little. Take it at a more manageable pace." Abercrombie spoke to the rest of the group, who had all gathered around to watch.

No. I'm so stupid. He wasn't blaming himself. *We're slowing down so Little Miss Thinks She's Perfect But Has Two Left Feet doesn't kill herself,* he seemed to be saying.

One by one, everyone stopped staring at me and started moving down the hill again. Backwoods Barbie led the pack while Abercrombie put away his first aid kit.

I unconsciously stroked my grazed palm with the tips of my fingers.

"You okay?" Quiet Wolf asked.

My palms and knees were skinned and bruised, but nothing hurt worse than my ego.

"I'm fine." I said. But it wasn't true.

"I told you the extra weight would throw you off balance. You still have your rocks, don't you?"

"It's not because of the freaking rocks," I snarled in a low voice. "The ground is slick. I just tripped." I looked over my shoulder. Abercrombie was only a few paces behind now.

"Why don't you just give them to him? We still have a few miles to go and it's not going to get any easier." He was talking full voice.

"Why don't you just mind your own business?"

Quiet Wolf shrugged with a *fine, but I told you so*, look on his face. Then he sped up and left me behind.

I glanced back. Abercrombie was keeping his distance and as soon as I caught his eye, he looked away. Who could blame him? There's really nothing worse than a person who thinks they're better than everyone else, and everything I had said and done since I first introduced myself sounded like I was that person. Covered in mud, I was as ugly on the outside as I felt on the inside.

I dropped my eyes and kept them fixed on the trail in front of me. Step after painful step I made my way down the steep path to the valley floor.

∞ ∞ ∞

The trail ended at a bus stop. The others chatted as we boarded the shuttle, half-full of tourists. I found an empty seat and took off my pack. Noah sat next to me. Everyone else stood watching the dark log buildings pass by.

118

"Finally!" I said, slouching down in my seat and resting my head against the window. "Could this day have been any worse?"

He didn't reply. It didn't matter. Caked in dry mud, I didn't really want to talk anyway. Tears were too close to the surface.

The other people on the bus were visiting Yosemite on vacation. It was hard to pretend I didn't care that the old guy in short shorts and long white socks was staring at me while whispering to his wife. Did he think I didn't know they were talking about me?

Abercrombie had his back to me now, facing a window and standing next to Backwoods Barbie right in the middle of the bus. They weren't talking to each other, but they were standing closer than they needed to on the mostly empty bus. I couldn't look at him without thinking about how he'd held my hand earlier. It stirred up all kinds of crazy emotions. Was he avoiding looking at me because the sight of me made him sick?

When we stopped in front of the Curry Village Pizza Patio, I didn't want to get off with everyone else. How much community service would I be sentenced to if I hijacked the bus?

"C'mon, guys," Pizza Face called, "real food."

It was no use. I had to go. The court had already given me my freebee. A hijacking would definitely go on my permanent record. But standing up wasn't as easy as you'd think. My legs were shaky, and my pack felt like it was full of boulders.

Because it was, actually.

The chain gang had almost reached a set of stairs on the side of the building when I was just barely stepping off the bus. A sign pointed customers of the Pizza Patio up the stairs. I didn't think I could eat due to my depressing life, but the smell of fresh bread and Italian seasoning changed my mind.

"The restrooms are down here," Backwoods Barbie said, looking directly at me. "Why don't we go wash up? Whoever gets done first can order. What do you guys like? A combo?"

"No mushrooms," Emphysema said.

"Or olives," Michaela added.

"Or green peppers," said Quiet Wolf.

"So just pepperoni?" Abercrombie laughed. "Sounds good. I'll get us a table."

We followed Backwoods Barbie inside, dropping our packs next to hers in a narrow hallway outside the restroom. I guess she wasn't worried someone would steal them. I shrugged. If somebody was stupid enough to want them, they deserved what they got.

I barely recognized myself in the tiny bathroom mirror. My face was pretty clean, but dirt covered my bare neck and the front of my shirt. I felt strangely sentimental about the existence of paper towels, as I did the best I could to clean myself off. And *running water*. How could I have taken it for granted? It was so beautiful.

Michaela and Emphysema went to join the boys upstairs before I was finished, but Backwoods Barbie stayed behind with me.

"Can you believe you've hiked over fourteen miles in the last three days?" she asked. "Doesn't it feel amazing?"

I glared at her out of the corner of my eyes. Was she saying that because she thought I'd never done anything physically hard before? Okay, maybe I hadn't hiked like this, but it wasn't like I'd just been sitting at home on the couch.

"How are you feeling?" she asked when I didn't respond to her first stab at conversation. "You've been so quiet all afternoon."

"I don't have anything to say," I told her. The paper towel I'd been using to scrub fell apart, so I took another from the dispenser.

"You've had a tough day," she said, "but I'm impressed. You never complain, and you really pushed through, even after you fell."

I stopped scrubbing at the dirt on my arm.

Glad you brought that up. Just in case I'd forgotten. I blew out a breath and started scrubbing again. Couldn't she just go away and leave me alone?

"You're the only one who decided to carry your rocks all the way down, you know." she continued.

So we were going to talk about the rocks. Now I understood. She wanted to know why I hadn't given them away.

"Firewalker said we could give them to him whenever we wanted…" I shut the sink off. "I didn't want to."

"Fair enough," she said, smoothing her ponytail. "I just wonder why anyone would want to carry around extra weight when it's so easy to give it up."

Why couldn't she just leave me alone? I knew what she was thinking. She was thinking I was too self-righteous to admit I had problems. Wadding up the paper towel, I threw it in the trash with a vengeance.

"Carrying extra weight is what I do." I charged past her, through the door. "Skinny people rarely understand." Slamming my hands against the door, I stormed out. But the door didn't swing closed behind me as I'd expected.

"Jasmine," Backwoods Barbie called, following me into the hallway, "wait."

Ignoring her, I pushed open the glass door.

"You're forgetting something," she said.

Forgetting what? Was she going to pass on some annoying Miwok wisdom? Or maybe she wanted to apologize for being skinny. I didn't really care.

This day just needs to be over. I continued on up the stairs without looking back.

Customers stood in line under the green and white striped awning, waiting to order at the window. Others sat at hexagon shaped picnic tables with green umbrellas. My group took up two tables in a corner near a tall tree. Its branches pushed over the railing, encroaching on the umbrella's space.

"Where's Monica?" Pizza Face asked, before I even sat down.

I shrugged and sat at the other table, next to Noah.

"Look at that," Quiet Wolf said, nodding toward a family that was just pulling apart a large Hawaiian. My mouth began to water as soon as I saw the stringy cheese. The sight and smell of it temporarily erased my disgruntled attitude toward life while the primeval desire to eat real food consumed me.

"How long until ours will be ready?" I asked.

"They said fifteen minutes, but that was about ten minutes ago," Pizza Face answered.

I expected someone to acknowledge Backwoods Barbie when she came up the stairs. She should have been right behind me. What was taking her so long?

I was starting to get nervous about what she might be doing. Did it have something to do with me? My question was answered all too soon.

"Monica?" Michaela stood up and looked from the stairs to me and back again. Everyone else stood too, except Noah. We both turned around to look at the same time.

Backwoods Barbie trudged up the stairs sandwiched between two packs—hers slung over her shoulders and mine in front with her arms wrapped around it like a jumbo paper grocery bag. Abercrombie rushed over to meet her, taking my pack. Everyone else turned their stink eyes on me. I wanted to crawl into a hole and die.

"Nice," Emphysema said. "You won't let Firewalker take your fifteen extra pounds, but you'll let Monica carry your whole pack up the stairs for you?"

"I didn't ask her to," I stammered. "I just…forgot it was down there."

Monica and Abercrombie dropped the packs against the rail. Next to all of the other packs I hadn't noticed at all when I came up the stairs. Abercrombie bent down a little and Monica said something in a low voice. He touched her arm above the elbow. Then he leaned in and whispered something in her ear. They smiled at each other. The "we've been through so much together, and we're going to come out of this stronger," kind of smile. I looked away, just in time to see the waiter bring out our pizzas.

Abercrombie and Monica sat next to each other at the other table. I wanted to explain myself, but nobody cared now. They were all too busy reaching for the pizza. When the vultures backed away, I put a slice on my plate. But my first bite went down like a rock. How could I eat when everyone had the completely wrong idea about me? I wasn't self-righteous. I wasn't rude and unfeeling. I wasn't the incompetent, clumsy person they all thought I was. People at home liked me. I had lots of friends. I was a good listener and I was extremely loyal. But how could I tell them all of that without sounding even more self-centered?

After the first slices of pizza were polished off, conversations started up again. But nobody was talking about me. Nobody was talking to me. Nobody was looking at me. Even Backwoods Barbie and Abercrombie talked and laughed like nothing had happened.

My situation was hopeless.

Thirteen

Nobody talked to me at all during dinner and the cold shoulder continued as we carried our packs down to wait on the curb for our ride. Even Noah was ignoring me, but I doubted it was because of the backpack thing. He looked like he didn't feel too hot again.

"The van will be here to pick us up in about ten minutes," Abercrombie said.

"We're meeting up with another group at the backpacker's campground at Tuolumne Meadows," Backwoods Barbie said. "They just finished the High Sierra Loop and tomorrow they'll start the Pohono Trail."

"So we're just swapping?" Pizza Face asked.

Backwoods Barbie nodded. "Our first two legs are going to be spirit walks."

The spirit walk was when we had to forage for food, right? Pizza Face didn't react, but I had an instant sinking feeling. How many days would it be before we ate another meal? No wonder they'd stuffed us full of pizza. I wasn't ready for this.

The van pulled up and we all piled in. I was the last to board, and they'd saved me the front row again. All to myself.

Perfect.

But on the bright side, sitting on an upholstered seat felt amazing. Sitting should always be done on upholstery. Abercrombie sat in the back, talking to Emphysema about classic rock bands. Pizza Face and Michaela argued with Quiet Wolf about the details of some first-person shooter game they all knew way too much about.

Noah looked horrible in the seat behind me, with his eyes pinched closed and his head pressed against the window. Maybe the pizza wasn't sitting right. Since nobody was talking to me, I stretched myself out on the empty bench and fell asleep.

∞ ∞ ∞

When the van stopped, the sun was low on the horizon. My window faced a big, open meadow with mountains off in the distance. I stretched my arms over my head.

"Go ahead and unload your bear canisters," said the driver. "They'll be waiting for you in the lockers at May Lake."

Abercrombie and Backwoods Barbie nodded. We followed them out of the van and took the canisters out of our packs. I was happy to see a legitimate campground with a store and gas station. Maybe it meant we would have real bathrooms too. The prospect was comforting, but I had to admit I was terrified of what the morning would bring. Hiking fueled by oatmeal and beans was bad enough. On an empty stomach, it would be unbearable.

The other High Sierra group had already pitched their tents in the mostly empty hikers' campground. They sat around a huge fire. We pitched our tents before joining them.

Abercrombie and Backwoods Barbie greeted the two spirit guides from the other group with hugs. Both guys were about Abercrombie's age, but not nearly as good looking. One of them had a full scruffy, black beard, and the other had abnormally skinny legs, like a flamingo. Blackbeard held a guitar. He sat down and started playing while our group filled in on the log benches around the fire.

The fire burned high and hot. Crackling logs scattered sparks above the flames. I leaned forward with my elbows on my knees and my chin resting on my hands. The bearded guy strummed familiar chords on his guitar, humming softly until he got to the chorus of "Collide" by Howie Day. One of my mom's favorite songs, but the words took on a different meaning.

Nobody's fallen harder than me since we've been here, I thought, touching the gash on my forehead lightly. The flames shifted in the breeze and Abercrombie's blurry face appeared. Our eyes locked, and the corner of his mouth drifted up sympathetically just as Blackbeard sang.

To my left, Pizza Face and Quiet Wolf burst out laughing. I whipped around and saw Pizza Face nudging Emphysema, who joined in the laughter. Laughing at me? Smoke clouded my eyes and I pinched them closed against the sting.

The laughing died off and the strains of Blackbeard's song faded, but I kept my eyes closed, trying not to choke on the lump in my throat.

"You should play for us, Bryce," Backwoods Barbie said after a few seconds of silence. My eyes opened slowly.

Abercrombie played guitar?

Abercrombie smiled, but shook his head, "Not sure if I remember how, it's been so long."

Of course he did. What didn't he do?

"C'mon," said Blackbeard. "It's like riding a bike." He handed the guitar over to Abercrombie, who ran his hand over the back of it before setting it on his lap. He played a chord, then readjusted how it rested on his knee. Finally, he began strumming a soft pattern, moving his hand smoothly up and down the fretboard.

And then he started singing, but his voice only vaguely resembled the one he'd used to rap during our game of name that tune.

"I am a child of God and he has sent me here. Has given me an earthly home with parents kind and dear." His deep voice caressed the words like he'd written them himself. The giant lump in my throat tripled in size. I wanted to look away, but my eyes were stuck on him like a magnet.

"Lead me, guide me, walk beside me, help me find the way." His eyes closed. "Teach me all that I must do, to live with him someday."

A child of God. The fire became a swirling sea of red and orange and my frazzled emotions sat exposed—like a fuse already lit.

Scanning the faces of the mangy hikers through blurry eyes, I blew out a slow breath, trying to make sense of it all and defuse myself. He continued to sing and play, but I couldn't process the words.

How nice for Abercrombie. His God was a loving father. What did having a loving father even feel like?

I had to get away from here before someone saw me. On the end of the bench nearest the trail leading back to the tents, I could slip into the darkness easily. All eyes were still on Abercrombie. I got up quickly and moved without breathing. The crunch of rocks under my boots was muted by the music and crackling logs as I tiptoed away.

Far from the uncomfortable warmth of the fire, the evening air was damp and chilly. Dim yellow light from the lanterns and fires at the campsites surrounding the bathrooms glowed in the distance. Our tents were up a hill in the opposite direction. I'd left my flashlight in my pack back at the tent. Several yards of pitch black stood between me and either destination.

There were no showers in the bathrooms, but I had to try to wash off as much of this day as possible. I needed that multi-purpose camping soap. Drying my eyes on my sleeve before heading up the hill, I hurried to go retrieve it.

But the farther I strayed from the campfire, the more unsure I became. My step faltered on the unstable ground. The shapes of the tents at the top of the small hill began to blend into the dark shadows of the trees. Insects, chirping in chorus, felt like the soundtrack to a horror film and every small noise had me searching the sides of the path for whatever was waiting there to eat me alive.

When I finally reached the tent, I found my flashlight right away but had to fish through my pack for the soap. Bent over, my war wounds throbbed lightly with my pulse. I touched the gash on my forehead. It was still tender and the raw skin on my palms stung.

Laughter rang out from the fire below. Blackbeard must have reclaimed his guitar. His gruff voice belted out the verse to "Yellow Submarine." Everyone else joined in when he got to the chorus.

Great. Why does the party always start as soon as I leave?

I finally touched the bottle of soap but lifting it out with my grazed palms was too much. I couldn't hold on, and it fell into the dirt.

Why? I wanted to scream.

I dug my fingernails into my palms until the pain felt like flames.

Why does it have to hurt so much to be me?

My eyes filled up and spilled down my face, making a trail through the grit and grime.

"Jasmine?" Abercrombie's voice cut through the dark before his headlamp came bobbing up the hill. "You up here?"

I didn't answer, holding my breath to try to stop the tears while madly wiping them away with my sweatshirt. But I didn't have enough time. His long stride rapidly closed the gap between us. I turned away just before his headlamp exposed me. I tried to think of a reasonable explanation for why I was facing away from him, staring at my shadow on a tree, instead of answering when he called me, but really, there wasn't one. And Abercrombie was about to see me at my absolute worst.

"There you are," he said. "I didn't see you leave the fire circle. You feeling okay?"

Feeling okay. That was it. I touched the gash on my forehead and shaded my eyes before turning to face him.

"Headache," I said, lowering my eyes dramatically toward the ground as soon as his light hit my face.

"Yeah?" He stopped where he was and did something to change the setting on his light to make it glow dim red. "We should probably take a look to make sure you're not showing any signs of a concussion."

"No!" I said, grabbing for the soap I'd dropped. "I mean, I think it was the smoke. It was bothering my eyes. I just want to wash my face and go to bed."

"Are you sure?" he asked, taking a few steps closer.

"I'm sure." Without looking up, I stepped out of Abercrombie's small circle of red light, back onto the trail, accidentally brushing his arm as I passed. I fumbled for the button on my flashlight while I tried to put him safely behind me.

"Hold on, I'll walk down there with you."

"Don't bother," I said.

"Maybe you should slow down a bit." His light, now bright again, bounced from the trees to the rocks on the trail ahead of me. If he caught up, he'd see my face for sure.

"I'm okay. Really."

"Hey, seriously." Gaining on me, he reached for me. The warmth of his touch spread rapidly through my arm from where he grasped it just above the elbow. "Slow down before you hurt yourself again."

I came to a dead stop. I was just a hopelessly clumsy, stupid girl to him. Clenching my jaw, I jerked my arm away.

"I don't need a babysitter," I growled through gritted teeth.

"Shhh!" Abercrombie grabbed my other arm.

"I'm not a kid!"

"Jasmine!" he whispered harshly.

His grasp tightened. I struggled to get free. What was he trying to do? Put me in a straight-jacket?

Suddenly, he let go and reached up for his light, switching it to red. I froze, and the hair on the back of my neck stood on end. His eyes were trained on the trees directly behind me.

Standing still, I heard what sounded like metal scraping against metal.

"What is it?" I whispered, terrified to turn around and look.

Abercrombie brought his finger to his lips. The scraping continued. Scratching. Claws against metal.

"Bear?"

He nodded but held completely still otherwise. Were you supposed to treat bears like bees? I wanted to run away as fast as I could, but Abercrombie was a statue. The scraping stopped. Had it seen us? Was it coming toward us? I slowly turned my head to look over my shoulder.

In the dim light, I could only see the rounded outline of the huge bear, perched on top of one of the big metal storage lockers they had at each of the campsites. Its face searched the inside of a pack that had been left out.

"What do we do?" My voice was barely audible.

Abercrombie moved slowly toward me without making a noise until his mouth was close to my ear. "She's got her cubs with her."

I glanced over my shoulder again. Two small bears sat on the ground near the locker. One of them reached up toward the mother.

The kids down at the fire started singing again, and the big bear lifted her head out of the backpack to see what was up.

"Can't we just run?"

Abercrombie shook his head. "Don't worry," he said. "Black bears come into these campgrounds all the time."

Abercrombie stood watching the bears while I tried not to pass out. My face was literally inches from his shirt, and his woodsy scent was the only thing keeping me focused— like some kind of medieval smelling salt.

Finally, the big bear jumped down from the locker. My hand came up involuntarily and clutched Abercrombie's forearm. After a few seconds, the bear moved into the trees and the two cubs followed her into the woods.

"What now?" I asked after they were out of sight for several seconds.

Abercrombie flipped his headlamp back to bright, exposing my dirty, smeared face.

"I'll walk you down to the bathrooms, and then I'll go report this to the rangers."

"What will they do?"

"The mother was tagged. I think they just like to keep track of sightings."

Abercrombie started down the trail toward the bathrooms. I hurried to catch up. Even if Abercrombie

could see what a huge mess I was, I had no desire to be alone
in the woods ever again.

Fourteen

The rain came off and on during the night. Sleep taunted me as I alternated between cold, uncomfortable misery, and dreams about bears attacking our tent.

When morning came, relief came with it. I was the first one up. Three nights down. Only 27 to go and I'd be like Pizza Face and Quiet Wolf. I shuddered. Would I ever sleep in my own bed again?

The scent of cooking bacon permeated the campground.

"Oh, man, that smells good!" Emphysema sighed, stretching her arms as she came out of the tent. "Where is that coming from?"

"It's the little restaurant up by the grocery store," said Pizza Face. "But don't get too excited. We're spirit walking, remember?"

Noah poked his head out of the tent after several minutes of coaxing from Abercrombie. His skin was as pale as the ashes in the fire pit, and his lips were completely white.

As soon as he stood up fully, he stumbled over to a tree and propped himself against it. How long did withdrawals last anyway?

The campground had flushing toilets, but I guess Noah couldn't make it that far. He staggered a few yards away and started throwing up in the bushes.

The others all seemed oblivious, rolling sleeping bags and packing up tents like they couldn't hear anything. It occurred to me that I should probably be helping too, instead of just standing there, watching Noah. Imitating what Backwoods Barbie was doing, I picked up the plastic ground cover from under the girl's tent and shook the dirt and pine needles off.

Noah wandered back just as the boys zipped the tent in its case.

"Where do we put these?" Quiet Wolf asked.

"The van's coming to pick up the other group," Abercrombie said. "Take them over to Windsong."

"The guy with the beard?" Pizza Face asked.

Abercrombie nodded.

I'd forgotten what Pizza Face had said about his first spirit walk. It wasn't just foraging for food. We were going to have to make our own shelter tonight too. I watched with a sinking heart as the boys took the tents to the other group and dropped them next to their gear.

Noah sat a few feet away from me. He must have been watching what was happening. He stood up, looking determined.

"I need to talk to you," he rasped, approaching Abercrombie.

Abercrombie smiled. "Sure, man," he said. "Feeling any better?" He was definitely playing it cool that Noah had finally broken his silence, but I could see that Abercrombie was excited.

"No," said Noah, clutching his stomach. He paused, looking across the way at the other group of hikers. "I have a fever."

Abercrombie put the back of his hand on Noah's forehead. "Feels normal to me."

"I can't keep anything down." Noah looked at the ground.

"I know," Abercrombie said, putting his hand on Noah's shoulder. "It's going to get better. Pretty soon the headache will go away. Your stomach will settle down. In fact, some of the stuff we're going to find on the trail will help."

Noah closed his eyes. "I'm slowing you guys down."

"It's not a race," Abercrombie replied.

Noah gritted his teeth and looked up with eyes blazing. "I can't do it anymore!" he said, throwing Abercrombie's hand off his shoulder.

Abercrombie stood silent, staring Noah down. "Well, I guess the decision's yours. I believe you can do it."

Noah's face grew pale, and his breathing heavy. It looked like rage and sickness were battling it out inside him. I guess the sickness won, because he doubled over and stumbled back into the trees.

I looked around. Had I been the only one listening to the hushed conversation? The others were packing up their stuff, talking to each other like nothing else was happening.

Abercrombie had said it was Noah's decision. If he could choose not to go on the spirit walk, could I choose not to? What would happen to us? Would we just be assigned to a different group?

I couldn't let this opportunity pass without asking. Stepping away from the tree I had been leaning against, I asked, "Is that really true?"

"What?" Abercrombie said.

"Can we really choose to hike or not?"

"Yeah." Abercrombie cinched up his pack. "The Great Creator doesn't force his children to do anything, and neither does High Sierra."

"So what, any of us could just walk away from this whenever we want?"

"If that's what you choose," Abercrombie said. His eyebrows came together. "But…I hope you don't choose to do that." And without another word, he turned away, walking toward Blackbeard in the other camp.

A million thoughts rushed my mind. Maybe I really could walk away from this program. If it was my choice, I could go over to the little store and ask to use the telephone. I could call my mom. I could apologize to her. I could convince her that this program wasn't the way to solve our problems. I could promise to be better. I might be able to salvage my summer vacation.

Abercrombie was still talking to Blackbeard. Whatever he was saying seemed serious. They both glanced at Noah, and then over to me. They were far enough away that I could only catch snatches of their conversation.

"Both of them?" Blackbeard asked.

"…more her. You know. It's just awkward." What was more me?

"I talked to Good Soaring Raven about it last night, but he wants you to stay put," Blackbeard said.

What? Abercrombie had been talking to Blackbeard about me last night? And he thought I was worse than Noah?

I stepped over to the picnic table where Noah's stuff was scattered and started shoving it into his bag. How could Abercrombie say that about me? Maybe I hadn't had the best luck, but wasn't it obvious I was trying?

Blackbeard chuckled and slapped Abercrombie on the shoulder. "I have faith in you. You can handle it, man." Abercrombie nodded and walked away. My ears burned.

Noah sat at the other end of the picnic table with his head on his folded arms. I cinched up his bag and grabbed the whole thing. "Here you go," I said, dropping the pack in front of him on the ground. He didn't look up.

I waited for a second, then sat on the bench next to him.

"Noah," I said. "You can do this. You have to."

No answer.

"This is hard for me too," I said in a strained whisper. "But we have to if we want to go home. C'mon. We can hike together." I put my hand on his back.

Noah shrugged it off.

"Seriously?" I raised my voice slightly. "Do you really want these people to think you can't hack it? That they're better than you?"

Noah finally looked up, rage burning in his eyes. "Just leave me alone!"

He might as well have punched me in the throat. "Okay," I choked. Standing up slowly, I turned toward my pack before he saw the mist in my eyes

For the first time ever, we didn't have to wait for Noah. When it was time to leave, he stood near Backwoods Barbie with his pack on, looking sullen but resolved.

I kept my eyes on the path as we left the campground, crossed the highway, and reached a parking lot and trailhead. Starting out, the terrain looked very different from the Pohono trail. The flat path through the meadow was wide and open, with no trees close to the trail for shade. The thick storm clouds from yesterday were gone, but smaller, fluffy ones blocked the sun until the wind blew them out of the way.

On the flat trail, we all stayed closer than usual. Even Noah was keeping pace. He still looked pretty pale, his feet dragged, and his head hung down, but at least he was walking. I don't know why I cared, since he'd made it clear he didn't like me.

The sunny weather and relatively flat trail would have lightened my mood yesterday, but I was at an all time low. I couldn't stop thinking about Abercrombie's conversation with Blackbeard. How could he think my attitude was even in the same universe as Noah's, let alone worse?

Compounding my problem, we'd skipped my favorite meal of the day. When we stopped to pick some edible greens and roots, it was a bitter substitute for eggs and bacon. Noah didn't even try them.

"We'll have fish for lunch," Abercrombie promised.

Pizza Face was chowing down on his wildflower salad like there was no tomorrow. Michaela seemed pretty excited to try the roots, but she couldn't pretend to like them. I had to hand it to her for not spitting them out. I tasted everything, but couldn't imagine that the number of calories I was getting out of it was worth the effort. I wanted to ask Abercrombie how many days of foraging we had to endure before we hit the bear lockers at May Lake the driver had mentioned, but I doubted he would deem my motives pure enough to answer.

We were on our way again a short time later. Soon, the sound of rushing water could be heard in the distance. The trail met up with a stream, moving downward over the rocky terrain. We followed alongside, on the shaded path. I might have been able to enjoy the beauty of it if it wasn't for the pains in my shriveled-up stomach. I was drinking water like a camel, trying to trick myself into feeling full, but it wasn't working.

The others must have been doing the same thing, because we had to stop several times for people to be alone in the woods. The wind picked up and ever thickening clouds began to crowd out the sun. Thunder rumbled in the distance. We'd only been hiking about five minutes after Emphysema's bathroom break when Noah said he needed to stop. It was going to be a long day.

"Twenty-seven!" Noah shouted as soon as he was out of sight.

We all stood on the trail awkwardly. It was weird to hear him call out his number.

"Twenty-seven," Noah called again, this time much softer. It sounded like someone had punched him in the gut.

Abercrombie and Backwoods Barbie exchanged a look. "This seems like a good spot to take a little break," Abercrombie said.

We all looked around at each other.

"But we haven't been going that long," said Emphysema.

"We're in no hurry to get anywhere today," Abercrombie replied. "Why not just sit out on those rocks for a while? Enjoy the water. Rest a little."

Quiet Wolf shrugged, then took off his pack. The others followed him out to the rocks near the river. I took longer unhooking my pack.

"Looks like he's having a breakthrough," I heard Backwoods Barbie say to Abercrombie.

Abercrombie smiled but raised his eyebrows. "Did something happen?"

"He's talking."

Abercrombie shrugged. "I think he still has some struggles ahead."

Finally! I was happy to hear Abercrombie giving Backwoods Barbie a reality check. Life isn't all peaches and roses, and three days of wilderness detox wasn't going to magically cure Noah.

"Twenty-seven," Noah's voice sounded even more pained and distant. The thunder rumbled in the distance again. I looked up at the sky, then over at the others out on the boulders. The water formed pools all around them. Probably not the safest place to be with a thunderstorm heading our direction. I didn't really need to use the restroom urgently, but with all the water I'd been drinking, I probably would soon.

"Maybe I should go check on him," Abercrombie said.

Something about his tone of voice put me on edge. Why was he suddenly so concerned about Noah? It was giving me a weird feeling in the pit of my stomach. Weird enough to cover up the hunger pangs.

Backwoods Barbie looked toward the area in the woods where Noah's voice was coming from. "Let's give him a few minutes. He just needs some privacy," she said.

Abercrombie shrugged but didn't say anything.

I decided to try. Might as well while we were stopped. I crossed over the trail and made my way into the trees.

"Twelve!" I called.

I stopped walking when I couldn't see the trail or the kids by the river anymore. I could still hear their voices every now and then over the sounds of the flowing water. After I finished my business, I leaned against a tree, listening for Noah. I was only about a hundred yards from where he had been calling from, but it had been ages since I'd heard his number.

What if something was really wrong with him? What if he'd collapsed? Would it be my fault since I'd pushed him into hiking today? I listened intently for rustling, dry heaving, anything that would reassure me he wasn't lying in a heap on the ground.

After several minutes of listening, with my body growing more and more tense, I realized I was being ridiculous. Noah didn't care about me. Why was I worried about him? He probably wasn't calling out his number because he was back with the others by the stream.

I started back toward the trail, but after only a few steps I heard Abercrombie.

"Noah?" he called. I froze. He was only a few yards away, but a large tree stood between us. "Are you okay, man?"

He didn't see me, continuing on farther away from the trail. I stayed behind the tree for a few seconds, then followed Abercrombie, careful not to make too much noise.

"Noah?" Abercrombie called again. He looked left and right. Still no response. He glanced back and forth from the trail behind him to the thick woods in front. Then he stooped down to examine the area where he was standing. It was my best guess that Noah had been somewhere in this area too. Could Abercrombie see footprints? What was he looking at? After a moment, he surprised me by turning back to the trail instead of continuing his search for Noah.

I moved slowly back to where I had been standing and called out my number again. I was making my way back to the trail when I heard Abercrombie talking to Backwoods Barbie.

"He's gone. I can see which way he took off, but he's got a lead. I'm going to have to hurry to catch up."

"What should I do?" Backwoods Barbie asked.

"Go ahead," he said. "We'll meet you at Glen Aulin. It's only a few more miles. Radio back-up and let them know we have a runner. I'll check in as soon as I find him."

Backwoods Barbie nodded then reached for the radio in her pack. Abercrombie threw his pack on and headed back into the woods, this time at a much quicker pace. He moved through the underbrush to the spot where he'd stopped before. Looking down, he seemed to be following Noah's footprints.

I stood frozen for a second then followed Abercrombie. My heart beat a million miles an hour. This wasn't smart. Backwoods Barbie would panic when she realized I was gone too. But I couldn't help myself. Noah was so desperate, he was willing to brave the woods alone. He wasn't thinking straight.

Abercrombie moved so stealthily through the trees, I could barely keep up. If he wasn't stopping every fifty yards or so to look down at whatever clues Noah had left behind, I would have lost him completely. The forest became even more dense and the sound of the rushing water faded as we climbed a hill. I looked over my shoulder. Would I even know how to find my way back if I turned around?

Suddenly, up ahead, the trees began to thin out. And then Noah's trail lead Abercrombie onto a smooth rock formation. I followed him to the edge of the treeline, trying to make a decision. If I kept following Abercrombie, he would see me out in the open. Or I had to turn around and find my way back on my own. But I'd completely lost track of how long we'd been walking, and I wasn't sure of my directions anymore.

Abercrombie scrambled up the incline with the determination of a mountain goat. What clue had he seen that made him decide to go up instead of around? It took me a second to spot Noah's green backpack about fifty feet above Abercrombie. Back pressed against the rocks, Noah peered down at Abercrombie as he approached.

"Don't come any closer," he yelled.

Abercrombie stopped climbing. I stepped behind a tree and pressed my face against the bark. It wasn't like he was standing on the edge of Crocker Point, ready to jump, but Noah's position wasn't exactly safe either. About ten feet to his left, the face of the otherwise smooth, yellowish rock cut off like someone had sliced it in half, dropping sharply into a ravine.

"Leave me alone," Noah called.

"What's up, Noah?" Abercrombie said. "Whatcha doing way up here?"

"I told you I can't do this anymore." Noah's voice faltered. He stepped closer to the edge of the ravine.

"Hold on, Noah. You don't have to do anything. Let's talk about this."

"I don't want to talk."

Abercrombie started climbing again. I held my breath, watching Noah inch closer and closer to the edge. What was he doing? Jumping off a rock into a ravine thirty feet down might break a few bones, but it wouldn't kill anyone.

"Why don't you come down here, Noah?" Abercrombie called, still climbing steadily toward him. "If you need to rest for a while, we can rest. If you're hungry, we'll catch some fish. It's not as bad as you think."

"It's worse than I think," Noah yelled back, scooting even closer to the edge. His shoe knocked a pile of pebbles down into the ravine, and he watched them until they stopped making noise with his back pressed awkwardly against the rock wall. Abercrombie was getting closer, but he was still several yards below. My palms were sweaty. Why couldn't Abercrombie hurry up? And why couldn't Noah just cooperate and come back down?

"I'm not doing this anymore," Noah reiterated.

"Okay," Abercrombie said.

"Stay away! You're coming up here to try to bring me back, but I'm not coming."

"I'm not trying to bring you anywhere," Abercrombie's voice became calmer and more controlled in response to Noah's growing frenzy. "Wherever you're going, I'm going with you."

Abercrombie climbed the last few steps, bringing him to the same ledge Noah was standing on. Only a few feet away now, he put his hands on his knees and took a few deep breaths. Noah's eyes darted back and forth between Abercrombie and the ravine. The sheer rock above him would take climbing equipment to scale. His only options were to follow Abercrombie back down the hill, or to jump. He wasn't really considering that, was he? Why wasn't Abercrombie saying anything?

Noah shuffled back and forth, knocking more rocks into the ravine. "I'm not coming down," he finally said.

"Totally your choice." Abercrombie stood up fully and taking a small step away.

"You're so full of it," Noah said. "None of this is my choice. This place is worse than prison. The trees are worse than bars." He was facing Abercrombie, but still rocking back and forth, only inches away from the ledge. *Just step away!* Even if he didn't really want to jump, he felt cornered. I reached a hand toward him.

"If you decide to walk out of here, nobody is going to stop you. I just have to come along," Abercrombie said.

"Yeah, right!" Noah said.

Noah rocked back and forth on his feet again, but his right heel was already hanging over the edge. When he realized, he shifted his weight, trying to regain his balance, but it was too late. Arms and legs scrambling, Noah tumbled to the ground, half of his body hanging over the edge of the ravine.

"Noah!" I shrieked.

"Hang on!" Abercrombie yelled, lunging toward Noah and dropping to his knees. I started running toward them too. Holding onto the rocks with his elbows, Noah slowly slid, struggling against the weight of his backpack. Abercrombie reached for Noah's arm, but Noah flailed desperately and slid even further until only his hands gripped the edge.

"I've got you," Abercrombie said, holding onto one of Noah's forearms. I was at the base of the rocks now, unsure whether to climb or stay put. By the time I reached them, it would be too late. Looking up, I watched Abercrombie lean all of his weight backward as he hefted Noah onto the ledge. When Noah's knees touched the rock again, he scrambled to stand up. I watched in horror as his struggle knocked Abercrombie off balance. The weight of Abercrombie's pack tilted him to the right, slamming him against the rock wall. Loose rocks beneath his feet shifted, and he tumbled forward. Over the ledge. I screamed.

His backpack hit another ledge with a thud. But the ledge wasn't enough to keep him from tumbling over again, this time rolling and bumping against the side of the drop off until he hit the floor of the ravine.

Abercrombie!

My view of him was blocked out by the thick underbrush. I pushed through it, barely aware of the branches tearing at my arms. Winding around trees and rocks, I finally saw the spot where he had landed.

"Jasmine?" Noah called, kneeling over the edge of the ledge above. I barely glanced up at him. Covered by his backpack, Abercrombie's body lay in a heap just a few yards in front of me.

"Bryce!" I didn't stop running until I reached him.

"Bryce?" I called again. He didn't move. I bent down to turn him over but hesitated. His back had hit pretty hard. Would it be dangerous to move him? What if I paralyzed him or something?

"Is he okay?" Noah called.

I had to make sure he was breathing, and there was no way I could do that when he was laying on his stomach. Grabbing his backpack with almost superhuman strength, I rolled him over.

He didn't respond. His face was all scratched up, blood trickled from the corner of his mouth, and a huge goose egg was forming above his left eyebrow.

"Bryce, can you hear me?" I begged.

"Is he alive?" Noah yelled down.

"Shut up!" I yelled back. Bending down I put my ear close to Bryce's mouth and nose. Was he breathing? It was so hard to tell with the breeze sweeping past.

Oh, please let him be breathing. I still couldn't tell.

What about a pulse? With my heart beating erratically, I reached for one of Bryce's limp arms. Wasn't I supposed to feel it near the artery on the outside of his wrist? Positioning his arm and finding the spot wasn't easy.

"Jasmine!" Noah called from above again.

"Why are you still up there?" I yelled. "He needs help!"

Was that it? I moved my fingers around. *Thump. Thump. Thump.* Yeah. That was definitely a pulse. I dropped his arm and put my ear on his chest. It heaved up slowly and sunk back down again.

"He's breathing!" I yelled. Noah didn't answer and his face wasn't peering over the edge anymore. Good. One of us was going to need to go for help.

"Bryce," I called. "Can you hear me?" My eyes swept over his body. Left pant leg. His knee. A deep red spot spreading across it. *Blood.*

Oh…oh….oh. No. What was I supposed to do now?

What if he bled to death before we could find help? I looked up again.

"Noah!" Where was he? My head spun and my eyes blurred.

Focus. I needed to see the injury to have an idea how bad it is. I cringed. How was I going to do that? Abercrombie's pants didn't zip off at the knee like mine.

But I could cut them off like they do on those trauma emergency room shows my mom liked to watch. Abercrombie's pocket knife was in the hip zipper of his pack. He'd used it this morning to close the lid on his bear canister before putting it in the van.

Unzipping the pocket while Abercrombie was still attached to the pack felt awkward, but it didn't take much fishing around to feel the smooth plastic knife case. The red and white Swiss Army symbol almost disappeared against the ever-widening circle of blood as I held it above his leg, searching for a blade that would cut through the fabric.

"Here goes nothing," I said. "Please don't let it be too bad." I looked up at the dark clouds blocking the sun. Could Abercrombie's God see what was happening down here?

Grabbing Abercrombie's pant leg, I carefully pushed the blade through, tearing the fabric.

The bone just below the knee had snapped like a twig and part of it was sticking out of the skin. The pocket knife fell out of my hand as I fought to keep my eyes focused.

"Oh my…" Noah came up behind me, stopping a few feet away when he saw the bloody mess. "What are we…how do we…"

"We have to stop the bleeding, and somebody has to go for help. "

Noah just stood there, shaking his head. I took the hole I'd made and ripped even farther. All the way to the seam. Then I ripped up the seam toward his torso. You're supposed to put pressure to stop the bleeding. I knew that much. But how and where?

"I can't look at this," Noah said. "I have to sit down."

"Stop thinking about yourself for two seconds," I said. "He's like this because of you."

"I didn't ask him to come up there."

"He saved you."

"I wouldn't have been up there if he hadn't followed me. Nobody would be here if he hadn't followed me," he said under his breath.

Unbelievable! What kind of alternate reality was Noah living in?

"You have no idea what might have happened if he hadn't followed you. You could be lying in a ravine instead of him—by yourself right now, or worse."

Noah cast his eyes on the ground. I focused my attention back on Abercrombie.

"Listen, Noah, we don't have time for this. One of us has to go for help."

He looked up and around. "Go where?" He was clearly lost.

"Do you know anything about first aid?" I asked, standing up.

He lowered his eyes again and shook his head. A low rumble echoed across the sky.

"Noah, you've got to go back and find Monica and the others. The trail is only ten or fifteen minutes away. Listen for the river. If you can find the river, you'll find the trail."

"What if I don't find them?"

"You have to find them." I reached for Noah's shoulders and forced him to look in my eyes. "Failure isn't an option here. You've got to run as fast as you can. Don't stop until you find them."

"Okay," he said, feet still firmly planted.

"Go!" I yelled.

Noah broke away and started running slowly in the direction of the treeline, but he stopped and looked back like he wanted to say something.

"You can do this, Noah," I said. "Don't stop until you find help."

He nodded and continued running, vanishing into the trees within seconds.

Sixteen

The thunder rumbled again, and I felt a small drop of rain.

Oh, please, don't let it rain now, I begged, looking up.

Kneeling back on the ground next to Abercrombie, I glanced at the leg again. *Uhhhh…breathe.* Without the pant leg to soak it up, blood was pooling around the gruesome wound. It looked like something right out of one of the *Saw* movies. *Okay, think.* Nobody would expect me to try to set the bone, but I had to try to stop the bleeding. I needed the first aid kit from Abercrombie's backpack.

But I had a huge problem. I had rolled Abercrombie's awkward, limp body over to make sure he was still alive and now he was lying on top of the pack. It had been risky to move him in the first place. I'd watched enough episodes of *ER* on Netflix to know I could have already messed him up for life if he had a neck or back injury. But was he in more danger of paralysis or bleeding out? How the heck was I supposed to know?

Finally, I decided to unstrap the pack. I couldn't count on Noah making it back before Abercrombie bled to death. I had to risk it. I would try to slide the pack out from under him carefully enough to avoid more injuries. Thunder clapped again in the distance, louder this time.

Abercrombie still hadn't moved. I put my ear to his chest one more time before pulling the tabs to loosen his shoulder straps and carefully pushing them off his arms. The ground below the pack was fairly level and covered with pine needles and leaves—still damp from the previous day's rain.

I looked up at the sky again. The rain was coming. If Noah didn't make it back soon, I would have to find a way to shelter both of us. The ravine didn't offer much in the way of protection, with only a few trees growing against the side of the rocks. *First things first,* I thought. *Stop the bleeding, then deal with the rain.*

Ever so slowly, I slid the pack out from under Abercrombie. He gasped softly when my final tug landed his left shoulder on the ground. Even though he was probably wincing from the pain, I was happy to hear him make any noise at all.

"Sorry," I said. "I'm just looking for your first aid kit. We've got to stop the bleeding on your leg."

He didn't respond. I took a deep breath and flipped the patch-covered pack over. My eyes immediately went to the shape of Abercrombie's walkie in the mesh outer pocket. Why hadn't I thought to look for it right away? I could call for help! Reaching into the pocket with trembling hands, I touched jagged plastic. The radio had been crushed by the weight of Abercrombie's fall. I pulled it from the pocket, praying it would still somehow work, but when I tried to switch it on, nothing happened. No noise, no lights. I turned it over. The battery pack hung open and they were missing. I reached into the pocket again, but it was no use. Only one of the two batteries was there with the broken pieces of plastic.

I uncinched his pack and began rifling around inside it. Finally, I touched the first aid kit. He also had one of the clear, plastic ground covers and his poncho inside the main part of the pack, along with his sleeping bag. As soon as I stopped the bleeding, I would try to make him comfortable.

Opening the red plastic kit, I found several large gauze packages toward the top. I glanced again at the jagged yellow bone poking through Abercrombie's skin just below the knee. I needed to put pressure on it. Did I need to worry about infection? I looked down at my hands. My fingernails were caked with dirt.

Better safe than sorry, I thought. I took the purple surgical gloves out of the kit and put them on before tearing open the gauze. Pressing it against one side of the wound, I awkwardly tore open another package and put it on the other side of the bone. Blood already saturated the first piece of gauze and was smeared all over the glove when I let go to reach for another package.

This isn't going to be enough, I realized, panicking. I opened several more packages and pressed them all against the wound. Was I pressing too hard? Not hard enough? What if I made the wound worse somehow?

I'm not sure how much time passed while I knelt over Abercrombie's body, but I couldn't help looking toward the trees. How long ago had Noah left? Had he found the trail yet? Would he know which direction Monica was going?

"Uhhhh…" Abercrombie moaned.

"Bryce! Can you hear me?"

His eyes twitched, then opened slightly. I saw the whites for a few seconds before they closed again.

"Bryce! Wake up. Talk to me." Regaining consciousness had to be a good sign. And if I could get him to wake up, he would be able to tell me what to do.

The wind swirled around us, rattling the leaves on the trees in the distance. I shivered.

"Can you hear me, Bryce?"

"Mmm…" he moaned without opening his eyes.

"Noah went to get help," I said. "Just hang on. You're going to be okay."

Abercrombie didn't respond, but a strange chill ran down my spine and tears filled my eyes. It was the kind of reassuring statement you were supposed to make in a situation like this, and I felt a weird power in the words. There was no way I could really know what was going to happen, but I wanted it to be true. I wanted him to be okay.

Light flashed across the sky. The patter of rain against rocks reached my ears and the first few heavy drops fell on us. I looked down at the gauze. It was completely saturated with blood. Was I doing any good at all? I let go just long enough to grab the sheet of plastic from the top of Abercrombie's pack, shaking it open and spreading it over him. I climbed underneath just before the drops multiplied and turned into a downpour.

"Help will be here soon," I promised. Why did I keep talking? I must have been trying to convince myself.

"Jas…" Abercrombie wheezed through barely parted lips.

"I'm here!" I said. His eyes twitched again. A few seconds later his pale lips quivered, and his teeth chattered against each other. With the sheet of plastic blocking the wind and rain, I felt uncomfortably warm. Could Abercrombie be cold?

I let go of the wound again and shifted around under to the plastic to reach for the sleeping bag. Leaving a trail of bloody handprints all over it, I unrolled the bag and spread it across Abercrombie's torso.

The rain continued to fall, and I kept applying pressure. Abercrombie was still shivering. My arms were getting sore and my knees hurt. There was no way to know how much time had passed, but it felt like hours.

Please come soon, I pleaded.

When the rain finally let up, I was relieved to come out from under the plastic. The breeze refreshed me, but I found myself looking toward the treeline almost constantly. Nagging thoughts kept creeping into my mind. What if Noah had gotten lost? Or worse, what if he had decided not to look for help at all?

More time passed. The bleeding seemed to be slowing down. I hadn't changed the gauze for quite a while. Abercrombie's shivering stopped too. I leaned in several times to listen to his breathing. It sounded normal. I tried to convince myself these were good signs. Finally, I decided that the bleeding was under control enough to wrap up the whole disgusting mess with an ace bandage.

The break from the rain was only temporary. Thick clouds swirled above us, and lightning lit up the sky. The narrow ravine channeled the wind through the rocks. What would I do if help didn't come before nightfall?

Lightning struck somewhere close enough that the sound of the thunder followed almost instantly. I jumped to my feet. We weren't safe here. The rain was coming again. We needed some kind of shelter.

The treeline was about thirty yards away on either end of the ravine. I had to find a way to move him to the trees, or I would spend the night as a human tent pole with the plastic draped over me.

Standing over Abercrombie, I assessed my options. Why did he have to be so tall? I was going to have to drag him, but I had to be careful, especially with his leg.

"You'll be cold and uncomfortable for a few minutes, but we've got to move you someplace more sheltered." Explaining what I was doing to an unconscious person was totally illogical, but I felt like I should run it by him anyway.

Abercrombie didn't react at all when I pulled the sleeping bag off. I unzipped the bag and laid it on the ground, then reached under his arms, awkwardly tugging him until he was completely on top of it. He groaned when his leg inched forward.

I was such an idiot! This wasn't going to work unless I could keep his leg from moving. I needed something sturdy to use, but I didn't have time to go hunting for sticks. It was already starting to sprinkle again. I opened the pack and dug through the stuff inside. Nothing long enough or sturdy enough.

Except the backpack itself! I stood up when the idea struck. The sturdy plastic between the pack and the padding would be just long enough to support the break. Dumping everything out onto the open sleeping bag next to Abercrombie, I moved the straps aside before lifting his ankle and sliding the bottom of the pack underneath. Slowly and gently, I move the pack upward toward his hip. I had to sit down for a few seconds when it was in place. My chest burned with each breath I took in. I'd been holding it like an Olympic diver.

Now I had to decide which direction I was going to drag him. We were almost smack in the middle of the ravine. It would probably be easier to drag him down the slight incline, but for some reason I decided to pull him uphill, even though it would mean pulling him around a big boulder that stood in our way. Maybe it was because those were the trees Noah had disappeared into. It was the direction we had come from. It would bring us a few feet closer to help.

After double checking to make sure the pack was secure around Abercrombie's leg, I picked up a corner of the sleeping bag and used all of my force to tug it toward the treeline. Twelve inches on the first tug. Six or so on the next two. Three inches on the fourth, and then I needed to take a rest. We were almost to the boulder. The wind was picking up and the trickle of rain increased steadily.

With a deep breath, I took hold of the corner of the sleeping bag again. At this rate, we would both be soaked before we reached the trees.

If you're real, and you're there, Abercrombie's God, I could use your help right about now, I thought.

Lightning flashed across the sky just as I tugged against the bag. My adrenaline surged and I pulled again—this time moving him almost twice the distance of the first tug. Fear of being struck by lightning fueled two more good tugs. We were almost around the boulder now.

After adjusting my grip on the bag for another pull, my hands slipped, and I fell backward. My tailbone hit hard against a pointy rock before the back of my head struck another.

My eyes instantly swam in salty tears—but not from the pain. It was the utter helplessness I felt. Why did I have to be so small and weak? Quiet Wolf or Pizza Face would have been able to drag Abercrombie to safety easily. Backwoods Barbie and Emphysema probably would have come up with some other way to shelter him until someone came to help. Why did Abercrombie get stuck with only me to help him? *Weak, helpless, incompetent me.*

I have no idea who I was trying to hide my tears from, but my hands covered my face and I rolled over onto my side. Pulling my knees up toward my body, I began sobbing. But my pity fest didn't last long. The wind swept through the trees and larger raindrops splashed against the side of my face.

"Mmmmm," Abercrombie moaned.

"Bryce?" I said, opening my eyes and pushing the tears away. I had fallen just beyond the boulder. A pine about the size of a Christmas tree was growing on the other side of it, right next to a small overhang on the rock wall.

"Jasmine?"

"I'm here," I said, scrambling to push myself to my feet. "You fell."

He lifted his head slightly and looked down at his body. "My leg." He set his head back down against the sleeping bag. "How long…?" he asked, his voice trailing off.

"I don't know," I said. "A couple of hours. I sent Noah for help."

But Abercrombie's eyes closed again.

"I wasn't sure what to do." I glanced from the treeline back to the small opening in the rocks behind the boulder. "I was trying to drag you somewhere to get a little shelter from the rain. It's another fifteen feet to the trees," I said, "But maybe that little cave behind the boulder would be better."

Abercrombie didn't respond.

"Hang on," I said, taking up the corner of the sleeping bag closest to the cave. It took five good tugs to get him to the tree in front of the cave entrance, and another six or so to get him positioned under the overhanging rocks. The cave was just big enough to shelter us from the rain, with a spot for me to sit near his head.

It felt good to be out of the downpour. I was breathing hard and sweating, but Abercrombie was shivering again.

"You're cold," I said.

It was much easier to pull the sleeping bag out from under Abercrombie than it had been rolling him on top of it.

Looking up at the thick clouds, I tried to picture how far down the sun had dropped in the sky. It must have been close to noon when we left the trail. How many hours did we have until nightfall?

Seventeen

After a long period of silence, listening to the rain tapping against the rocks, I hugged my knees to my chest and glanced at Abercrombie. His eyes were open. His breathing seemed labored and his brow knit together.

"Are you in a lot of pain?" I asked, softly touching his forehead. When he didn't respond right away, I wanted to slap myself. Why was I touching him? And of course he was in pain. His snapped bone was sticking out of his skin. What a stupid thing to say. He tried to smile, but the pain was even more obvious now in the dull whites of his eyes.

"Fire," he rasped.

"Fire?"

He nodded slightly.

Was he telling me to try to get a fire started? Now was probably not the best time to remind him that he'd blown me off instead of teaching me how to use the bow drill. But

Emphysema had learned quickly. What did I need? Some rocks for a ring? Some wood?

"I think a break in the clouds is coming," I said, looking off into the distance. "I remember passing by some fallen trees. They shouldn't be too far from here."

"Dry pine needles…" he said. "Twigs and grass for kindling."

A few minutes later, the rain let up.

"You're okay while I go look for wood?" I asked.

Abercrombie nodded.

Hurrying toward the treeline, I didn't have to go far to find one of the fallen, rotting trees I'd passed earlier. Some of the smaller branches broke off easily, and I was able to kick off a few big pieces of bark. After a few minutes my arms were full of mostly dry wood. I dropped the pile next to the cave before looking inside to check on Abercrombie. His eyes were closed again.

The clouds moved quickly in the wind. I needed to find more wood before the rain started back up. I returned to the fallen tree four more times, breaking off branches and bark until I had a decent sized stack. Then I made a small ring of rocks like the one we'd found that first night on Crocker Point. Finally, I ducked into the cave.

"Bryce," I called.

He didn't answer.

"Bryce," I said, louder this time. "I have the wood."

"Mmmmmm." His eyelids twitched and opened slightly like he was trying to wake up, but I could only see the whites for a few seconds before they closed again. His shivering continued.

Great. I had to try to get it started alone. The rain wouldn't hold off forever.

My eyes searched through the items I'd dumped out of the backpack onto the sleeping bag earlier. The bow drill was near the middle of the pile, half covered by a folded pair of wool socks. It was lashed to a wooden plank like the one I'd seen Quiet Wolf and Emphysema using that first night.

I moved the pile of stuff onto the rocks and took a second to pull the sleeping bag up and tuck it in around Abercrombie's shoulders before moving out of the cave.

It only took a few minutes to arrange some of the smaller pieces of bark and a few twigs into the shape of a teepee, like the one Quiet Wolf had built for Emphysema. Then I began looking around for dry pine needles and grass to make a kindling nest. It would have been much easier without all the rain. Everything that wasn't covered was soaking wet. Finally, I began digging through the pile of bark I'd collected. If I couldn't find kindling, maybe I could make my own. I opened Abercrombie's knife and began chipping away at a flat, dry piece of bark.

The knife rubbed uncomfortably against my knuckle, and the blade came dangerously close to my other hand a few times. Abercrombie had made wood carving look so easy.

Abercrombie hadn't budged since the last time I'd tried to wake him up. His teeth weren't even chattering anymore. I stopped shaving away at the bark several times to make sure his chest was still moving up and down.

When I finally had a nest of shavings that looked big enough, I set the bow and drill awkwardly on top of the plank with the notch. Positioning and repositioning myself with one foot on the plank, my left hand on the flat rock at the top of the drill with the other end resting in the notch on the plank, and my right hand holding the bow, I began slowly moving it back and forth.

Not too bad. This looked right. I was doing it. I just had to keep going long enough to heat up the board with the friction. I glanced over my shoulder, wishing Abercrombie was awake to see this.

After a few minutes, I expected to see smoke coming from the little notch in the wood, but nothing was happening. My arms were getting tired. My back was already sore from hunching over Abercrombie all afternoon. I stopped and set the bow aside for a second, inspecting the inside of the notch. No smoke. No red glow. It didn't look like anything was happening at all. I touched it to confirm. It wasn't even warm yet.

I stretched my arms and legs and took a deep breath before trying again. It needed to be faster. The stick jumped and wobbled wildly with the first few pulls of the bow, and then flew off the board completely. I picked it up quickly without glancing over my shoulder at Abercrombie.

Starting back up again, I made sure to put enough pressure on the top of the rock this time. It took a few seconds, but I was able to get it moving faster without having it jump out of the hole.

I kept it up for quite a while, still with no sign of smoke. This wasn't rocket science. Primitive man had figured this whole thing out with less technology than I was using. *Just keep going. It has to work eventually.*

But my back ached. My shoulders burned. My palm hurt from pressing against the stone. I felt a blister forming on my other hand from pulling the bow back and forth. And the wind was picking up again, moving the thick clouds ominously across the sky. I had to get this fire going before nightfall—otherwise, Abercrombie's headlamp would be the only light we would have. And no heat. I kept working, despite my agony.

Finally, after what seemed like forever, the board began to smoke. But it was only a tiny bit. Did I need to keep going, or should I dump whatever was smoking into the little nest of shavings right away? I couldn't remember how long Quiet Wolf and Emphysema had waited.

"Bryce," I said, still drilling away.

No answer.

"I think I got it," I said. "It's smoking. What do I do now?"

No response. I glanced back at him. He was completely still, and his complexion was grey. Was he breathing? My whole body tensed up. What was I doing? What good was a fire going to do Abercrombie if he...

No! I dropped the bow and lunged into the cave, ripping the sleeping bag off of Abercrombie's torso.

"Uhhhh," he moaned, his eyes opening wide.

"Sorry!"

"What..." He looked around the cave with glazed eyes.

"I just," I said, instantly fumbling to try to cover him back up. "I couldn't...I wasn't sure."

His eyes came into focus, and he grabbed my trembling hand. "It's okay," he said. "Take a breath."

"I almost had it," I said. "It was smoking." I nodded toward the board, which had completely stopped smoking now.

"Good," Abercrombie said, squeezing my hand before letting it go. "You'll get it." His eyes closed, and he began trembling again.

I pushed the sleeping bag up around him before returning to the bow drill. This time, it only took a few minutes to get the board smoking. My fingers trembled when I lifted the board and dropped the tiny coal into the nest of shavings and pine needles. After awkwardly setting the board back on the ground, I began blowing gently into the nest. The coal glowed red and smoke swirled around me.

I inhaled, getting ready to blow again, but a wind gust blew the smoke back—right into my face, burning my throat and choking me. Coughing and sputtering, I dropped the nest on the ground. With tears streaming down my face, I reached for Abercrombie's water tube. A long sip cooled the burning and silenced the cough. It was the first water I'd had all afternoon. I took another long drink after the choking was completely done. I was dehydrated. The water revived me.

Abercrombie hadn't had any since the accident either. But he was still sleeping, which worried me, since my choking fit was loud enough to wake the dead. As soon as I got this stupid fire going, I would try to get him to drink.

I picked up the nest and started blowing on it again, but by now, the nest had stopped smoking, and the coal was completely cold. I had to start over. From scratch. I picked up the bow and drill and placed them on the plank again. Thunder in the distance warned me that time was short. Sundown and rainfall were both coming for me.

Moving the bow with determination fueled by desperation, I mentally begged the smoke to start. When it did, I dropped the coal into the nest and immediately began blowing on it. This time, I turned slightly to let the breeze help. The warm glow and smoke increased with each breath I blew. Finally, the center of the nest ignited and I jumped, nearly dropping it. The flames grew steadily as I set the nest in the middle of the rock ring, near the teepee of larger sticks I'd built. The flames quickly lapped up the nest and the sticks weren't catching fire. I reached for more shavings, hoping to keep the kindling going long enough to spread the fire.

Slowly, but steadily, each twig and shaving I added to the nest built the flames until the larger sticks caught fire above them. I wanted to jump up and down and dance around. I'd done it! Now all I needed to do was keep it going.

The flames burned steady and hot after adding a few bigger pieces of bark, and I felt like I could take a break. Back inside the cave, I sat down next to Abercrombie. His face and lips were still grey, but the shivering seemed to have calmed down a bit.

I touched his forehead with the back of my hand. He felt cold.

"Bryce," I said softly.

The wind rustled through the trees.

"Bryce," I said again, "I got a fire going. Help is coming soon. You've just got to hang on."

He didn't open his eyes, but his breathing changed slightly.

"You need to drink some water," I said, reaching for the tubing and bladder. Abercrombie's eyelids flickered. "Here." I pressed the end of the tube to his slightly parted lips. "Can you drink?"

Abercrombie seemed to be expending every ounce of energy to lift his eyelids. He focused on my face for a split second, then opened his mouth. I had to guide the tube in, but once he had it there, he took several sips. When he let it go, he took a long breath.

"Thank you," he said.

I smiled. "Is there anything else I can do for you? To make you more comfortable?"

He closed his eyes and shook his head.

Eighteen

The rain came again, but the branches from the little tree and slight overhang of the rocks protected the fire just enough. The heat from the flames barely reached us, but whenever the wind shifted, the smoke came swirling into the cave. It choked me, and there was no place I could go to avoid it. I did my best to fan it away from Bryce with one of his t-shirts, but the effort had me panting for breath like a sumo wrestler running a marathon.

My pile of dry wood faded just slightly faster than the daylight. From our little cave, I couldn't see the entire treeline, but I listened intently for someone, anyone, to call out our names. They had to be looking for us. Noah had to have found someone by now.

When I only had two pieces of bark left, I thought about venturing back out of the cave to the fallen tree, even though the rain hadn't let up. A few rays of blood red sun pierced the clouds on the horizon. If I waited any longer to restock, it would be completely dark.

By the time I reached the trees, my clothes were already damp. All alone in the eerie, low light, I moved quickly, filling my arms with the driest branches and bark I could find. When my arms were full, I hurried back toward the cave but tripped over my own feet and dropped my bundle after only a few steps. The pouring rain sounded like thousands of hands clapping, but they weren't cheering me on—they were mocking me.

As I hurried to pick up the scattered wood before I was completely drenched, I thought I saw something moving near the treeline in my peripheral vision. I froze, then stood up slowly and turned toward the shape.

A. Huge. Brown. Bear. Several inches taller and at least 100 pounds heavier than I was. A green tag with the number ten hung from its right ear. It stopped moving and turned, looking straight at me. Then it growled, exposing its razor-sharp teeth.

I wanted to drop my stack of wood and run back to the cave. But I held my breath instead, standing perfectly still as my mind raced. What if it chased me? Bryce was completely helpless. I would be leading it straight to him. Were bears attracted by the scent of blood, like sharks? Oh no, oh no, oh no.

Tears mixed with the rain pouring down my face. I knew what I had to do. Bryce had shown me last night. I had to just stand here and wait until it went away. But last night he'd been standing next to me. And this bear looked bigger. And hungrier.

Leaning back on its haunches, the bear watched me like I was a juicy pork chop. It stretched out its long paws, clawing at the ground, then licked its lips.

My heart ticked like a clock, marking the passing seconds as they turned into minutes. My shoulders burned from the weight of the wood bundle in my arms. If the bear was going to eat me, wouldn't he have done it by now?

Move along! I wanted to shout. But the bear seemed to be thoroughly entertained by my Statue of Liberty impersonation. And the daylight continued to slip away. How long would it take for the bear to lose interest? Didn't it have somewhere better to be?

Soon, the wind began picking up again, but that didn't seem to bother the bear. Probably because it was cozy and warm, wearing a nice fur coat. The burning muscles in my shoulders were the only part of me that felt remotely warm. The rest of me fought to control waterlogged, fear-laced, miserable trembling.

After what seemed like ages, I decided that the bear had no intention of leaving. Ever. So what was I supposed to do now? Wait until it fell asleep, then tiptoe away?

I couldn't do that. Without me, Bryce and the fire were both in danger of dying. My heart drummed hard in my ears. I'd already been away too long. Whatever the consequences, I had to get back to the cave. I slowly took one step backward, intending to keep backing up until I reached the cave. But he was watching me. He'd know where I was going. He might follow me. I had to do something.

"Just go away, bear!" I shrieked, lifting the stack of firewood above my head like I was going to throw it. The bear rocked forward onto all fours. "I don't have anything you want!" The bear seemed startled, taking several small steps away from me.

"That's right! Get out of here! Go away!" I stepped toward it again, when every bone in my body should have been running the other direction. "Rrrrrrah!" I yelled in the most primal, bizarre voice I'd ever heard come out of a human being.

"Grrrrrrr," the bear responded, but it had already retreated several more steps toward the treeline. It didn't stop to look back at me, and I didn't wait for it to. As soon as it reached the trees, I turned, practically tumbling over myself to get to safety.

∞ ∞ ∞

The fire was almost out. I dropped the stack of wood under the overhang.

"Mmmmmm," Bryce moaned.

Squatting at the mouth of the cave, I huffed and puffed, trying to catch my breath. I couldn't keep my eyes off of the treeline in the distance, desperate to know the bear hadn't changed its mind and followed me.

"Jasmine?" Bryce called from the dark shadows of the cave. "Are you okay? You were gone for a long time."

My shoulders heaved up and down. I'd never been happier to hear a human voice in my life. I opened my mouth, but words choked in my throat.

Bryce reached out and touched my sopping wet shirt, "Jasmine? What happened?"

"I'm…okay," I managed.

"You're soaked."

"I…" Crossing my arms, I rubbed my palms against my biceps to try to get some feeling back in them. "I'm fine. I need to get the fire going again."

"You need to dry off." He rustled the sleeping bag completely off of his arms and tried to push himself up on his elbows.

"Don't!" I said. "I'm fine. Really. I'll dry off as soon as I get the fire going again."

The whites of Bryce's eyes glistened in the dim light.

"Try to relax," I said, pushing myself back out into the drizzling rain. Bryce didn't lower himself, watching me as I reached for some of the wood from the bottom of the stack and set it in the coals. A poof of smoke and ashes jumped out of the fire ring and blew away from the cave.

When the air cleared, I waited for the wood I'd added to catch fire, but aside from the increased smoke, nothing seemed to be happening.

"You need some smaller kindling to get the flames going again." Bryce's words immediately made my stomach drop. It had taken forever to make my nest of shavings earlier, and even if, by some miracle, there was dry grass to be found out in the trees, there was no way I was going looking for it.

Oh, please…Abercrombie's God, I'm begging you. You've gotten us this far. If it's not too much trouble…

Before I could even finish the thought, one of the embers in the middle of the fire seemed to glow a little brighter. I immediately dropped to my knees and began blowing softly. The smoke stirred, and the coals in the path of my breath glowed deep red. I reached for the smallest stick from the pile and placed it right on top of the brightest coals, then kept on blowing.

"The wood must be pretty wet," Abercrombie said.

"Please…please," I whispered.

Suddenly, the breeze shifted, pushing the smoke toward the cave and into my eyes. I turned away and pinched them shut. Abercrombie coughed and the sleeping bag zipper jingled. When I turned back toward the fire, distinct, orange and yellow flashes danced across my eyelids before I opened them and saw the flames.

"Yes!"

I placed another small piece of wood on the flames.

"I got it!" I looked over my shoulder at Abercrombie, who was still coughing softly.

The heat from the little fire thawed my fingers immediately. I wanted to hold my hands over it until the stinging stopped, but my body trembled and I couldn't be still.

"You can't stay in those wet clothes," Abercrombie said, searching the pile of gear next to him with the hand that could reach it. "Where's my first aid kit?"

I knelt down and reached over his feet, feeling for the box with the red cross where I remembered leaving it—right next to his flashlight. I found it after a moment of fumbling around in the dark, but holding onto it with my shaking hands wasn't easy.

"Here it is," I said, scooting awkwardly toward Abercrombie's face.

"Good. There should be a survival blanket in there. Do you see it?"

I set the kit down and searched for the switch on the flashlight. It clicked on, with the beam shining directly into Abercrombie's eyes. He squinted and covered his face.

"Sorry," I said. The kit had been much easier to unlatch earlier when my hands hadn't been made of jello. The emergency blanket was in a small package, between the last of the gauze and some packages of antibiotic ointment. It looked like a tiny, folded sheet of tinfoil. "Here it is. You want me to open it?"

"I'll close my eyes while you take off your wet stuff," Abercrombie said. "I had an extra t-shirt somewhere in here. It's pretty big. You can use it like a nightgown, or whatever you call it."

I sat trembling in the dark, staring at Abercrombie. He wanted me to strip down? Right here in front of him?

"Oh…I don't…"

"Jasmine," he said. "You can't spend the night soaking wet. Hypothermia is no joke."

"You think we're going to be here all night?"

"It looks like it."

My jaw tightened and I lost any control I had over my chattering teeth. It was somewhere on the level of those skeletons that show up at Mickey Mouse's house in that black and white cartoon.

"Do you have enough room?" Abercrombie was already trying to move himself farther into the cave, but he was practically against the back wall already.

"Don't," I said. "You're fine where you are. I can figure it out."

How stupid was it that I was only slightly less terrified of Abercrombie seeing me undressed than I was of being mauled by the bear? I couldn't think about it. He wasn't the type of guy who would look. His face was already turned away.

The wadded-up t-shirt was right where I'd left it after using it to fan the smoke away from Abercrombie. I started by untying my shoes and stripping off my damp socks, but before I started undressing, I switched off the flashlight. I struggled to get out of the clinging, dry-fit shirt in the dim light from the fire with only a few inches of space above my head. I kept bumping my arms, but I finally managed it. I threw the t-shirt on before stripping off my pants.

The struggle must have warmed me up a little, because my teeth stopped chattering. I switched the flashlight back on before spreading my wet clothes out on the rocks above our heads.

"All clear?" Abercrombie asked when I settled back into my spot near his shoulders.

"Yeah," I said, already shivering again.

"Open up the blanket."

"Will it really make that much difference?"

"Trust me." Abercrombie shifted his upper body until he was facing me.

Tearing off the plastic, I unfolded the foil sheet. The tiny wrapper was deceiving. The thin, metallic material crinkled and rattled until the blanket was as long as I was.

"What now?" I asked.

"Tuck your knees up as close as you can to your body." Abercrombie reached toward me and straightened the blanket out. "This will hold in your body heat."

I pulled my knees into my chest and wrapped the blanket tight around me, but my bare feet still peeked out below.

"I should have a spare pair of socks somewhere in this mess too." Abercrombie turned back toward the heap but winced. His leg must have moved.

"Are you okay?"

A long breath hissed through his gritted teeth before he answered. "I haven't looked at it yet. Is it pretty bad?"

I hesitated, not sure what to tell him. "The bone came through the skin, but I stopped the bleeding."

He took another deep breath. "Can you see those socks?"

I found the socks with the flashlight before leaning carefully over him to get them. They were thick and wooly, and long enough to reach my knees, leaving only a small gap between socks and the long t-shirt.

"Should we check on it?" I asked. "It's been a long time since I changed the gauze."

"Naw. If you stopped the bleeding, we should keep it covered. Less chance of infection."

I set two more pieces of wood on the fire then pulled the thin metallic blanket tightly around me. It instantly began to warm me, offering protection from the chilly wind. If only Abercrombie had something in his emergency kit that would save him from the invisible threats that had us both frozen with fear.

Nineteen

The wind eventually died down a little. The only other sound we heard was the steady rainfall until Abercrombie finally broke the silence.

"Can I ask you a question? I'm a little confused from the fall."

I lifted my chin from my knees. "Sure."

"I remember following Noah into the woods, but I thought you were back with everyone else at the stream. How'd you get here?"

My jaw tightened. I should have been back at the stream. What could I say to explain myself? I was too tired to try to gloss over the truth.

"I heard you and Monica talking about Noah. I followed you," I said. "I was worried about him. I don't know what I was thinking. I should have told someone…asked someone…"

Abercrombie's smile pierced the darkness. "It's okay. I'm glad you didn't."

"You are?" I couldn't breathe.

He pulled the sleeping bag up tighter around his neck. "If you'd have asked Monica, she wouldn't have let you follow me, and that would have left Noah in a really bad place when I fell."

I couldn't help smiling. He was glad I was here? Glad I had broken the rules? But I knew I was being stupid. He was just glad he hadn't fallen with only Noah to help him. I might not be the most competent person, but Noah was even less competent than I was.

"Do you think Noah made it back to the trail okay?" I whispered.

"I hope so."

My eyes blurred, staring at the fire, and I shivered. What if Noah was out in the wilderness all alone right now? He didn't know how to make fire yet either. Maybe I should have been the one to go for help. Abercrombie knew how to survive out here. He was conscious now. He could have helped Noah.

"If he didn't make it, if he got lost, how long will it take for them to come looking for all of us?"

Abercrombie shrugged. "Monica should have radioed for backup as soon as she realized you were missing."

"I heard you tell her to go on. I thought Noah would have to chase them down. You think they're already looking for us?"

Abercrombie was silent, but hope grew inside me. No matter where Noah had ended up, they were already looking for us. They had to be.

"We can't be that far from the trail," I said, thinking aloud. "It can't be long before they find us."

"Unless…"

My rapidly inflating bubble burst with his one soft word. "Unless what?"

"You disappeared around the same time Noah did."

"Yeah," I said.

"Monica thought you kind of had a thing for Noah. Maybe she thought you ran with him."

"Psha!" I hissed. Heat rushed to my cheeks and I sunk down deeper, hiding my face inside the emergency blanket. Monica thought I had a thing for Noah? I hated everything about that statement, but most especially, I hated knowing they *had* been whispering about me—thinking they understood something they obviously had no clue about. "You can't be serious. None of you get who I am," I muttered.

"What's that?"

"Because I'm the only one who gives a crap what happens to him, you automatically assume I have 'a thing' for him?"

"I didn't assume anything…" Abercrombie pushed himself up on his elbows again.

"This program is so twisted." The pitch of my voice escalated. "You people have done nothing but assume since I got here. But guess what, you're all wrong! I'm a normal teenager! I don't drink. I don't do drugs. I'm not even depressed and that's a miracle after everything my mom's done to me…all the programs she's shoved me into. I don't have a thing for Noah. I wouldn't even talk to him, much less run away with him, if we weren't stuck out here together!"

I threw my arms up, pushing the emergency blanket off my shoulders, and reached for one of the last few hunks of bark, tossing it on the fire. An explosion of sparks punctuated the night air.

"I'm sorry." Abercrombie's voice was irritatingly calm. "I guess we all assume stuff, whether we're trying to or not. We judge people by the part of them we can see." He paused. "The part they show us."

The chill air encircled me. Abercrombie had seen exactly two days' worth of clumsy mishaps and diarrhea of the mouth from me. I hadn't shown him anything but my worst.

"Well, it needs to stop!" I said. "Try listening to what I'm saying instead of reading into what you think you see."

"Fair enough. But you're the one that said you followed me into the woods because you were worried about Noah."

No! I wanted to shout. *I was worried about Noah, but I followed YOU into the woods!* "Well I don't have a thing for Noah and if I wanted to run away from the program, I would have done it back at the campground when you said it was our choice to hike or not. I'm not stupid. I would have done it near a phone."

"I'm just saying that you care about him." He interlaced his fingers and put them under his head as a pillow. "There's nothing wrong with that. It's a good thing to care about people."

"Well, I don't care about him like that! He has serious problems. I would never be dumb enough to let myself fall for someone like that."

A frigid blast of wind pushed underneath the emergency blanket. I was already trembling with anger, but it intensified with the fresh cold. Abercrombie let my words hang in the air.

"'Someone like that?'" he finally said. "You've only known Noah for three days. How do you know what he's like?"

"I think it's pretty obvious."

"What's obvious?"

I turned, meeting Abercrombie's eyes. "He's a user."

"Really?" The flames from the fire reflected in his eyes. "I'm not sure I know what you mean by that."

"Seriously? They don't call them users in Utah? Or do they not have people who do drugs at all there?"

He didn't answer.

"C'mon. You can't pretend you don't know that Noah's been in withdrawals. I heard you talking to him this morning. You said we'd find stuff on the trail that would help him feel better."

"He told you he does drugs?"

I looked away. "He didn't have to. Any relatively intelligent person could figure it out."

"How?"

Why was he pressing me like this? He knew Noah did drugs as well as I did.

"You know…the pale skin, the sunken eyes, the throwing up." My voice faltered.

"Oh, so you assumed he was a user because you were reading into what you thought you saw?"

My breathing stopped for a second like the wind had been knocked out of me.

"Noah hadn't really talked to me at all until this morning," he continued. "I don't know anything about him yet. I don't know about his family. Does he live with both parents? Does he have any siblings?"

My heart pressed hard against my ribcage.

"I don't know."

"Oh," Bryce said, "what about school? What kind of student is he? Does he struggle? What about friends?"

I shrugged my shoulders. "You know he didn't talk to me much more than he did to you."

"Well, you knew he was a user just from watching him. I thought maybe you knew why too."

I closed my eyes. "Okay. I get it," I choked.

"Get what?" he continued to press.

"I get it! I judge people too! Is that what you want me to admit?"

"I don't—"

"You want me to tell you that you're right. That I have problems too. You want me to admit I belong here?"

"I don't have some big secret agenda. I'm not trying to get you to say or do anything." Abercrombie closed his eyes. "What do you think this program is for?"

My mind raced but when I opened my mouth, I was at a loss for words. "Wilderness therapy…"

"Yeah?"

"I guess it's like rehab. For drug addicts. Sex addicts. Cutters. I don't know. Kids with big problems."

"And you don't have big problems. You don't belong here? Is that it?"

It was exactly what I'd been saying since day one, but when Abercrombie echoed my words, I knew they weren't true.

"You're not a drug addict or a sex addict or a cutter. You're a normal teenager?"

"I…"

"And how does that work exactly? Is somebody a user the first time they do drugs? That's it for them? They're labeled for life? No more normal teenager?"

"No! Of course not. People make mistakes."

"Well, what about Noah?"

"I mean, just because I said he's a user doesn't mean he's labeled for life. I wasn't trying to say that people can't change."

Abercrombie shifted around in his sleeping bag. "Yeah, I agree, but changing isn't easy, especially if we believe the labels—see ourselves the way other people see us."

Chunky Monkey. Pain washed over me like a salty wave. He was right; it's hard not to see yourself the way other people see you. "Especially when those 'other people' are your mom," I muttered.

"Your mom?"

"Labels," I whispered. I couldn't remember when her label had turned painful. It started out as a nickname.

"She labeled you?"

"She called me 'Chunky Monkey,'" I said. "You know, in the same tone of voice that other moms say, 'Sweetie Pie.'"

He laughed. "I've heard worse."

"Yeah, no big deal, right?" My eyes lost focus. "Until I hit puberty and she stopped thinking it was cute." I took a deep breath and threw a small stick on the fire. "She started counting calories for me and monitoring my exercise. And when that didn't work, she sent me to "Fresh Image Teen Camp."

He shrugged. "What's that?"

"Fat camp," I said.

"Huh?" His expression read sincere confusion.

"I mean, nobody used the word 'fat' outright, but that's what it was." I pinched my eyes closed, trying to shut out the memories. "It was a special kind of hell. Nothing but carrot sticks and treadmills. Chunky kids with pit stained grey sweat suits. The counselors kept telling us the sweat was just our fat crying."

He choked a laugh, then tried to recover. "I can't picture that—you like that. At all."

"Well, good. I guess that's because her little plan worked." I pushed my face under the thin blanket. "And as long as I keep those 15 pounds off, I'll be fine."

"Wow. That's rough," he said.

"Not really. I've kept it off for almost a year."

"No, I mean the whole thing. Feeling like your mom thinks of you that way."

He had no idea. How no matter what the numbers on the scale read, I was always in danger of becoming a Chunky Monkey, and it would never be cute again. No matter what I looked like on the outside, I would always be fat on the inside. Tears pushed very close to the surface, but I cleared my throat and shook them away. "So you think wilderness therapy is the answer? Hiking around out here is somehow going to make us forget the labels?"

He didn't answer.

"You know some secret trick? Is it easy, like using a bow drill?" I pulled the thin blanket closer around me, but it was a poor shield against the cold wind.

"I don't think it's so much about forgetting labels as it is realizing they don't define you. Behaviors aren't who you are. Believe it or not, I know how you feel."

"Well, sorry if I don't believe you. What labels have you ever had to overcome? What did they call you in Argentina? Saint Bryce?"

Abercrombie sucked a breath of air through his gritted teeth, obviously in pain. Seriously! I'd completely forgotten I was picking a fight with a guy who'd been unconscious most of the afternoon.

"Sorry," I said softly. "Can I do anything to help?"

"Hang on…" he said without opening his eyes. Even in the dark, I could see that his body was rigid.

"You don't have to talk. You should be resting." I reached for his water and put the tube near his mouth. "Here…"

He opened his eyes and forced a smile. "Talking has been distracting me from the pain. But every once in a while, it's intense." He took a sip of the water and seemed to relax slightly.

"Maybe you should try to go back to sleep."

"It's going to be a long night."

I turned back toward the fire and the tiny stack of wood that was left. We still had hours until the sun would rise, and it was only going to get colder.

"I wasn't trying to avoid your question," Abercrombie said, his voice sounding steadier now. "You're right about Argentina. Being labeled as a missionary was one of the best experiences of my life. Part of me didn't want to come home."

Abercrombie pushed the water toward me, his nod indicating that I should take a drink. I'd hardly had any all afternoon, trying to conserve it for him. A long sip of the cold water eased the burning in my throat.

"I guess I was afraid to come home. I liked hiding behind a name badge for two years."

I set the water down. What did Abercrombie have to hide from? "Weren't you excited to see your family after all that time away?"

"Sure, don't get me wrong. I love my family," he said. "I'd just changed so much. Nobody knew me in Argentina. The mission let me forget everything from before and I could be whoever I wanted. I was afraid when I came home it would be easy to fall into old habits…old friends…my old ways."

"You make it sound so terrible. I have a hard time believing you were ever anything less than perfect."

He chuckled. "That's cool. But you wouldn't have liked me five years ago."

"Right…" I said. "I'm sure. What were you five years ago? Mafia?"

"Worse—" He laughed. "I was a user."

Twenty

I had no idea how to react. The image of Abercrombie shooting up in a dark alley was so opposite the male Mother Teresa I had painted in my brain.

"You were a user?" I repeated.

"Well, that's what people would have said about me." He shifted in his sleeping bag.

I didn't want to take a breath for fear he would think I was gasping. My brain burned almost as much as my lungs, wishing I could suck the entire conversation we had just had back in. How could I have said all of those things? My cold, holier-than-thou attitude about Noah now transferred to Abercrombie. There was no way to disconnect the two.

"This isn't really something I usually tell people about," Abercrombie said.

"I feel like a huge idiot."

"I didn't tell you to make you feel bad about yourself."

"Why—" *did you tell me then?* I stopped myself, but left that one word hanging in the air.

"You want to know why I started doing drugs?"

"No…I mean, I'm sorry." Asking why made me sound like the world's biggest hypocrite. "You don't have to talk about it."

"It's okay. I don't mind."

I pulled the foil blanket tighter around me. "I know it's none of my business."

"It's kind of a long story," Abercrombie said, shifting around on the rocks, "but I'll tell you. Only while I'm telling you, I need you to do something awkward for me."

I looked up from the tiny fire. Could I take more awkward? I was barely holding it together now.

"Don't worry," he said. "It's nothing I wouldn't do for you if the situation was reversed."

"Okay."

"I can't feel my foot." He sat up slightly and pushed the sleeping bag aside. "I need you to check for a pulse."

"Seriously?" I said. "You have one. That was the first thing I checked for after you fell."

"Seriously," he said, touching his tattered pant leg. "I should have had you check this right away, but I didn't want to look at it."

"A pulse?" I set my blanket on the ground and knelt on it next to his leg.

"Yeah. We need to find out if there's any circulation happening below the break."

"What if there isn't?" I couldn't stop myself from asking stupid questions. My filter was broken or something.

"Well, it's not good." He touched the bare skin on his calf. "The color doesn't look great. If the circulation's cut off, I might lose my leg."

What the? Might lose his leg? He said it as casually as I might if I was telling my mom we were out of Cocoa Puffs.

"What do I do?"

"Loosen my boot. Check for a pulse in my ankle."

I nodded, but couldn't move right away—frozen in every sense of the word.

"So my long story," he said, laying back down. "You remember I told you my dad used to like hunting and fishing when I was little?"

"Yes," I said, reaching for the laces on his boot…because it totally made sense to talk about hunting and fishing while I tried to figure out if his leg was alive or dead.

"He would take my brother Aaron and me up to this little cabin my grandpa built in the mountains. He started taking us when my little sister, Laurie, was born, so Aaron would have been about ten and I was eight."

"How many kids are there in your family?" I asked, finally managing to untie the knot with my stiff fingers.

"Five."

I slid my fingers under the laces and gently loosened them.

"We went up there three summers in a row. My dad taught us how to fly fish and he gave us both pocket knives and made us gut our own fish." He took a breath. "I'll hold my leg steady while you take off my boot. We don't want to move it at all."

The lace was completely loose, but his foot must have swollen some—the shoe was still snug. I nodded.

"We were really looking forward to the third summer up there. I was eleven. Dad had given us both pellet guns and he was going to let us shoot rock chucks. He set up a bunch of cans out behind the cabin for target practice."

Abercrombie paused, bracing himself as I moved the boot right and left as carefully as possible. It didn't budge. I was going to have to pull the tongue back.

"Anyway. We'd been up there for three days. Dad was going to let us go out by ourselves after breakfast. He was cooking bacon and eggs. I was sitting at the table and Aaron was still getting dressed in the loft."

Abercrombie gritted his teeth when I reached for the heel of the boot. If I pulled gently on the back and the tongue at the same time, it had to come off eventually. He nodded like he knew what I was thinking and held his leg steady below the knee.

Slowly, I eased the boot forward and back until it finally slipped off.

Abercrombie took a deep breath and let it go slowly.

"Now what?"

"Pull my sock down below my ankle. Feel for a pulse on the inside, just behind the bone."

I did what he asked but I couldn't keep my hands from trembling.

"My dad had all of the guns leaning against the wall. He usually kept his locked up in the safe."

Pushing the sock down to his arch, I looked at the swollen ankle before putting my fingers behind the bone. I couldn't feel anything but my own racing heart.

"I was kind of obsessed with that gun—a Marlin 336 with a scope."

Maybe I wasn't pressing hard enough. My fingers shifted around, searching—hoping desperately to feel something.

"Nobody was watching. I wasn't allowed to touch it, but I couldn't help myself."

Abercrombie exhaled on the back of my neck. His hands still gripped his leg below the knee.

"The safety wasn't on. My dad blames himself for that."

My eyes finally broke away from the swollen ankle. Abercrombie's face was stoic.

"I've relived that moment so many times, but I still don't know how it happened. My dad startled me. The gun went off. Aaron was coming down the stairs."

"You…"

He let go of his calf and sat up straight. "I couldn't live with myself," he said. "I was the reason."

My fingers still rested behind his ankle, but I stopped moving them. *He was the reason. His brother.* Silence sat thick between us as I searched his pain filled eyes.

"It was an accident. I was a little kid. My parents taught us to believe that death isn't the end." He paused, choking back his emotions. "But how do you live with yourself?"

"I'm so sorry—" Tears filled my eyes. Sorry for what he'd lost. Sorry for his pain. I wanted to throw my arms around him and beg him to forgive me.

"Everything was different after…" his voice trailed off again. "They sold the cabin. My dad stopped hunting and fishing. My mom was like a robot around me, but she cried in her room every night. And I was the reason—for all of it."

We returned to silence. I tried to imagine what that must feel like. I'd never experienced the loss of someone I loved like that, but I knew what it was like to blame myself for other people's misery. When it came right down to it, my birth—my existence, was the reason for most of my mom's stress and unhappiness. I felt it in everything she said and did. A familiar, dull ache started in my chest. Emptiness that could never be satisfied, not with a thousand Doritos.

Abercrombie cleared his throat. "It sounds cliché, but I was looking for something…anything to dull the pain."

"And drugs dulled the pain?"

"It sounds stupid."

"No. Doritos are stupid."

"Doritos?"

"To dull the pain. I ate Doritos to dull my pain."

A wide smile spread across his face. "Does that work?" He laughed. "Which flavor—nacho cheese or cool ranch?"

We both laughed until he winced in pain.

"Sorry," I said. "I know it's not the same. And you had a way more valid pain to dull."

"No—" His smile faded. "I didn't mean to say that. Pain is pain."

I smiled.

"What do you feel now?" he asked. "Anything?"

My heart pressed hard against my ribs. I wanted to tell him about my mom, but where should I even start? Her obsession with my grades…my clothes…my fingernail biting? Maybe it would sound stupid, but all the small things contributed to the big feelings.

His eyes dropped to my fingers on his ankle. "If you don't feel it, you don't feel it."

Right. His pulse. I pulled my hand back. *We're talking about his leg.*

I shook my head. "I can't feel anything."

"Okay. We're going to have to try to set it."

"Your leg?"

"Seems like the most reasonable choice."

Seriously! How could he be so calm. Had he set a broken bone before, because it seemed like a big deal to me.

"How?" I asked.

Looking down, directly at my makeshift bandage covering his protruding bone, he blew out a breath. "Traction. You've got to pull on my leg until the bone moves back into place."

My mouth fell open. "You can't…I can't…you don't even…"

"You can do this, Jasmine." Abercrombie took my trembling hand in both of his. "You know—maybe you don't belong here. Maybe you didn't deserve to be sent here. But maybe you are supposed to be here. You followed me. You sent Noah for help. You started that fire on your own. It took me three days to learn how to use a bow-drill."

"But— "

He pulled my hand to his chest. Warmth spread through me.

"You can do this. I need you to do this for me."

I nodded. As terrified as I was, I had to try. Abercrombie had no other options.

Twenty-One

Abercrombie had me move to the small space at the end of his feet. The ceiling of the cave was slightly lower there, so I had to hunch over.

"It's pretty simple," he said. "You're just going to lift my leg up gently, and then pull on it. Not a tug, but a firm, solid pull."

Sure. Just yank on his broken leg. My stomach flipped. What if I screwed it up even more? My jaw ached from trying to stop my teeth from chattering.

We sat in silence for a few moments while I stared at the leg and tried to put on my big girl panties.

"Have you ever had a broken bone?" He was trying to calm me. Distract me from what I had to do next.

I shook my head. "My mom wouldn't allow it."

He laughed. "Allow what? The bone to break, or you to break a bone?"

"Both, I guess." I forced a smile.

"She's the one who sent you here, right?"

I nodded.

"Have you ever gotten along with her?"

"As long as I do everything she tells me without questioning, we get along just fine." I laughed, trying to be sarcastic, but my shivering made me sound like a maniac instead.

"What about your dad? You haven't said much about him."

"Shouldn't we be worrying about your leg?"

"I was just curious to know if he thought sending you here was a good idea."

Why did he have to ask about this right now? Was this really the time and place to get to the bottom of my daddy issues? "He's just like me. He didn't know anything about it."

The hint of frenzy in my voice should have told him to change the subject, but he either didn't notice or he ignored it. "So you're more like him?"

"Maybe!" I blew out a puff of steamy air. *Maybe I am just like him. Maybe that's why she sent me here. Because I'm no good. Just like him.* "What does it matter?" I turned away.

"Oh," he said. "I didn't know it was like that. Sorry."

We sat in silence for a few seconds while I tried to pull myself together. What was wrong with me? I wanted him to understand where I was coming from. I wanted him to get me. Just a few minutes ago, I'd wanted to unload my feelings about my mom on him. But my dad had nothing to do with that. Nothing to do with me.

"I guess my questions don't matter right now. I'm just prolonging the inevitable." He shifted, and I looked away from the wall of the cave to see what he was doing. "In the movies, they give you something to bite down on." He reached for a stick from the small stack of firewood that was left, just above his head.

"Is that where you learned how to set a broken bone? From the movies?"

"No. Don't worry, I've had lots of first-aid training." He laid back against the rock again.

"What if I screw this up?"

"You won't."

"I screw everything up," I said. "I don't mean to. Bad things just happen to me."

"It's okay. Bad things happen to everyone, Jasmine. It's part of life."

"You wanna know why I'm here? It's because I screwed something up."

Bryce lifted his brows.

"I got arrested on prom night." Our eyes locked in the dim light. "My friends were drinking in the car, but I wasn't. I was driving. I was trying to keep everyone else safe. I was following the rules. I always follow the rules. But I'm the one who got in trouble."

"You weren't drinking, but you got arrested?"

"There were open containers in my car."

"And you think that's why your mom sent you here?"

"Yeah. She's been weird about everything ever since it happened. Checking in a million times a day. Like she doesn't believe I'm going where I say I'm going. Questioning everything I do."

"I know that feeling."

"It was one mistake, and she's acting like I'm a completely different person."

Abercrombie nodded. "Sounds like she's worried about you."

"But it's ridiculous! I've always done exactly what she wants me to do! I'm an honor roll student. I'm involved in every after-school club known to man. I don't have time to get in real trouble, even if I wanted to."

Abercrombie was thoughtful for a few seconds. "Then what do you think she's worried about?"

The question sat on me like a two-ton elephant. The one in the room that nobody wants to talk about. What *was* she worried about? *Stand up straight. Pull your shoulders back. Read the news. Hold your tummy in. Show your teeth when you smile. You're too quiet. But don't talk about that*…she had been trying to mold and shape me into something I wasn't ever since I could remember. The truth I had wanted to spill for years brimmed on the edge of my tongue.

"Maybe she's afraid I'll turn out like him."

"Who?" he asked.

"My dad."

"Is that such a bad thing?"

My eyes blurred, watching the black drops fall from the sky, illuminated only momentarily by the dim firelight before they reached the ground. "Well…apparently she'd rather risk having me die out here in the wilderness than end up like him—" I tried to dry my eyes on my shirt, but my hands were shaking from the cold. "He's pretty much a no good. He left her all alone to raise a kid. A kid who doesn't even look like her. People don't even think I'm hers."

He let silence fill the cave for a few seconds. "That's heavy—"

"I didn't ask for this. I didn't ask to be this way." I couldn't stop the tears from streaming down my face.

"What way?"

"Too ugly. Too loud. Too clumsy. Too tan. Too fat."

"What? Are you serious?"

"I never wanted to ruin her life," I sobbed.

"You think that's how she feels?"

I nodded, too choked by my tears to speak. Why else…if she doesn't, why would she…do everything she does? Say everything she says?

Bryce put his hand softly on my shoulder. "Have you ever told her how you feel?"

I shook my head and pressed my eyes against my knees.

"I can't imagine *anyone* thinking or saying those things about you, let alone your mom."

"Are you blind?" I sniffed. "I've proved her right over and over again in the last few days. I can't do anything right."

"Having a few accidents doesn't make you 'no good.'"

"Just clumsy," I sniffed.

"You're not always clumsy—and anyways, clumsy can be cute."

"Well, I'm never going to look like her."

"So? Why's that important?" Abercrombie asked. "What's so great about how she looks?"

"Beautiful. Tall. Blonde. Skinny."

His hand slid off my shoulder. "You can be beautiful without being any of those things." He looked at me, focusing on my eyes. "I mean you are…"

Beautiful? Whatever. He was just saying that to try to make me feel better. There was no way Abercrombie thought I was beautiful, especially how he'd seen me—covered in mud and looking my worst. *"Right,"* I said.

"What? You don't believe me? I'm not the only one who thinks so."

He'd been talking about this to someone else? Somehow it didn't bother me at all like it had when he'd been talking to Backwoods Barbie about me and Noah. It was like someone suddenly shoved a cork in my tear ducts and I couldn't do anything except stare at him with my lips slightly parted.

"You probably overheard me talking to Windsong this morning. I was trying to change groups because of you."

"Because of me? Why?"

He shifted around. "It just seemed like…well we're not supposed to—you know, I just had a hard time keeping my eyes off you at first, and then the more we talked…the more crazy stuff you said and did…I was having a hard time focusing."

What was he saying? I understood the words, but could he really be talking about me? His voice sounded sincere, but he was looking at the ground. Maybe he was talking about a rock down there.

"You—" I stammered. "I thought it was because I annoyed you."

He shook his head. "Maybe I'm crazy," he continued. "But last night. With the bears…and you were standing so close. I mean, it's not just because you're beautiful. But you are—beautiful."

Wait. Was he kidding? The glances and smiles. His refusal to teach me how to make fire. When he'd let go of my hand so awkwardly after my fall. Maybe it wasn't because I repulsed him. There was no reason for him to joke about something like this. Especially right now. My whole body warmed like someone lit a fire in my chest, fanning the flames outward to my extremities.

"I shouldn't be saying any of this to you." He took a deep breath. "But you can't go one more night thinking…believing that about yourself."

A twig snapped on the fire, but neither of us looked away. I didn't want to move. The day had been misery layered on top of torture, and now it seemed like a dream I didn't want to wake up from. But I couldn't just sit here, staring stupidly into his eyes forever.

"Thank you," was the only thing that made sense to me to say.

"Thank *you*— "he whispered.

"I guess, we'd better…I'd better."

Abercrombie blinked slowly, then looked down at his leg and nodded at me. "I know you're afraid, but you can do this. You're tough and smart. Just keep steady traction until it straightens out."

"You'll tell me if I'm doing it wrong?"

He shook his head. "I'm not going to be able to tell you anything. I'm going to do my best not to scream like a little girl before I pass out."

I started to laugh, but quickly realized he wasn't joking.

"Once it looks straight, use my bandana to tie my ankle to those branches. Not too tight, but enough to keep it stretched out. Then give it a few minutes and check for a pulse again."

I nodded. "What if I don't find one?"

"There isn't much else we can do. I'm praying you find one."

The rain stopped tapping against the rocks around us, and silence sat heavy on the chill air.

"Is that what you were doing that first morning when I saw you out on the rocks?" My voice seemed loud, but I was barely whispering. "Were you praying?"

Abercrombie lowered his head. "I feel so close to Him when I'm out here. I found God up there on that mountain. Sending me here was the most amazing thing my parents could have done for me."

"Wait…what?" I said. "Sent you here—like how I was sent here?"

Abercrombie nodded.

A lump formed in my throat. "So what do you do? I mean, how do you do it?"

"What?" He looked confused for a second. "Oh, you mean pray?"

I nodded.

"It isn't complicated. You just talk to Him."

My heart began pounding hard. "About what?"

"Whatever you're struggling with. You can ask for His help. He's your father. He wants to help."

I am a child of God. The words to the song Bryce sang around the fire the night before played in my head. How many times had I secretly wished I had a father I could ask for help? Fresh mist filled my eyes.

"Does He talk back to you?" I whispered.

Bryce laughed. "Not so much in actual words. Usually it's more in feelings, or in things that happen. He finds ways to let me know He hears me, and He cares."

"That sounds so nice."

"It is," he said. "You should try it."

"I don't know. I would feel weird. I don't know what I'd say."

"Keep it simple for your first time. Maybe just ask Him to let you know He's there."

A chill ran through me. Could it really be that simple? It was what I'd always wanted to know. What I needed to know. I nodded. "Maybe I will."

"Good," he said. He let a few moments pass in silence. "Are you ready to do this?"

I nodded and wrapped my hands around his ankle.

"One more thing," he said. "I know this is going to sound weird after everything else, but when it's all done and I'm out, you need to curl up next to me and cover us both with the sleeping bag. It's the only way we're going to stay warm enough tonight."

I nodded like what he had just said was no big deal. Just going to set a broken leg, then spend the night curled up next to a guy who thought I was beautiful.

Twenty-Two

He didn't scream, but his face twisted in pain as I pulled on the broken leg. After a few seconds, the stick he'd been biting fell against the rocks. The leg felt like a ton of bricks, but I kept pulling.

Finally, the piece of bone that had been poking through his skin disappeared. I kept pulling until the broken leg stretched a few inches longer than the other one. It still looked crooked at the break, so I pulled at a slight angle. Finally, after several minutes, the leg started to look almost normal, aside from the swelling.

I set the leg down gently and followed Bryce's instructions, tying his ankle to the tiny tree at the end of the cave. I crawled back to my spot near Bryce's head, and caught my breath. It was done.

The cold set back in after just a few seconds of stillness. I reached for the last two scraps of wood and set them on the fire. The rain was only dripping now, punctuating the silence.

As the light in the cave increased from the fuel I had added to the fire, I turned to Bryce. His chest rose and fell steadily, and even though his face still drooped to the right, his features looked more relaxed. I guess passing out will do that for you.

It had been long enough—I should have been checking for a pulse in his leg again, but I hesitated. Bryce's invitation to talk to his God was replaying over and over in my mind. Did he mean I should do it now, or sometime later? I really wanted to do it now, but I wanted to make sure I did it right. Bryce made it sound so simple, but everything I knew about religion seemed to say the opposite. Wasn't there a certain way I needed to hold my hands, or specific words I should say? Candles? Sitting, kneeling, standing? What if I didn't get an answer? Would that mean I was doing something wrong, or that He really didn't exist? How would I know for sure? Maybe I should just wait.

But God had answered Bryce. What did that mean? Even though I hadn't experienced it myself, I believed him. And I wanted what he had.

What would it hurt to try? If it didn't work right away, I could always ask Bryce about it again when he woke up. Before I started, I pulled the sleeping bag back over his torso. There was no reason for him to freeze while I was trying to figure out the mysteries of the universe.

The rain stopped completely, and the wind was still. Bryce had been kneeling out there on the edge of the cliff, so I decided to kneel too. I fumbled with my hands in a few different positions before settling on the traditional interlocked fingers, pulled in at heart level.

I closed my eyes and lowered my head like everyone had done around the fire when thanking the Great Creator for their beef stew.

With my eyes closed, my mind became eerily clear. All I had to do now was just say the words. Ask the question. My heart thumped hard in my chest.

"Great Creator," I whispered. "Bryce told me you're there. He said you showed him you're his father. I know this is the first time I'm really talking to you, but it's not because I haven't wanted to."

I paused, thinking about the birthday cards from my grandparents, each with some small hint that they believed in God. I hadn't asked much about it because I knew it would hurt my mom. But I'd always wanted to know…just like I'd always wanted to know more about my dad.

"Anyway, you probably know what I want. If you're there, you must have heard our whole conversation just now. I'm not asking for some big sign or miracle. I just want what Bryce was talking about."

Tears filled my eyes and spilled out onto my cheeks. "Could you just let me know somehow that you're there—?" My voice cracked as I continued. "And if so, do you care about—me?"

That was pretty much it. I kept my head down and eyes closed while the tears ran from my cheeks to my chest. The fire crackled and I became aware of the slow, steady dripping again. A cold breeze encircled me, but I didn't move. Bryce said God had answered him through feelings. I waited for something other than the overwhelming self-pity that consumed me.

After a few minutes, the tears stopped. How long did this usually take? The soggy front of Bryce's t-shirt felt like it was going to freeze against my skin. I clasped my hands even tighter together to try to stop them from shaking. My legs trembled too, which made my knees rub against the uneven rock.

Why does it have to hurt so much to be me?

A huge wind gust rattled the trees in the distance then whipped through the cave, forcing me to open my eyes. *I should have waited.* As much as I wanted God to hear and answer me, I couldn't control my shaking. The pain and worry from the day weighed down on me and I just couldn't do it anymore.

Rolling off my knees, I reached my shaking fingers toward Bryce's ankle. *Please just let me find a pulse.* I touched his cold skin and almost instantly felt the steady rhythm. Warmth poured over me like a pot of warm honey, leaving my skin covered with prickly goosebumps. *Thank you!* Finally I had done something right.

I tucked the end of the sleeping bag gently around Bryce's legs. Before climbing under the covers with him, I grabbed the foil blanket, which had blown against the back of the cave, and spread it over Bryce as an extra layer. I wasn't sure if it would help, but I figured it couldn't hurt. Finally, I let my weary body drift down next to him, at first leaving several inches between us as I adjusted the covers and tried to get comfortable. The fire glowed low, reduced to a pile of bluish-orange embers.

How long had Bryce waited before getting an answer he recognized? His face was still tilted down, but perfectly relaxed and only inches from mine.

Abercrombie. I could never think about him that way again. He would always be beautiful to me, but not in a shirtless poster in the mall kind of way anymore. He was so much more than that. His tragedies made him more. The way he'd turned his life around made him more. The way he thought about and treated people. Listening to my lame problems. Telling me I was beautiful. When he should have been telling me to hurry up and end his misery.

I reached my hand out and brushed it across his cheek, eventually letting it rest against his warmth.

∞ ∞ ∞

I must have slipped into my own unconsciousness because it felt like I'd only closed my eyes long enough to blink, but when I opened them again, the glow from the fire was gone. The back of my palm had shifted from Bryce's check to his stubbly jaw, right below his ear. I quickly pulled my hand away.

I reached for the flashlight above my head and switched it on, careful to shine it away from Bryce's face. The beam cut through light mist, which now hugged the forest floor. With a hint of moonlight above, everything around me screamed horror story, but for once, I wasn't afraid. My breath crystallized in tiny droplets, but when I inhaled it was like I was breathing in the steam from a hot bowl of soup. I felt quiet instead of anxious. Peace instead of fear. Warmth in spite of the cold.

Turning the beam on Bryce's legs. I made sure the bandana was in place. I uncovered him long enough to check his bandage for blood and make sure he still had a pulse in his ankle. Everything looked as good as I could hope for. I tucked the sleeping bag around his feet and curled back up next to him, this time a little closer.

Exhausted, I should have fallen back asleep quickly, but my restless mind returned to the Great Creator and my as yet unanswered prayer. How had Bryce's prayers been answered? How had the Great Creator let him know in no uncertain terms that he was there, and that he cared? I should have asked for more details.

As I lay on my side contemplating, the clouds parted like a curtain, revealing the full moon above. In the distance, the shadowy treeline appeared. The treeline I had been watching all day. Waiting for rescue. Just like I was waiting now for an answer.

What if it neither ever came?

Tears pushed to the surface again and I let my eyelids slowly drop, too exhausted to have another full-blown pity party. But before they closed completely, my eyes caught a small movement in the shadows in the distance. Adrenaline surged through me. Could it be someone out looking for us? Or was it just the branches moving in the wind?

I turned slightly and watched the limbs of the little tree. They weren't moving at all. The night air was still.

I glanced back at the trees, holding my breath. Maybe I had just imagined it. I waited a few seconds, then saw it again—a heavy shadow, much shorter than the treeline, pacing slowly back and forth near the area where I had taken the wood from the fallen tree. My excitement turned to fear as the silhouette became more distinct.

Bear.

Paralyzed with fear, even my heart tried to stop beating. In the dim light, I saw the tag dangling from its right ear. I couldn't read it from this distance, but I knew instinctively it was number ten. The bear from earlier.

What was he doing? He took five steps to the right, paused for several seconds and turned back—taking five steps to the left. Then he did it all over again. When he paused, he seemed to be looking in our direction. Was he thinking about what kind of veggies he wanted on his Jasmine sandwich?

I curled into a ball and waited. The fire was out, and I didn't have anything but the small stones around the fire ring to use as a weapon if the bear decided to charge. Bryce and I were defenseless. And the bear seemed to know it. Why else would he keep pacing back and forth? He was stalking his prey.

Twenty-Three

Warm breath on the back of my neck and a single bird chirping in the distance jarred me awake just as the sun erased the last few stars above and changed the sky from deep blue to soft pink.

I'd fallen asleep? How? But we were still alive. That was good. My eyes went immediately toward the treeline, in search of my furry friend. He was still there. And still pacing. Five steps and pause. Five steps and pause.

I watched him for several minutes before turning to check on Bryce. His peaceful, sleeping face bolstered my confidence, even before I pulled back the covers to check on his leg. The swelling had gone down quite a bit—it almost looked normal. I found his pulse easily. As I was tucking the sleeping bag back in around his feet, he took in a deep breath, and groaned softly.

"Are you okay? Did I hurt you?"

"Where am I?" He opened his eyes slowly, blinking a few times, looking groggy and confused.

"You fell, remember?"

"Oh. Yeah." He rubbed his temples and cleared his throat. "You did it? You set the leg?"

I nodded. "Pulse is good. The swelling seems to have gone down a bit too."

He smiled. "I knew you could do it."

My cheeks burned like they'd been lit on fire and I had to break eye contact, looking down at my folded hands like some demure Victorian chick. "It wasn't a big deal."

"Sure. You do this kind of stuff all the time." His gravely morning voice almost made me forget our impending doom lurking in the distance.

The lingering mist dissipated as the sun came filtering through the trees. The bear continued his patrol, but I only glanced in his direction every now and then, debating whether to tell Bryce about him or not. He would probably reassure me that I was in no danger, or that I could handle it—just like he had with setting his leg. But he was in a very vulnerable position. If the bear charged, I could at least run away.

"I've been wondering something," I said, careful to avoid looking in the direction of the bear. "You know the other night with the bears?"

Bryce raised his eyebrows. "Uh-huh."

"You said the mom was tagged. Do they tag all the bears here?"

"No. Not all of them."

I paused, considering how to ask what was worrying me without worrying Bryce. "How do they decide which ones to tag?"

"I'm not one hundred percent sure, but I've heard they tag the problem bears."

"Problem bears?" I said. "You mean because they're aggressive or something?"

"Nah. Black bears aren't usually aggressive unless they're protecting their young. They just tag the ones that are getting a little too comfortable around humans." Bryce pushed himself up on his elbows. "You were really spooked the other night, weren't you?"

I nodded. "So it's not because they hurt or killed somebody?"

"No! Nothing like that. I should have explained a little better. They probably tagged that bear for exactly what she was doing when we saw her—getting into people's stuff. I think that's why they tag most of them."

Well, that was a relief. I let out a long breath.

"Wow. You were really worried about the bears, huh?" Bryce reached out and touched my shoulder. "Don't worry, Jasmine. Nobody has ever been seriously injured or killed by a bear in Yosemite."

"Well, that would have been useful information to give us at orientation," I muttered.

Bryce laughed.

"Just one more question," I said, nodding toward my furry friend near the treeline. "What does it mean when a bear paces?"

"Paces?" Bryce had to sit up a bit more to be able to follow my gaze. "Oh! How long has he been there?"

"All night," I said, my empty stomach churning.

"All night?" Bryce's eyebrows furrowed as he watched. Five paces to the right. Pause. Five paces to the left. "That's weird. He was doing that all night long?"

I nodded.

We continued watching.

"I've never seen a bear act like that in the wild," Bryce said softly. "I mean, in the zoo, for sure."

"What do you think it means?"

"I don't know," he whispered. "Doesn't it seem like he's looking right at us when he stops?"

A chill ran down my spine and I nodded vigorously. "What should we do?"

Bryce glanced at his leg, still lashed to the tree with the bandana. His eyes darted around the cave, and eventually landed on the stones around the fire. "I don't know. Maybe he's trying to show his dominance. But bears are usually easily scared. If you stand up as tall as you can and yell at him, he'll probably run away."

"Yeah! That's what I did yesterday," I said. "But I guess it's not a very permanent solution. What if he keeps coming back?"

Bryce was silent.

"Do you think he knows you're injured?" I whispered.

"To be honest, he makes me a little nervous." He cleared his throat, his face somber. "I don't really know what we should do."

My psyche felt like a rubber band, stretched to capacity. Bryce not knowing what to do was about to make me snap.

Bryce turned his attention from the bear and locked eyes with me. "Are you cool if we say a prayer?"

"Sure," I said. "But you'd better say it. I tried last night and that's when this guy showed up in the first place."

"You tried praying?"

Heat rose to my cheeks again, but I didn't break eye contact. I shrugged and then nodded. "I don't think I did it right?"

"Why do you say that? It doesn't matter how you did it."

"I don't know," I said. "I didn't get an answer."

"Sometimes the answers take a while." Bryce gave a half-smile then glanced back at the bear. "What did you pray for?"

I hesitated, not wanting to sound silly—which *was* silly, since it was Bryce's story that had encouraged me to try praying in the first place. "I just asked Him to let me know if He's there."

Bryce's eyes seemed to fog over, but he was still smiling. "And nothing happened? You didn't feel anything different?"

A lump formed in my throat as I shook my head. I wanted to be able to tell him that I'd seen a light or heard a heavenly choir, but I couldn't.

"Don't worry. It will come." Bryce sat up completely and folded his arms over his chest.

"That's right," I said. "I couldn't remember what you did with your arms."

"Seriously, the arms don't matter. You can pray anywhere and anyway you want. I've prayed in my head on the back of a motorcycle before."

"Okay," I said, folding my arms across my chest anyway. Bryce smiled, then lowered his head and closed his eyes. I followed suit.

"Heavenly Father," he began, "we're so thankful for the help you've given us so far. We're thankful to be alive, and to have had a good rest—under the circumstances." He paused. "I'm really thankful for Jasmine, and her calm, level head. I'm thankful for her willingness to try new things that would really scare most people. I'm thankful she followed me into the woods yesterday. And I'm thankful she sent Noah for help and stayed behind to take care of me."

Tears flowed and the warmth that had burned my cheeks now filled my entire being.

"Heavenly Father, we're both feeling unsettled about the bear. And we know my leg needs professional attention. Please—just watch over and protect us, and send help soon."

He finished off the prayer in the name of Jesus Christ— another person I knew very little about—and then said "Amen."

When I opened my eyes, he was staring at me. Was he waiting for me to say how I felt? I uncrossed my arms and pushed the tears off my cheeks.

"That was nice," I said.

He touched my arm, then looked over at the trees.

"Can you see him?" he asked. "Is he gone?"

I turned, searching for the bear, who seemed to be MIA. I should have been panicked—maybe the bear had taken the opportunity to sneak up on us when we weren't looking. But I felt a strange calm. Bryce's Heavenly Father wouldn't let that happen. Not when he'd just asked Him for protection.

"Where did he go?" Bryce said after a few seconds.

I shrugged. "Maybe your prayer worked. Maybe He changed the bear's mind about eating us for breakfast."

Bryce forced a laugh, but it was strained. He seemed more nervous now than he had been before the prayer.

"Something's not right," he muttered.

I didn't respond, wishing I could hear the thoughts that were making Bryce's forehead wrinkle.

"I hate to ask this," Bryce said, hesitating.

"Ask," I urged.

"I feel like you need to go look for the bear."

"Wait, what?" I said. "You want me to look for the bear?"

"I know it seems weird."

It did seem weird, but an urgent pressure in my gut told me to do as he said. I scrambled to my feet.

"What do I do if I find it?"

"I don't know," Bryce said.

I took a deep breath and a step away from the cave. "Okay."

"Be careful."

"I will," I said.

Taking several shaky steps toward the boulder blocking the rest of our view of the treeline, I said a back-of-the-motorcycle prayer that the bear wouldn't be standing on the other side of it. Luckily, that prayer was answered. I paused, now that my view was unobstructed, and surveyed the trees in the distance.

Nothing.

Where did he go? I did a 360, scanning every inch of the surrounding area. He was gone. Why would he suddenly disappear like that? Especially after his predictable behavior all night long.

Feeling oddly frantic, I rushed toward his patrol area. A path had been worn through the tall grass, down to dirt patches in several places. But I wasn't any sort of expert, and I couldn't tell where his tracks led.

"Jasmine?" Bryce called.

"He's gone," I shouted back.

"Hello?" a third voice called from the trees behind me.

I whirled around, heart beating a million miles per hour. It took several seconds to see where the voice had come from. A skinny blonde guy in a tan ranger hat came striding toward me through the trees. Could it really be? Maybe I was just seeing things. I waved my hands over my head.

"Hey there!" he called as he got a little closer. "You're pretty far from the trail. Are you camping out here? I'm going to need to see your permit."

I started laughing hysterically, realizing how ridiculous I must look in only a t-shirt and long socks.

"Are you okay, ma'am?"

I opened my mouth to try to explain our situation, but laughing turned to sobbing, and I couldn't get any words out. We were safe! We were rescued! Bryce was going to be okay. My eyes swam in grateful tears.

"Did you have a run-in with a bear?" the ranger asked. "Are you hurt?"

He'd reached me now, and he put a hand awkwardly on my shoulder. I shrugged it off, and grabbed hold of his arm, pulling him toward the cave, still unable to form complete sentences.

"My friend. Over here." I panted. "Needs help."

The next few minutes were a blur. Bryce calmly explained what had happened and the ranger radioed for help. He assessed Bryce's injuries and complimented the job I'd done with first aid. He gave us each an emergency blanket and a protein bar. And then we sat there, waiting for more help to come.

"So you weren't out here looking for us, were you?" Bryce asked.

"No," the ranger replied. "If they have search parties out for you, I must have missed it."

"Do you usually go this far off the trail?" Bryce asked.

"I go where the bears go," the ranger said. "I'm part of the bear team. I've been tracking one for the last couple of days and I thought maybe something had happened to him."

"The bear," I said.

"Did you see him?" the ranger asked.

I nodded.

"He's one that's been a regular around Tuolumne Meadows for several months now. Then he suddenly took off yesterday. He was running for a few hours almost like he was being chased—and then suddenly he just stopped. Somewhere right in this area."

"Yeah," Bryce said, "We saw him just a little while ago. He was pacing back and forth up there by the trees all night long. Then he just disappeared."

"I was looking for him when I saw you," I said.

The ranger grinned. "Lucky thing you were," he said. "I doubt I would have seen you back here."

"Might have been more than luck." A thick Nutella smile spread across Bryce's face.

Twenty-Four

The area swarmed with rescuers. A few were rangers, but it seemed like most were people from the High Sierra team. Jabba arrived just before a helicopter landed in the ravine.

"You gave us a good scare," he said to Bryce as they loaded him onto a stretcher.

"Did Noah make it back?" Bryce asked.

Dave nodded. "He walked all the way back to the campground at Tuolumne. He tried to lead us to you, but he was confused. Our search perimeter is over a mile from here."

With Bryce secured on a stretcher, a couple of paramedics turned their attention to me. Blood pressure cuff. A light in my eyes. A thermometer under my tongue.

"Everything looks good," one of them said to Jabba as he ripped off the cuff. "We can take her in for observation if you'd like, but she seems normal."

"How are you feeling, Jasmine?" Jabba asked.

I stood up as two of the paramedics lifted Bryce's stretcher and moved toward the helicopter. I hadn't stopped to consider what was going to happen next. Of course they were going to take Bryce away. He'd be rushed to a hospital. They'd do what was necessary to save his leg. Set it? Surgery? A cast? Whatever was going to happen to Bryce, he was leaving. And he wasn't coming back anytime soon.

"Jasmine?" Jabba said, touching my arm. "Are you okay?"

I nodded, but inside I was shaking my head, wishing I could erase this sad new reality and go back to last night— warm and safe next to Bryce. The helicopter swallowed Bryce's stretcher and its blades whirred to life, creating frenzied wind and deafening noise.

"Can I say goodbye?" I shouted.

"Oh, sure!" Jabba yelled, waving his arms and pulling me toward the helicopter. "Don't worry! He's going to be just fine!"

The paramedics re-opened the doors of the white and red chopper, and Jabba helped me step up. Bryce was wearing a headset, looking pretty comfortable and relaxed. Everyone turned and smiled at me. One of the paramedics handed me a set of headphones too. I pushed them over my ears, relieved to dampen the noise.

"Is everything okay?" Bryce asked. "Are you coming too?"

I shook my head. "I'm fine. I just wanted to say goodbye…and thank you." I kept my mouth open, wishing I could say more without all of the ears connected to these headsets hearing. My eyes misted over.

"Hey!" Bryce said. "This isn't goodbye. I doubt I'll get to hike with your group again before you graduate from the program." He smiled. "But I'll definitely stop in to see how you're doing."

I couldn't help smiling back at him. That was all I needed to hear. I was going to see him again.

We sat staring at each other for a few moments without saying anything until I finally realized everyone was waiting awkwardly for me to say or do something.

"Okay. Well, see you then." I turned away and reached for my headphones.

"Jasmine," Bryce said. I looked back up at him. "Keep trying. Keep asking. He's there and He'll answer you."

I nodded slowly, tears brimming. "I will," I promised.

∞ ∞ ∞

I told Jabba I could walk, but he insisted I ride back to Tuolumne Meadows on a ranger's ATV. The ride was just long enough to relive every minute of the previous day. We passed through an open field, similar to the one where we had eaten our roots and greens yesterday. It felt like a year had passed since then instead of just twenty-four hours. I felt so different now.

I hadn't even paused to consider what would happen when we got back to the campground, but I wasn't expecting the reception waiting for me. Quiet Wolf, Pizza Face, Michaela, and Emphysema stood in a clump at the trailhead. Backwoods Barbie stood a few feet away with the walkie-talkie in her hand.

They didn't even wait for me to get off the ATV before rushing at me. Patting my back, touching my shoulder, and peppering me with questions. So many that I couldn't answer any of them.

"How's Firewalker?"

"We heard you set his broken leg yourself!"

"Did you get caught in the flash flood?"

"Are you okay?"

"Have you eaten?"

"Guys! Guys!" Backwoods Barbie pushed into the circle that had formed around me. "Give her a little space."

The hands on my back and shoulder slipped away, but the circle didn't widen, and I didn't want it to. Yesterday, these kids hadn't seemed to care about me at all. Or maybe it was that I didn't care about them. Now, they looked like the family that Quiet Wolf had described to Emphysema. I wanted to tell them every detail about what had happened. Details that would never mean anything to Hilary and the other kids around the pool back home.

"You guys look so beautiful," I said.

"Ha!" Emphysema laughed. "I wish we could say the same for you!"

"Yeah, I'm sure I'm a hot mess."

Emphysema smiled. "Nothing a shower and some plastic surgery won't fix."

"Geez!" Pizza Face said, elbowing Emphysema's arm. "Cut her a break for two seconds."

"Where's Noah?" I asked.

The whole group lowered their eyes to the dusty ground in unison.

A second wave of ATV's came buzzing up the trail behind us—one of them carrying Jabba.

"Hey, guys!" he said, jumping off the machine and coming toward us.

"Where's Noah?" I repeated, addressing the question to Backwoods Barbie directly this time.

"He's not with us anymore," she said.

Not with us anymore? My heart thumped hard against my ribs.

Jabba must have followed my train of thought. "He's safe and fine, Jasmine. Don't worry. His parents just decided to check him into an inpatient rehab program last night."

"We want to hear your version of what happened," said Quiet Wolf.

"Yeah," Michaela said. "I mean, one minute we're all out there sunning on the rocks, and the next everyone's gone missing."

"Hold on, hold on." Jabba interrupted before I could set the record straight. "Jasmine can give you guys the gory details on the way back to the lodge."

"We're going to the lodge?" Pizza Face's jaw dropped.

"Yep," Jabba said. "You guys can meet Firewalker's replacement and then head back up to the trail tomorrow morning."

"Wildcat?" Backwoods Barbie asked. "Why not have him meet us here? We could still make it up to Glen Aulin before sunset."

"You could do that," Jabba said. "But I just got word that Jasmine's mom landed about twenty minutes ago. She's on her way to the lodge, and it doesn't sound like she's very happy. I thought it might be nice to let you all have some time together before she arrives."

"She's coming to get me?" *No!* It was stupid of me not to have considered the possibility. Now that I didn't want her to, she was going to cut my stay in the program short. "Does she know I'm fine? Can't someone just tell her she can go back home? False alarm?"

"We tried to reassure her, but she seemed very resolved."

"She's already made up her mind that I'm going home?"

Jabba shrugged, "She didn't say…*exactly* that."

I didn't need to ask any more questions. The picture of what had happened crystallized in my mind. My mom had gotten the call that I was missing and had completely flipped out. She must have called Jabba and chewed him up one side and down the other. My mom was a force to be reckoned with when she was mad. And she was known for making rash decisions in the heat of the moment. That was probably how I'd ended up here in the first place.

"What do you think guys?" Backwoods Barbie asked.

"I say Glen Aulin will be there tomorrow," Quiet Wolf said.

"Yeah," Pizza Face agreed.

The girls both nodded, and Backwoods Barbie smiled. "We were all really worried about you," she said, stepping back like she was bracing for whatever comeback I was going to throw at her. *Poor Monica.* She'd never been anything but nice to me.

"I'm really sorry," I said. "I never should've taken off like that without telling you."

She tilted her head to the right and raised her eyebrows like she was wondering if I'd been abducted by aliens. But then she smiled and simply said, "Thanks."

Our little crew turned down the dusty trail toward the big white van and piled inside. Pizza Face opened the door for me, and I parked myself on the middle bench. Everyone filled in around me—all five of us on the middle two benches.

They waited till we were on the road to bombard me with questions again.

"Just start at the beginning," Emphysema said. "How did you conveniently end up in the exact spot where Firewalker fell if you weren't with Noah when he ran off?"

Why did Emphysema have to make it so hard to be nice to her? I took a deep breath and started filling in the details. But I started back at the campground that morning and pointed out how I'd been keeping an eye on Noah's situation the whole time. I skimmed over some boring stuff about putting pressure on Bryce's wound and keeping the rain off of him, and I tried not to make too big of a deal of dragging him up the hill. But when I got to the part about building the fire and the bear, I didn't hold back.

"That's crazy!" Pizza Face said. "You seriusly had a stare down with a bear?"

I nodded. "At first, I thought if I held perfectly still, he would just go away. But he wasn't budging."

"I would've peed my pants," Michaela said.

"Well, I finally just lost it," I said. "I went all ape crap crazy and started yelling at it to go away."

Monica turned around, "Wow! That's really cool."

"It is?" I laughed.

"Yeah," she said. "That's exactly what the rangers teach people to do when they run into bears here. We usually wait to teach you that until we run into one."

Tingles from head to toe. That *was* pretty cool. I'd tried doing what Bryce had done the night before and it hadn't worked. Yelling at the bear was nothing that my instincts should have told me to do.

"So what else?" Emphysema urged me to continue.

I picked up the story where I'd left off, skipping the conversation Bryce and I had had, and the part about me praying. But I was thinking about it when I told them about the bear patrolling.

"That's so weird," Michaela said. "Weren't you terrified?"

"Kind of."

"You must be exhausted," Monica said.

"I'm a little tired. But I actually slept pretty well."

"You slept? With the bear watching you like that?" Emphysema didn't believe a word I was saying.

"I guess adrenaline does weird things to people," I said. "And now that I think back about it, even though I was scared of the bear, maybe I knew all along that he was there to help."

Everyone looked at me, waiting for an explanation.

"He's the reason we were found this morning," I said. "He was tagged and cuffed. The ranger that found us had been tracking him. The bear basically led him straight to us."

The hair on the back of my neck stood on end. The bear had shown up right after I'd prayed. Could the bear have been my answer?

The van slowed as we started down the bumpy gravel road to the lodge. All eyes turned to the sleek, black airport limo parked right in front of the building, blocking the way to the small parking lot behind where they kept the vans.

My mom had arrived.

Twenty-Five

She stood in the corner of the main room, examining the group photos pinned haphazardly to the walls. Arms folded tightly across her chest, she didn't seem impressed. As we entered, my crew was uncharacteristically quiet.

She didn't seem to recognize me for a second, and when she finally did, she looked like she was going to blow a gasket.

Her heels clicked against the cement floor and she almost knocked Michaela over. She took hold of my arms like they were dirty diapers and stepped back. "You look terrible!"

"Welcome to High Sierra, Ms. Fuentes." Dave came into the room with a big smile on his face.

"Mr. Richardson?"

"How was your flight?"

Her full lips pulled into a straight line. "Jasmine will need clean clothes and a shower."

"Of course. Her personal items are in her cubby," Dave said.

"Good. I want to get out of here as soon as possible."

"Mom," I squeaked.

"Is there paperwork I need to sign?"

"Mom," I said again, a little louder this time.

"Jasmine, go get cleaned up."

Pressure built steadily inside me until my ears rang. I stepped backward and yanked my arms away.

"Mom!"

"What?" she snapped, finally making eye contact with me.

"I want to stay."

Her blank expression didn't seem to register what I'd said.

"Which cubby is yours?" She scanned the room.

"Did you hear me?" I asked. "I don't want to go."

Dave moved between us. "Why don't we step into my office to talk about this?"

"I don't think that's necessary. We have a plane to catch."

"You don't want me to finish the program *you* signed me up for?" I said.

"This is *not* the program I signed you up for."

Pizza Face leaned over and whispered something to Quiet Wolf. The others moved farther into the room, looking unsure where they should go and what they should do.

"Please, Mom. Can we go in Dave's office and talk about this?"

"There's nothing to talk about." She straightened the buttons on her fitted suit jacket, then took several steps toward the door. "I'll wait for you in the car."

If she walked out that door, she wasn't coming back in. I had to do something. My chances were slipping away.

"Wait! You were right."

She stopped but didn't turn around.

"You were right. I need to change. I don't want to turn out to be no good." My voice cracked and I blinked back tears. "I don't want to be like him."

"Jasmine!"

There was no turning back now. "I know that's what you're worried about. I know that's why you sent me here. I remind you of him…and I'm sorry."

All noise in the room swirled to a stop, like we were in the eye of a hurricane.

"You weren't wrong about this program. I need to be here. I've seen what it can do for people. But you have to give it time. I have to finish this."

She didn't move. I couldn't see her face. Why wasn't she saying something?

"Please, Mom."

She pulled her shoulders back and turned toward Dave's office. "Will you please excuse us?"

Dave rushed to open the door before my mom came storming through it. I followed her, with the low chorus of whispers resuming behind me.

Please…please help her understand.

She sat in one of the chairs across from Dave's desk and drummed her fingers against her folded arms. She looked about as friendly as a spine on a cactus.

"Can I get you both something to drink?" Dave asked.

"I doubt you have anything strong enough," she muttered.

"I'll take some water," I said, sinking into the chair next to her. "I think I'm still a little dehydrated from yesterday."

She glanced at me and narrowed her eyes.

Dave handed me a glass of water, then pulled out a large rug from behind his desk. He unrolled it and spread it on the floor next to us.

"We haven't had the opportunity for a sitting yet, Jasmine." He sat on the rug and held out his hands. "Will you join me? The Miwok—"

"What did you mean by that out there?" my mom snapped.

"Which part?"

"About not wanting to be 'no good, like him.' What were you talking about?"

"We both know what I was talking about," I breathed.

"I've never said you reminded me of him. Where would you get an idea like that?"

"Well, I don't look like you, so I figured I must take after someone."

"*Jasmine.*"

"Well, what am I supposed to think? You slather me up with sunscreen, put me on a diet, and correct my every move. I get it. You don't want me to be like him."

Her eyes widened and her mouth fell open, but she didn't speak.

Dave glanced back and forth between the two of us. Several uncomfortable seconds passed, and I started to wonder if I should say something else. But what else was there to say? She couldn't keep pretending my father didn't exist.

Dave cleared his throat. "Those are some strong feelings you've expressed, Jasm—"

"That is *not* why I sent you here," my mom interrupted. She looked at the ceiling and blew out an exasperated breath. "I don't know how you can think that. I've *never* said that."

"You didn't have to."

"You're being ridiculous." She stood up. "You don't remind me of him, Jasmine. You remind me of *me*. You always have."

"What?" My brain felt like someone had pulled the plug on it. There was no way she actually believed what she was saying.

"You're smart, and driven, and ambitious. Just like I was in high school. The future's wide open to you." She took a breath. "As long as you don't screw it up like—"

She bit her lip, cutting herself off.

"Like you did?" I whispered.

My mom glanced at Dave, then made full eye contact with me. "Okay. *Yes.* Is that what you want to hear? I thought I knew better than my parents. I threw their rules out the window and I made a mistake that changed everything."

"Hhhh." My fists clenched. "You mean *me?*"

She stepped backward, stumbling on her heel. As she regained her footing, I thought I saw a flicker of mist in her eyes, but she pinched them closed and pulled her shoulders back. When she reopened them, fire doused any hint of emotion I'd glimpsed.

"We're not talking about me. None of this has anything to do with why *you're* here."

Of course. We were just about to get somewhere, and she was going to cut me off again. She didn't want to talk about it—but *this* had everything to do with it. I stood and stepped toward her.

"Why am I here, then? Prom night?"

Her brows arched.

"It was one mistake."

"That mistake could have cost you everything."

"I wasn't even the one who was drinking."

"You are who you associate with."

So now my friends weren't good enough? How would she know? She hadn't even met some of them until the prom night incident, and she had barely spoken to them then. I wanted to rage. I wanted to scream all of the things I'd been thinking for years. I wanted to tell her how unreasonable and judgmental she was being, but I had to bite my tongue.

"I said I was sorry. I finished my community service. What else do I have to do?"

"'Sorry?'" She shook her head. "You still don't understand how serious this is."

"You're right. I guess I don't. I thought I made a one-time mistake. I thought I would pay for it and move on."

"Well, sorry to break the news to you that life doesn't work like that. Consequences don't just magically go away because you're sorry." She paced toward Dave's desk. "Believe me. I learned the hard way." She turned and paced back to where she'd started. "And you don't just pay once and move on. Consequences are endless."

She stopped pacing and dropped her hands to her sides. "One mistake—" Her voice faltered. "I would have graduated valedictorian of my class. Instead my diploma came in the mail. I opened it at a card table in a basement apartment. Wearing a spit-up covered t-shirt."

My mom had never been one to let me look through her scrapbooks. Now I knew why. As she pulled back the curtain a crack and let me see into her window of pain, it was blinding.

"I may have what I want now, but I had to fight to get it." She folded her arms again. "'Sorry' didn't let me graduate with my class. 'Sorry' didn't help with midnight feedings. And doing the 'right thing' didn't fix my problems."

I backed up until my hand touched the chair. I tried to picture it. She must have been so humiliated, giving up everything for some guy, just to have him toss her aside. I sunk slowly into the chair. It must have been devastating to have her dreams crushed and be left with all the responsibility.

"I...I'm sorry that happened to you."

"Don't be sorry." Her eyes bored into me. "Just don't repeat my mistakes. You don't want to have to move thousands of miles away and leave everything and everyone behind just so you can start over." Her voice became so soft, it was barely audible.

The corners of my mouth dropped, and my brows came together. *Move thousands of miles…so you can start over.*

"Wait. You left, not him?"

Her breath stopped short and she turned slowly away toward the window. The branches of an aspen tapped against the glass and the leaves rattled in the breeze.

"Mom?"

"It was…I had…"

"You did, didn't you?"

She was silent.

"Did he know you were leaving?"

Her folded arms dropped down around her waist. "We both knew it was over."

So much pain. Her words hung in the air like a puff of smoke I just couldn't grasp hold of. My mother had left my father. She. Left. Him. Not the other way around.

"You…has he…ever tried to contact me?"

She didn't answer, staring blankly out the window.

I rose up out of my chair.

"He has, hasn't he?" I demanded.

"I knew this would happen. I never should have started talking to them again. None of this would have happened."

My heart pounded in my ears. "Who? Never should have started talking to who?" I stepped toward her. "Does he know where we live? When did he try to contact me?"

She finally turned around but hesitated when our eyes met. "Not until after I started talking to my parents again. I think they're the ones who told him how to contact me."

I fought to control the stream of thoughts that wanted to come out. How could she have let me believe it was his fault all these years?

"Do you know where he is now?"

She nodded slowly, staring at the wall behind me. "He lives in the same small town we grew up in. The same neighborhood as my parents. They all go to church together. Apparently, he has a big family and owns his own business." Her voice trailed off.

My father lived near my grandparents? I closed my eyes and took a deep breath picturing the address on my birthday envelopes.

"I made the mistake of telling my parents about prom night. I told them I was researching wilderness therapy programs. They're the ones who suggested this place."

Tingles passed through me. It was like this whole crazy thing had happened just so I could know the truth. *You are there. And you do care.* I closed my eyes and a wide smile spread across my face.

"Jasmine?"

I opened my eyes and met my mom's concerned look.

"It's okay, Mom," I said in a clear, crisp voice. "You did the right thing. You needed to send me here."

I couldn't stop myself. I threw my arms around her rigid shoulders and squeezed.

"I—" She seemed to want to say something, but I squeezed tighter. Dave smiled at us from the blanket.

"Mom," I whispered, with my cheek pressed against her shoulder.

"Yes?"

"I think I'm old enough now."

She stiffened and pulled away from me.

"Old enough for what?"

"Old enough to decide for myself what I believe and who I want in my life."

Twenty-Six

"I think we should work this out at home," Mom said.

"Mom, I'm begging you to let me do this."

Almost an hour of talking with Dave on the rug and I still hadn't been able to convince her to let me stay. She was being completely unreasonable. There was no real reason I had to go home with her now. We both knew what had happened wasn't High Sierra's fault. Every word she said, every concern she brought up, every excuse she gave betrayed her biggest fear. I was almost 18. Now that I knew the truth, she was afraid she was going to lose me.

The light was fading outside Dave's window. I was tired.

"You know," I finally said, "I don't ask for much. And, aside from the prom night incident, I think I've tried to do what you want me to do. I've finished every single one of the programs you've put me in. I didn't want to go to any of them—but I finished them for you."

She folded her arms across her chest, staring at the diploma behind Dave's desk. She didn't say anything. I was wearing her down.

"Please," I said again. "I didn't choose this program, but I want to finish it. I have to finish it."

We were both tired, and there was nothing else to argue about. The only thing left for her to say was yes or no.

She cleared her throat. "Okay."

"Okay?" We'd been in this room for a long time. Maybe I was hearing things.

"Yes," she said. "Fine. You can stay."

It took every bit of energy I had left to keep myself from jumping up out of my chair and dancing like a maniac. "Thank you! Thank you! You won't regret it. I promise."

"That's wonderful!" Dave said. "And we'd love it if you came back to walk with Jasmine during her final week."

"Me?" my mom asked, like there was someone else in the room he might have been talking about.

"Yes. We invite parents to come experience for themselves what their children have been doing—to walk every step of the last leg of their High Sierra journey with them. It'll be a great opportunity for Jasmine to show you what she's learned."

"Camping?" she asked.

Dave nodded. "We call it their rite of passage."

"It's okay. You don't have to come," I said.

"No." My mom cleared her throat. "I'll be here."

I was stunned. Maybe she was too emotionally exhausted to realize what she was agreeing to, but I wasn't going to argue with her. I sat in silence as Dave reassured her again that she'd made the right decision. Honestly, I'd completely tuned them out—my mind too full of excitement and gratitude. She was really letting me stay.

When we finally came out of Dave's office, my little crew was sprawled around the room—some on folding chairs, others on sleeping bags on the floor. They sat up, all eyes on me—waiting for a verdict.

"I'm staying!"

They cheered and everyone rushed me except Emphysema. She hung back a bit, but it looked like she was sort of smiling.

"You're welcome to stay the night," Dave said to my mom.

She shook her head. "I can't. I have an important meeting tomorrow afternoon."

I nodded.

Dave and I followed her out to the limousine, and she hugged me awkwardly before climbing inside.

∞ ∞ ∞

Wildcat joined us the next morning before we packed up the van. He was an average guy with an average build, just barely taller than Monica. He was no Bryce, but he seemed pretty cool. Monica had obviously been on the trail with him before. They talked like old friends.

When we reached the trail, I took up the rear. The sight of the dusty path and everyone's boots and packs in front of me filled me with contentment.

The day flew by. We passed the spot along the stream where Bryce had gone after Noah. I smiled but didn't say anything. We reached the backpacker's campground at Glen Aulin just before sunset. The stream we'd been following along the trail all day became a waterfall, tumbling into a sparkling pool.

We dropped our packs and followed Wildcat and Monica up a small hill to watch the sun slip below the horizon between two cliff walls, the winding stream, and about a thousand pine trees. I took a deep breath and thanked the Great Creator for letting me see it.

That night around the fire, I sat listening to Quiet Wolf and Pizza Face argue about movies with a stupid grin on my face.

"We should get to bed early," Wildcat suggested. "The hike to May Lake is pretty intense." He stood up and stretched.

The others followed, scattering one by one, except Emphysema, who was still staring into the fire.

"You heading to bed?" I asked.

"In a minute."

I nodded and stepped back from the light of the fire.

"Can I ask you a question, though?" she said.

"Sure," I replied, a little nervous.

"What happened to you out there?"

"What do you mean?" I said. "I told you guys what happened."

"Yeah." She hugged her knees to her chest. "But what really happened? You're like a completely different person."

I shrugged and sat back down on the log opposite her.

"It might sound kind of stupid," I said. "Do you promise not to laugh at me?"

She raised her eyebrows. "No. But tell me anyway."

I took a deep breath. "Well," I said. "I guess I just had time to think. I realized that I have problems, just like everyone else. I realized that I need help too."

"What made you realize all that?"

I stared into the flames for a few seconds, trying to decide what I should tell her. "I guess it was something Bryce said."

"What did he say?"

"He just helped me realize that everyone has a story. And you can't judge a book by its cover."

She rolled her eyes. How did I make this not sound cliché? "I thought Bryce was all perfect, and that he'd always been that way. But he went through the program just like us."

"He did?" Her voice was soft.

"Yeah. You should ask him about it the next time you see him."

She shrugged. "Maybe."

"You know what?" I continued. "I think we all have more in common than we realize."

"Right," she scoffed. "Like the two of us?"

"Especially us," I said.

"How?"

"You were talking the other day about not having a family—I guess you probably figured out from the conversation with my mom that I've never had a dad. I mean, I have one, but I don't remember him. We've never talked."

She nodded. We were both quiet for a second.

"I don't know," I said. "I guess I just like the idea of what Quiet Wolf said to you. I like the idea that any group of people who love you can become your family."

"Yeah, it's a nice idea," she muttered, "but what about forgetting all the stuff that's happened to us in the past? What about all the stuff we've done that makes us feel unlovable? The stuff Michaela was saying at the talking circle."

The crackling fire filled the silence between us.

"I don't know," I admitted. "But there must be a way to get past it. Firewalker knows how. I bet Jabba does too."

"Jabba?"

My face flared up, and it wasn't because I was too close to the flames. Why did I have to be such an idiot? "Sorry," I said. "I meant Good Soaring Raven."

Emphysema laughed. "I like Jabba. It's less wordy."

"Naw. It's not cool. It's a bad habit I have—that I'm going to try to break."

"What habit?" She raised her eyebrows.

"Giving everyone nicknames."

"You have a nickname for everyone?"

My gut rolled up in a ball, but I slowly nodded my head.

"Nathan?"

"Pizza Face."

She snorted.

"Todd?"

"Spud Boy."

"Ha! What about your little boyfriend, Noah? Did you have one for him too?"

Boyfriend. It still made me cringe that everyone thought that. I cleared my throat. "It wasn't very nice—" I said. "Quasimodo."

She laughed so hard, tears ran down her face.

"You pretty much pegged everyone," she finally said, wiping her eyes. "I probably don't want to know what you call me."

I sat silent, not sure if she expected me to tell her, or if she really meant she didn't want to know.

"Which was it? Skank, ho, or slut?"

"What? No!" My chest tightened like she'd knocked the wind out of me. "I told you I'm not a nice person, but I didn't think anything like that."

"Well, you should have," she said. "I'm not the same as the rest of you with your cute little suburban problems."

I didn't know what to say.

"I'm sure you figured out I was living on the streets."

I shook my head.

"When Samuel Chavis picked me up on the corner of University and Fairmount, this wasn't what I expected."

"Stormi, I—"

"Don't worry about it," she said. "It might as well be written on my forehead. Changing my clothes and my environment doesn't change who I am."

"Seriously, I had no idea."

"Oh, come on," she said. "You saw it the first day. That's why you treated me different."

"Not true," I said. "I treated you different because you were a total jerk. I had no idea you were a prostitute."

Stormi laughed so hard it triggered a coughing fit. "Nice," she said when the choking was under control.

"I'm really sorry," I said. "I mean, I'm really sorry for what you've been through. I'm sure it sucked."

"I guess you could sum it up like that."

"Those names…people have called you. That's not who you are."

"Really? Then who am I?"

Good question. Bryce would know what to say. I tried to remember what he'd told me, but I didn't know quite how to translate it over to Stormi's situation.

"It's okay," she said. "You don't have to think *that* hard about it."

"No. I'm not…I mean…I know who you are."

"Oh, really? You gonna tell me the nickname you have for me?"

"No, not a stupid nickname. You're the same as me. I just found out who I am. You see it. You know I'm different."

"Yeah, okay. Who are we?"

"You remember that song Abercrombie sang around the fire at Tuolumne?"

"Abercrombie? Seriously?"

"Bryce…anyway, that's who I am—and who you are too."

"Who?"

"A child of God." I said it so loud and clear that every hiker in the campground probably heard.

She smiled like she was about to laugh, but she must
have realized I was dead serious because the smile faded to
a squint.

"And you figured that out exactly how?"

"I prayed and asked Him," I said softly.

Saying it out loud to someone else gave me the strongest
tingles I'd ever felt in my life. Tingles that made my eyes fill
with tears.

"Sorry if I don't believe you," Stormi muttered. "But
that's the stupidest thing I've ever heard."

Twenty-Seven

I made a point to hike with Stormi after that. I couldn't blame her for not believing me, but I wanted her to understand. At first, she acted annoyed, but each day, she opened up a little more about her past. She didn't remember much about her parents. Or maybe she didn't want to remember. They'd both been on drugs and would sometimes leave her at home alone for days at a time.

"I'd been eating dry spaghetti noodles and ketchup for two days straight when the police showed up at our apartment."

The dysfunctional families she stayed with in foster care after that hadn't been much better.

"The group homes were the worst," she said. "They never had enough staff to supervise the messed up kids in there."

"Messed up?"

"You mean more messed up than me?" she rolled her eyes. "I'm actually one of the lucky ones. There are worse things than just being really, really neglected."

"Do you keep in touch with any of those other kids?"

She shook her head. "One of those other kids was the reason I ended up on the streets."

I was at a loss for words.

"It wasn't really his fault. When people do that kind of stuff to you, it's because somebody did it to them."

"I'm sorry," I whispered.

"Why are you sorry? It's not your fault." She blew out a breath. "See why it's hard to believe there's a God? I mean, why would you let that kind of stuff happen to your kids?"

She made a very tough point, and I didn't know the reason why. I only knew He was there.

Over the next seven days, we covered about fifty miles, completing the entire High Sierra Loop. On our last night, the entire crew sat around the fire, feeling the satisfying exhaustion that comes after a long hike.

"We're going to head back to the lodge tomorrow," Monica said. "It's time to switch rotations. You guys will have new spirit guides. And I have a feeling you're going to be losing Quiet Wolf and Runs on Wind."

"You think so?" Quiet Wolf said solemnly.

Monica nodded. "Good Soaring Raven said you have some special guests waiting for you."

"Rite of passage!" Runs on Wind could barely contain his excitement.

"What about the rest of us?" Stormi asked.

"We've got two new groups starting tomorrow," Wildcat said. "You're at a place now where you can help someone else in their walking."

"Don't we need trail names?" Michaela asked.

"True," Stormi said. "I mean, without their trail names, these two would have seemed like a couple of clowns to us. We never would have taken them seriously."

Monica laughed. "How about it guys—have these ladies earned trail names?"

"Yeah, I've had one for you for a while, Stormi," Quiet Wolf said. "I was just afraid to tell you."

"Afraid to tell me? Why?"

"You're kind of intimidating," he laughed.

"Well, if it was a nice name, you wouldn't be afraid to tell me."

"It's nice…I just didn't want you to take it the wrong way."

"What is it?" I asked.

"You know those red flowering plants we saw toward the beginning of the week? The ones that can't grow on their own, so they get their nutrients from fungi that attach to the roots of trees?"

"Snow flowers?" Wildcat said.

"Nice," Stormi said. "You think I'm a parasite?"

"No! Shut up and listen to the whole thing," Quiet Wolf continued. "I was just thinking how you're like the flower. You add color and beauty to the group, and you've blossomed since you've been here. You just needed to be attached to some roots."

Stormi smiled and punched Quite Wolf's arm. "Snow Flower." She let it drip off her tongue. "I like it."

The boys had a name ready for Michaela too. "Forest Water," because she pushed forward, disregarding her own pain. Giving freely to anyone who asked.

When everyone settled into quiet again, I waited for someone to offer a name suggestion for me, but the minutes passed, and no one spoke up. It stung a little, but these things couldn't be forced. Trail names had to be earned.

"Well, I'm going to head to bed," I said with a yawn.

"Don't you want your trail name too?" Monica asked.

"I wasn't sure—" I stuttered. "I mean, I didn't know if you had one for me."

"I mean, it seems kind of obvious it needs to have something to do with the mysterious bear that saved you and Firewalker," said Stormi. "If that's not your spirit animal, I don't know what is."

Monica nodded. "Bears symbolize strength and confidence…and standing up against adversity."

Looks and nods passed between my little crew.

"The spirit of the bear also uses its abilities to heal itself and others," Wildcat added.

"How about Bipolar Bear, since she's made such a huge personality swing?" Stormi joked.

I laughed along with the others.

"If she hadn't been watching Noah, things might have turned out way different," Michaela said. "I mean, none of us had a clue what was going on with him."

"And didn't you say that's what the bear did all night long—just pace back and forth and watch you?" Stormi said.

I nodded.

"What about Watching Bear?" Monica suggested.

Everyone smiled, looking to me for approval.

I liked it.

∞ ∞ ∞

Quiet Wolf and Runs on Wind's parents weren't the only special guests waiting for us at the lodge. Bryce greeted us on crutches, with a cast that went clear to his mid-thigh. Seeing him again felt unreasonably good. But I tried not to act too weird or familiar. It was enough to just sit back and enjoy the Nutella smile he spread around on the others as they told him what he'd missed over the last week.

When they reached a lull in conversation, it was Bryce who approached me.

"I heard you had a nice talk with your mom," he said.

"Is that how Good Soaring Raven described it? Nice?"

He laughed. "Okay, he said a bit more than that, but it sounds like the outcome was good."

I nodded. "She's coming back for my rite of passage at the end."

Our conversation got cut short when Good Soaring Raven announced that it was time to break off into our new groups. The folding chairs were filled with terrified-looking kids in their street clothes. Michaela and Stormi were going with the group on the right side of the room, and I was assigned to the group on the left. I found a seat next to a girl with an especially sarcastic look on her face.

Bryce stayed at the back of the room while we all went around and introduced ourselves. He looked so proud when Stormi and Michaela announced their trail names, but I didn't look at him when I said mine.

I helped Melissa, the sarcastic girl, pack up her bear canister, and pretty soon it was time to load up the vans. In the chaos, I hadn't noticed Bryce slip out of his chair at the back. I wanted to make sure I said goodbye before he left.

"I'll be right back," I told Melissa.

I searched the lodge and Good Soaring Raven's office but didn't see him. *What if he already left?* My group was being guided through the back doors, but I didn't follow. Instead I ran to see if he was out front.

He stood alone on the front porch, leaning against one of the log posts. I caught my breath and tried to will my heart to slow down.

"We're heading out," I said. "I just wanted to say goodbye before we go."

"I'm glad you did," he said. He shifted around on his crutches.

"How long until you're back on the trail?" I asked.

"Only six weeks in the cast," he replied. "But I'm not going back out on the trail this summer. I was able to get in on a session at school. I leave in a couple of days."

"Oh."

"Hey," he said. "Don't look so sad about it. This isn't how I'd planned on spending my summer, but it's probably a blessing in disguise. Everything happens for a reason, and if it weren't for you, I'd probably be hobbling around on one leg, or worse."

I smiled. The muffled sound of the kids loading the vans around back beckoned me, but I didn't want to go yet.

"What are your plans?" Bryce asked. "I mean after you go home?"

"Senior year."

"Applying to colleges?"

I nodded.

"East Coast schools?"

"I haven't decided for sure."

"You should check out BYU."

"Is that where you're going?"

Bryce nodded. "It's a really good school. Kind of a little-known secret."

"Where is it?"

"Provo, Utah. Only about thirty minutes from where I grew up."

Provo, Utah. The birthday envelopes from my grandparents.

The van horn honked.

"I'll check it out," I promised. "I've gotta go."

"Enjoy your walking." He reached out like he was going to touch my arm but changed his mind and waved at me instead.

I nodded and waved back. Turning away quickly, I stumbled down the porch steps and ran toward the corner of the building. Almost out of Bryce's view, I stopped. What if I never saw him again?

"Bryce," I called, spinning around.

"Yeah?"

"Thank you. Thank you for everything you told me that night."

He nodded. "You're welcome."

I stared at him stupidly, wishing I could run back and throw my arms around him.

"I got an answer," I said breathlessly. "I know He's there."

A wide smile spread across his face.

"I knew you would."

∞ ∞ ∞

My summer on the trail flew by. I looked forward to weekly meetings with Good Soaring Raven. Sometimes he came out with us for "sittings" on the trail, and sometimes we came in to the lodge between hikes. Now that he understood my situation, it was easy to talk to him.

Before I knew it, I was meeting my mom at the lodge for my rite of passage. Stormi was there too, looking fit, suntanned, and content.

"It's so good to see you!" I said, giving her a huge bear hug.

"I can't believe you're still here," she said. "I thought you would be done already."

I smiled, ignoring her backhanded compliment. "It seems right to me that we're finishing this together."

Just then my mom came walking up in her designer hiking gear, looking completely lost and a little terrified.

"Mom, this is my friend, Stormi."

"Hello, Stormi." She wrinkled her nose and gave a slight nod, then reached down to adjust her shoe.

241

"Stormi started the same day I did."

"How nice," my mom said.

"It was nice." Stormi rolled her eyes at me. "Remember how you almost started a fight with me in the bathroom?"

Still tying her shoe, my mom glanced up, raising her eyebrows at me.

"You were afraid of me. You couldn't get out of there fast enough," I said.

"Right," Stormi laughed, "That's not how I remember it."

"How did you say you two met?" My mom finally stood up.

"Stormi was in my first group. We started together and now we're finishing together."

"Are your parents coming for your rite of passage, Stormi?"

I cringed. How did she always manage to find the most painful paper cuts to pour salt on?

"My parents are probably in prison." Stormi laughed. I joined in, watching the judgy wheels turn in my mom's head.

∞ ∞ ∞

Two days on the trail with my mom was eye opening. It was nice to have her in an environment where I felt more comfortable than she did. For the first time in my life, she was on my turf.

Stripped of all of the distractions from our normal lives, we actually had to talk to each other. There was nothing else to do. Eventually, we started to really communicate about things that mattered.

"I can't put my finger on it exactly, but it's more than just your confidence that's changed out here," my mom said one night as we sat around a fire I'd built.

242

"It's everything," I said. "I know who I am. I know why I'm here, and I know what I want."

"Wow," she said. "Do you plan to enlighten me?"

"Well, this is my senior year. I want to go all out. I'm never going to get the chance to do this again, and I want to make you proud."

She smiled.

"I'll need to start applying to schools in a few months."

"Have you decided on a major?" she asked. "Are you still thinking about PR?"

"I'm keeping my options open," I said. "I know it was great for you, and I'm still thinking about it, but being out here has opened my mind to some other possibilities."

"Really? What are you thinking about?"

I cleared my throat. "I kind of like the idea of helping people the way Good Soaring Raven does. Not necessarily in a program like this, maybe in a private practice, or social work or something."

"Hmmm," she said, eyebrows raised. "Yes. I think it would be good to keep your options open."

We sat in silence for a few minutes while I thought about how to introduce my next bit of news. I had no idea how she would react to the idea, but at the very least, I knew it would take some time for her to adjust.

"I'm also thinking about applying to a couple of schools out here in the West."

She didn't look up from the fire.

"Which schools?"

"I don't know. Maybe a couple here in California. One of my spirit guides is studying psychology at the University of Washington, so I've thought about that one. And maybe BYU."

"Ah," she said, finally looking up at me.

"If it's okay with you, I'd like to start talking to my grandparents…" I said, hesitating to add the next part. "And my father."

She nodded. "I knew you'd want to."

∞ ∞ ∞

Two days later, I joined Good Soaring Raven on the heavy wool blanket for one final sitting. Pride shone in his eyes as we discussed what I'd accomplished.

"What's the most important thing you've learned here, Watching Bear?"

I thought for a moment. It was a tough question. I'd learned so many important things. I'd learned to see people for who they really were. I'd learned that it didn't matter who you'd been or what you'd done in the past—you could change. All you had to do was get on the right path and begin walking forward. But before I could open my mouth to say anything, my mind took me back to that first day in Good Soaring Raven's office when he'd hinted that making fire was the most important thing we would learn to do.

"It's the fire, isn't it?"

Good Soaring Raven raised an eyebrow. "I'm not looking for a specific answer. There's no right or wrong here."

"No, I know that. But I get it now. The fire is the most important thing. Everything revolves around it. It cooks the food and boils the water, and keeps you warm at night."

He smiled, waiting for me to continue.

"But you can't take it with you. You have to build it new each day. And it's work. You have to gather the fuel and get a spark, and then tend the flames."

His eyes gleamed.

"No…I totally get it," I continued, the connections continuing to form in my brain. "The most important thing we learn out here is how to make fire. No matter what happens after this, I'll always have that. Nobody can take it away from me. Whenever I need a fire, I can build one."

"You're very wise, Watching Bear."

Epilogue

With the tools High Sierra had given me, I took my senior year by storm. Sure, it wasn't perfect, and my mom and I still clashed, but we both understood what it took to keep the fire going and to keep walking in the right direction.

In January, my acceptance letters started rolling in. NYU, Pepperdine, University of Washington, and finally BYU. I'd already made up my mind, but I left all of the envelopes sitting on my desk for a few weeks so my mom would know I'd really thought it all through.

By then I was having weekly phone conversations with my grandparents and my father. They were all making plans to fly out for my graduation, and though she seemed a bit nervous, my mom acted cool about it.

I hadn't quite worked out how I was going to find Bryce once I got to BYU. I didn't have any of his contact information, and if he had social media accounts, they were well hidden. Finally, I resolved that if the Great Creator wanted us to see each other again, he would find a way to make it happen. I kept the brochures under my pillow and looked at them every night. Only 33,000 students. We were bound to run into each other eventually.

Just when I thought I couldn't get more excited about my future, a follow-up email came from Good Soaring Raven. It wasn't the first time I'd heard from him. He checked in about once a month to see how I was doing. But this was something different.

I'm excited to hear that you're considering a career in counseling. I don't know if you've ever considered working as a spirit guide, but we've had a position open up for this summer. If you're interested, this could be a great opportunity to share some of the skills you learned while you were on the trail. And many schools work with us for internship credit.

My hands were trembling with excitement, and I couldn't stop myself from jumping up and down. This was exactly what I wanted to do.

Graduation and the celebrations that followed were a blur. Things went surprisingly well with my grandparents. My mom even agreed to stay with them when she came out to drop me off at school.

My father and his wife were nice too. His big extended family all wanted to meet me, not to mention my four half-siblings. I wasn't really sure I was ready for all of that, but my father seemed to understand, and didn't push anything.

Before I knew it, I was landing at Merced Regional Airport. My plane was met by the same driver who had taken us to the Pohono trailhead.

Orientation started the next morning with a group of ten new spirit guides. It was pretty cool to be on this end of the process. Good Soaring Raven explained High Sierra's philosophy about letting our young walkers choose. We were supposed to set good examples and be there when they wanted to talk. We were never supposed to coerce or force our young walkers to do anything.

I'd be lying if I didn't admit that I wanted to ask Good Soaring Raven about Bryce from the second I arrived, but somehow I exercised self-control and waited until the next morning.

"He's doing great!" Good Soaring Raven said. "He's out on a two-week rotation. You guys will just miss each other. He comes back in while you're out with your first group."

"That's cool," I said, trying to act nonchalant. "I wasn't sure if he'd still be working here."

"Oh, he's here," he said with a weird grin on his face. "And he's excited you're a spirit guide."

"He knows I'm here?"

Good Soaring Raven smiled, "He likes to think it was all his idea to offer you the job."

I practically floated to my tent that night and I could barely sleep, looking forward to meeting my first group of young walkers the next morning. Knowing Bryce believed in me and had recommended me for the position intensified my desire to be the best spirit guide possible.

Rotations for spirit guides were two weeks on and one week off, so it took three weeks before I ever even ran into Bryce at the lodge. I was getting ready to go out with my second group, and he was just coming in.

I was glad it wasn't the other way around. Bryce was dusty and rugged looking, just like I remembered him from the year before. His hair was a little longer, and his stubble more filled in, but his sparkling eyes and deep smile were exactly the same.

I, on the other hand, looked dramatically different than the last time he'd seen me. I was freshly showered and looking very put together in a hiking outfit that fit like a glove and didn't have any zippers or drawstrings in weird places.

"Jasmine!" he called as his group entered the lodge.

I made my way through the sea of kids and threw my arms around his neck. "How are you?" I asked. "Everything good with your leg?"

Bryce lifted his leg in the air and bent it at the knee. "I never told you what a great job you did of setting it."

"Really?"

"They didn't even need to reset it." he said. "Maybe you should think about a career in medicine."

My cheeks burned. "I've got to get going pretty soon here," I said. "Hopefully we can catch up for real sometime."

He nodded. "For sure. I need to hear the whole story about your answer."

I smiled and hugged him again. "Looking forward to it."

I'm not sure if it happened by accident, or if Bryce pulled some strings, but we were assigned to the same group on my next rotation.

As luck would have it, our group was starting the High Sierra Loop at Tuolumne Meadows, heading to Glen Aulin. Our young walkers were spirit walking, so when Bryce started telling them the story about what had happened to us, they were happy to have the distraction from their hunger.

The day passed without incident, and we watched an incredible sunset from the cliff overlooking the canyon at Glen Aulin. Another High Sierra group coming from the opposite direction came into the campground just after dark and joined us around the fire.

One of the spirit guides was a friend of Bryce's. They sat across the fire from me, laughing and talking. I was just about to call it a night, when Bryce stood up and turned to me.

"Hey, Jasmine. Brian said he'll make sure our kids get to bed. You want to come with me to go check in with the ranger? Somebody messed up our permits, and we need to make sure everything's good before we take off in the morning."

I stood up and brushed off the seat of my pants. Bryce led the way through the dark campground to the ranger's tent, where he took care of the issue in about two minutes, completely without my help.

"We should walk over to the waterfall for a little while," Bryce said. "You promised to tell me something, and it took a lot of work to get you alone. We may never have another chance."

I laughed. "Lead the way."

We sat on a rickety bench someone had placed a few feet away from the pool the waterfall emptied into. Millions of stars twinkled above us, and the slightly chilly air felt refreshing after our long hike.

It wasn't hard to tell Bryce about how my prayer had been answered. I'd replayed it so many times in my head over the past year.

"It's amazing what a difference knowing makes," I said. "I kind of feel like He hasn't stopped showing me He cares since that first prayer."

Bryce draped his arm behind me on the bench. "That's so cool."

"I just can't imagine how things could have worked out any better. I mean, my relationship with my mom, my father, my grandparents. School. Everything has totally fallen into place."

"I can't believe you listened to me about BYU. You'll love it. It's going to take a week to show you all of my favorite places there."

My heart kicked into overdrive. "Just a week, huh?"

"At least," he said. Turning toward me, his face glowed in the light of the half-moon. "You know, I never really got to thank you the way I wanted to for saving my leg, and my life."

He leaned toward me, erasing the short distance between us.

"I think you're the one who saved mine," I whispered.

His soft lips touched mine, creating the same warm tingle that I'd come to recognize over the last year as God's way of letting me know when something was good.